All the Days After

Foothills #1

Carrie Thorne

Thorny Books

Dedication

For you. Seriously. I started writing for me, only to find out how much I enjoy being able to share this. I truly hope you enjoy!

1st in the Foothills Romance Series

ALL THE DAYS
After

Navy SEAL.
Irresistible grin.
Whiskey Eyes. Epic Abs.
And... her best friend's
heartbreaker brother.

CARRIE THORNE

Chapter One

T-Minus 21 Days

S itting on the edge of his bed in the moonlit room, Asher inhaled in slow, measured breaths. Wiping the sweat from his brow, he shook away the nightmare and tossed on his running clothes. The offensively bright red numbers on the clock cast an eerie glow across the room like a sub on red alert.

No matter how hard he tried, he just couldn't sleep in late. SEALs had drilled it into him. Awake before dawn. Every day. PT for an hour, minimum. Drills, meetings, planning for the next mission.

Not anymore.

Burning off the nightmare with a punishing run around his parent's property and beyond, his lungs burned, his muscles tremored from exertion. As he rounded the final bend, the house came into view, the predawn glow casting off the dark windows. Despite the early summer heat, a sharp chill brushed over his sweat-soaked skin like razorblades.

Anything less than the five-mile run, and the unspeakable shit in his head followed him like a wicked shadow all damn day. He almost felt like himself when he pushed his body to the limit like this. If he even knew who that was anymore.

Or ever, really. Eight fucking years in the navy, and he still didn't know what he wanted out of life. Never did. Maybe never would.

Not like his sister, Pippa. She'd known exactly what she wanted since kindergarten. *I'm going to be a teacher when I grow up. I'm going to marry Lincoln, have three kids, and we'll live next door to you in Foothills.* What kid figures it out that early?

Turning the shower on lukewarm to cool his throbbing muscles in the stinging spray, he rinsed off the thick, salty sweat like a damn workhorse. He didn't linger, not wanting to miss his favorite part of the day. With a quick teeth-brushing and an attempt to tame his past-due-for-a-trim hair, he considered shaving to fully present himself as an upstanding citizen.

Nah. He rather liked his stubble. Maybe he'd grow a full beard one of these days, but that just seemed so cumbersome. Would irritate his dad nicely, though. Maybe that uptight sister of his while he was at it. Yikes, old habits rearing back up. All grownup, nearly thirty, remember?

Tossing on yesterday's jeans, he smelled a shirt he found in a laundry bin by the door. Huh. Fresh and clean. Folded too. His mom was taking it way too easy on him.

Paul was glad he was home like Mom was; he was almost sure of it. When his dad continually pestered him to take over the family business, asking when he was going to do something with his life, what he really meant was *I love you, son.*

Sure. Keep thinking that. As if finishing a four-year degree in three years, then eight years as a Navy SEAL wasn't meaningful. What his dad really meant was, *when are you going to be more like me?*

Asher had been home a few weeks. Or had it been a month already? Two? He'd totally lost track of time. All he knew for sure was that therapy at the VA was every Monday, then group therapy every Wednesday. He was working his ass off to feel normal again. If that was even a realistic ambition. Had he ever been normal?

Had done pretty well for himself, considering the shit he'd gone through, but he was a work in progress. He didn't like being unemployed any more than Paul liked it. But his dad didn't seem to understand that Asher needed to get his head on straight before he could consider becoming a productive member of society.

He had set the coffeepot to be done just as he finished his run and shower each morning. His parents wouldn't be up for another hour or two, thank goodness. They were great parents despite his dad's highhanded nature; he knew he was lucky. But sometimes it was nice to savor the peace and qulet of the mountains.

Sneaking across the living room with his piping hot cup of coffee in hand, both to avoid spilling and to not risk waking his parents, he slipped silently through the glass slider to the front deck. As he had made the habit since coming home, he sat on his favorite Adirondack chair to watch the sun rising over the mountains. Shades of pink, purple, and orange fingered across the craggy peaks as the sun awoke, rising behind the Cascades. Each breath filled his lungs with crisp mountain air, each sip of the robust brew calmed his thoughts.

It would be hot this afternoon. He couldn't remember the temperature going over eighty much when he was grow- ing up, and that wasn't until August. June had barely begun, and the National Weather Service was predicting sunny and eighty-two today. Would be drought conditions and nearly a hundred degrees by August, or so they said.

All too soon, the moment came to an end, as it did every day. Coffee drained, sun burning brightly in his eyes, he headed out to the garage. Soon, he'd start work for his dad.

Not today. Not that he could put it off much longer. He'd already been putting it off for twenty-nine years. *I just got home... give me a month... let's plan on after Pippa's wedding... I should be able to start by mid-July.* Paul had to know he was stalling, but he also had to know that Asher had no desire to work at the hardware store.

At no point had he ever indicated to his father that he wanted to take over the family business. Ever. His degree was in political science and his only real experience was in combat. When had he ever indicated an interest in running Sutherland's Hardware?

Popping the hood of his antiquated pickup, he got to work. This old truck would run, whether it wanted to or not. The rust-bucket had gotten him through high school, college, and eight years with the navy. It couldn't give up on him yet.

Not with all the damn new parts he'd put in it; it was becoming quite the bionic rig these days. He wouldn't be surprised if it stood up and declared it was an alien here to save Earth from the Decepticons. Wasn't owning a Transformer every guy's fantasy?

C lutching her official license in her hands, Sophie twirled a sprightly jig around the room. Carefully, to avoid tripping over the neatly stacked boxes which made up the complex maze that used to be her living room.

Sophie Jones, Certified Public Accountant. Master's graduate, financial genius, successful businesswoman. Okay, maybe let's not go that far just yet, but Sophie couldn't seem to reign in the thrill of recognition for her accomplishments. It had been a long haul.

"Pip, where are you? It came. I passed," She hollered across the apartment, grinning so wide she could feel the warm breeze from the open windows blowing across her teeth.

"What? In here." Pippa Sutherland, her best friend and roommate of the last four years, called back from her bedroom.

"Can you send me your Aunt Jane's number? I want to send her a pic, so she knows her protégé is official." Sophie tried to calm her prancing feet to show Pippa the certificate, but she couldn't seem to stop the happy dance in progress.

As a child, she'd never dreamed of being an accountant. But after tightly managing the household finances, lest her aunt blow their limited income on manicures and highlights, she'd discovered she had knack for it. Years of working in coffee shops, the bank, then the vigorous internship at the investment firm in Seattle, led to today's overjoyed response.

Prying the certificate from Sophie's eager hands, Pippa admired the page and squealed, throwing her arms around her friend. "Congratulations. I'm so excited. I'll text you Jane's info; she'll be anxious to hear from you."

As soon as Jane had heard that Sophie was planning a career in accounting, she'd been begging for her to come join her at Foothills Accounting. *Begging* maybe was too strong of a word, but she'd been asking *meaningfully*. From the moment she'd laid eyes on Foothills, Sophie had wanted to make the move.

Foothills was aptly named, charmingly settled on the talus of the Cascade Mountain Range, just before the elevation rapidly inclined. It was a charming town with delightful people, of which the Sutherlands were a household name. And it was tucked neatly away from the hustle and bustle of the bigger cities that surrounded Puget Sound.

Seattle had been a great change of pace from Los Angeles, but still too much for Sophie. Foothills was just right, with the population just over eight thousand. Large enough to be able to hide in the crowd, but small enough to not get lost, either.

Tossing her long hair behind her shoulders, she attempted to tame the mass of locks. Neither blond nor brown, but an odd mix of both. Although they were natural highlights, the variety looked like she couldn't decide what color highlights to add and tried a sampling of every shade of blond and light brown at the salon. With a flourish, she finished the happy dance with a bow and plopped down onto the foot of Pippa's bed.

Grin as wide as Sophie's, Pippa dropped onto the wooden chair across from her friend and teased, "I don't think I've ever seen you quite so bouncy before. How much coffee have you had today?"

"Just two or three cups so far." She bugged her eyes out in dramatic punctuation.

Pippa's legs did their own goofy wiggle around her backwards desk chair. "The teacher and the accountant, ready to take on Foothills by storm. We're quite the sensational pair."

Rolling her eyes, Sophie chuckled over the irony. Although Pippa could honestly say she'd always epitomized the prim and proper, albeit fun, schoolteacher, Sophie couldn't exactly say the same. But it sure felt good to now have a fancy certificate that announced to the world she was Ms. Stability.

"Shouldn't Lincoln be here soon? I'm sick of living out of boxes. The fridge is completely empty aside from last night's pizza. Which, I already had for breakfast." Sophie grabbed her gurgling stomach and groaned, a pitiful scowl drooping over her face.

Pippa handed her back her certificate and rested her chin on the back of the chair. Studying her watch, she scrunched her face in careful calculation. "Twenty minutes. They gave him the runaround at the rental truck office. He actually read every last line of the agreement, proving himself the tenacious attorney already."

"I can't stop fretting: your parents don't mind me crashing at their place for a few weeks? Even while you're away on your honeymoon?" Although she'd asked the same question dozens of times over the last few weeks, she still didn't want to be a burden. Never wanted to be an inconvenience. Not that she had a complex or anything. Okay, she totally did, but she was really working on that.

Pippa kicked her across the narrow aisle between the bed and her spot on the backwards chair. "Stop asking. Trust me, they love having you around. I think they've put in for an adult adoption. Your picture is on the dang mantle. Mom brags about you on Facebook as much as she does Asher and me."

Trying to not bite her fingernails, a nasty habit she officially quit five years ago, Sophie settled for letting her knee vibrate at a critically high frequency. "But Asher just got back what, a month ago? They must have their hands full helping him get settled now that he's back from the navy."

Rolling her eyes lovingly, Pippa reached her foot over to still Sophie's frantic knee jiggle. "It will be a full house, but that's the way they like it. I worry more about you having to live in the same house as my reprobate brother."

"He can't possibly be the lecher you've made him out to be. Besides, you know I have too good of self-restraint these days when it comes to men. If it helps you relax a bit, I promise to not have sex with him." Sophie crossed her heart and raised her hand in a heartfelt salute.

Despite her many trips to Pippa's parent's house, she'd never met Asher. According to Pippa, he maintained an almost laughable affinity for women–particularly Pippa's friends.

A picture of him in his uniform resided next to hers on the mantle. She could certainly understand the fuss. Maybe, just maybe, on lonely nights, she let her imagination wander and allow a fantasy or two about the sexy SEAL. Not that she'd ever tell Pippa, and she told her best friend everything. Hell, their periods were synced to the day.

"Before he joined the navy, every friend I brought home just ended up straight in his bed. I'd like to be able to make and keep a friend that is just mine. You can be friends with him, just please don't fall for his charms." She feigned a teasing smile, but Sophie knew it was no joke. Pippa and her brother had butted heads enough over the years, and the loss of a few friendships due to Asher's dating habits had been a huge strain on their relationship.

Rising from the bare mattress, Sophie grabbed her certificate and reassured her friend. "I would love to take offense that you think I would choose one night with your brother over a lifetime of friendship with you, but I know you have a bit of a complex about the whole thing—"

Mouth open to defend herself, Pippa couldn't get her thought out. Sophie talked right over her friend, holding her finger up to silence her.

"Which I really do understand. And I'll pretend you didn't just imply that I'm a faithless friend and a slut." Sophie rolled her eyes and nudged her friend. Yeah, he was absurdly handsome, with a body that made her imaginary love life that much more interesting, and deliciously creative, but she didn't let her libido rule her life.

"I don't think you're a slut or a faithless friend." Pippa raised an eyebrow and nodded plottingly. "Actually, I suspect you may just be the one to put Asher in his place. All gorgeous with those long lashes and long legs. A heartbreaker that will finally leave the desperate single men of Seattle in peace, so they may spend their nights pining away for some other supermodel disguised as an accountant. When you refuse his come-ons, can you film it? I can't wait to see the look on his face when a woman doesn't fall at his feet."

Billy Idol's *White Wedding* blasted from Pippa's phone. With a squeal of delight, she hopped out of the chair and answered, "Hey, my sexy fiancé. Come on up. Our muscles are primed for heavy lifting." Ending the brief call, Pippa gazed about the room. "Let's get out of this dump."

It wasn't exactly a dump, but the apartment was in the untrendy section of the university district, far from the ritzy shopping centers. Although their apartment may be musty and tiny, she'd miss it. End of an era.

She blinked back the threatening tears. The best friend she'd ever had was getting married in three weeks to a great guy. Yes, precisely three weeks; Pippa had shared her digital calendar which included a daily countdown alert. Sophie was really happy for her. Not even that awkwardly jealous, smiling-and-nodding happy. She was genuinely thrilled for her friend.

Pippa had planned their futures as she planned everything else, meticulously and boisterously. Sophie didn't mind; uncertainty was far scarier than a well-mapped plan. Being included in Pippa's life and family over the last few years had been huge for her. Gave her the sense of belonging she'd been desperate for. Plus, she was excited about her fresh start in an adorable hometown with a great job already lined up.

Sophie needn't have bothered fighting the tears. After greeting her fiancé briefly, not quite overdoing the PDA, but close, Pippa turned and looked around the apartment. Tears streaming down her face, Pippa ran across the apartment to Sophie. "I don't want to go. I'm going to have to be a grownup now and go home to a smelly boy every night."

"Right here." Lincoln waved from the kitchen. "Don't worry about me. I'm not offended. I do stink sometimes." The women ignored him. In a loving way. He was good-natured and a good fit for Pippa's wound-too-tightness.

Wiping away the pesky tears that soaked her cheeks, she hugged her friend. "You get to work your dream job as a teacher and live with the man you love. Maybe make a few adorable babies soon. Even if he does smell sometimes." He didn't, but he was an easy, affable mark.

After a few sniffles and another round of tears, Pippa pulled away. Lincoln knew his fiancé well and had already started carrying boxes out to the moving van. Returning from load number one, he was now followed by his very handsome friend, Grady, who was carrying a stack of pizza boxes.

Lincoln put one arm around Pippa and kissed the top of her head. "I hope you don't mind, I dragged Grady up from Foothills. I figured we could use a hand."

Mustering up her appetite, Sophie endured yet another meal of pizza. She loved pizza, but it might be time for a break. Grady made eyes at Sophie immediately, as he seemed to be more and more flirty each time she saw him. Glancing to Sophie subtly over her folded slice, Pippa raised her eyebrows suggestively.

Sophie rolled her eyes and shook her head *No*. Grady was ridiculously handsome. Ocean blue eyes, surfer blond hair, incredible body he'd toned to perfection. An attorney that had graduated from law school last year, he was a great conversationalist. And, rumor had it, was good at *everything*.

He was an old friend of Lincoln's from Foothills and his business partner, so she'd only met him a few times. She'd be seeing a lot more of him in the future. The pair had just opened their own law firm in Foothills with an office a block or so down from Foothills Accounting.

Pippa seemed to think he was her soulmate. She liked him. A lot, really. Maybe once she was settled, she'd give it a chance? She'd already put him off once, claiming she wanted to get to Foothills before she started anything.

Stalling. She knew what it was. Trying to think of a nice way to refuse him, as she really did like him. Hell, he was perfect. Everything a woman could want.

He just... she didn't get that heat deep in her belly when he walked into a room. Her heart didn't skip a few beats, forgetting its rhythm, when he winked at her. She'd never felt those things, but knew they were imperative when considering a permanent mate. Maybe she would react differently when the stress of the last few months was gone?

Love at first sight was a stupid notion anyway, one she did not buy into. Not even in response to a few stupid photographs of a man she couldn't–and wouldn't–be with that had burned into her brain.

Chapter Two

F our hours on the road and Sophie was sick of white and yellow lines on asphalt. It should only have taken an hour, two at the most, but, thank you Seattle traffic, it had taken four. She was sick of living in the city. Case in point. Although she'd always lived in the city, she was a country girl at heart.

You didn't have to be raised in the country to know it was for you. The first time she'd stayed at Pippa's folk's place in Foothills, as usual, she'd been the first one out of bed. Sitting and watching the sunrise, the glow over the mountains illuminating the trees lining the high peaks, she'd fallen in love.

Despite the crazy traffic, she hadn't lost sight of the moving van. Lincoln was easy to follow, ensuring there was always room for all of them. That included Pippa's car being towed behind the moving truck, and Grady following in Lincoln's car behind hers.

In their cozy caravan, they'd made a dusty wedding and grad-school graduate parade across Western Washington. Lincoln had been staying with Grady in Foothills for the past two months since he'd finished law school, but after the wedding, he and Pippa would move into a rental house, just the two of them for once. High school sweethearts reunited by no mere coincidence; they were eager to start their little family.

Pippa was habitually a pragmatic planner and, Sophie suspected, she was born that way. She and Lincoln had broken up after high school, not wanting to sacrifice their careers for young love. Pippa went away to UCLA for her undergrad, where she'd met Sophie. When Pippa discovered Lincoln was going to Seattle U's law school, she'd dragged Sophie with her to get some experience under their belts, then attend grad school together at UW, conveniently located fifteen minutes away from Lincoln. Well, if one avoided I-5.

Ever the good-girl, Pippa had wanted to wait until they were married to move in together. Which generally meant Sophie got to know Lincoln well, as he crashed at their place at least two nights a week. Sophie wouldn't miss needing to turn her headphones up to drown out the sound of the lovebirds.

At last, they pulled into the driveway. She'd been here several times over the years. Since leaving LA, she hadn't been back to that over-populated metropolis.

Refused to go home to LA for the holidays, as her aunt didn't care to see her any more than she cared to see her aunt. Unless she was flush from a recent deposit from her trust fund when dear Aunt Yvette decided they needed some quality girl time.

Denise and Paul Sutherland had welcomed her into their home instead. When Pippa had shared Sophie's sad history, they fixed up a special bedroom just for her. They had plenty of space; had built a massive four-bedroom home expecting tons of kids, but they hadn't been able to have more after Pippa was born.

They had always tried to make up for Sophie's lack of family. Fresh flowers, cozy sheets, a thoughtful birthday present sent to her every year. The first Christmas she'd joined them, they even had a stocking hanging up for her with her name embroidered on it. To this day, Sophie couldn't figure out what she had done to deserve them.

The moving van kicked up quite a bit of dust that seeped into the air vents of her little SUV, but even her dust-encrusted nostrils couldn't take away from the beauty of the drive. Wildflowers were densely scattered along the sides of the driveway. Grandfatherly maples and cedars made a canopy through the first hundred feet of the rural drive, as if welcoming her to the magical homestead hidden within.

As the trees thinned, a clearing sprawled out before her, with neatly mowed green lawn to the left, an oversized shop-garage combo up ahead to the right, and the house beyond. Behind the house, to the right, lay an expansive concrete patio, a great entertainment setup including a hot tub with a waterfall that poured into the heated pool. To the left, east, she supposed, was a sizeable wooden deck no more than a few feet off the ground, with a propane outdoor fireplace and expansive seating that overlooked the bulk of the property. Her favorite part was the view off the deck, with a small, heavily vegetated valley leading to the rugged mountains that dominated the vast landscape.

Pippa hopped out of the moving truck and motioned Sophie to park her car into the garage. Theatrically waving her arms for Sophie to the last of the four bays, Pippa guided her in with gusto. Her friend was as giddy as she'd ever seen. Quite the pair, they were way too excited to be done with a long, long trudge through academia.

Sophie rolled down the window of her well-loved, high-mile CR-V and hollered at Pippa. "Are you sure? I can park wherever."

Skipping like a carefree kindergartener as she approached the car, Pippa leaned into the open passenger window and winked. "Not to worry, it's not prime real estate. Mom and Dad park in the double-sized first garage bay, I get the second, and I see Asher has claimed number three. So, you get to stash your stuff, and your car, in number four. Lincoln is bringing all of my stuff to our house."

"What? I didn't know the house was ready." Holding her foot steady on the break, Sophie leaned across the center console to hear better, convinced she must not have heard correctly.

"It's not, but Lincoln is handling the landlord's divorce, so he's letting use move stuff into the garage while he finishes up with painting and new floor installation." Beaming, Pippa was clearly excited to have a spiffy new place. Or brag about her fiancé doing some real work.

Either way, Sophie was excited with her. "That's awesome. Okay, I'll unload my boxes into my very own garage bay." Before pulling her foot off the brake, she locked eyes with Pippa. "Don't think you get to keep that coffee table. In fact, I'm going through all your stuff after you unpack to steal back all of *my* stuff that I know you tried to pilfer."

Pippa tapped the roof of the CR-V, the metallic thud echoing through the car, and backed away to let Sophie park. "We'll see. That coffee table looks great with my couch."

Sophie continued in reverse until she'd backed neatly into the garage. Turning off the ignition, she stepped out into the unseasonably arid June day. She attempted to smooth her road-wrinkled skinny jeans and white t-shirt, shook out her tired feet in her black Toms, and pulled her windblown hair into a loose ponytail. She felt almost presentable.

A shrill, grinding sound pierced into her brain. She covered her ears reflexively. Wincing, she walked around the back of her car and caught sight of the racket in the neighboring garage bay.

No wall separated the three single bays of the garage. Just tool benches, boxes, and automotive equipment that formed an unofficial, mobile divider. A pair of legs covered in oil-stained jeans and ratty combat boots stuck out from an antiquated Ford pickup.

Assuming this was the notorious Asher, Sophie attempted to sneak away. Not that she was a fraidy cat, but she didn't feel an overwhelming need to meet him just yet. Not after

Pippa's warnings about him. Not when she was tired and likely wouldn't be very witty or quick on her feet to deal with the rumored Casanova.

Too late. The screeching halted, leaving a thick, deafening silence in its stead. The body connected to the legs shoved out from under the truck and rose to stand.

Oh. So that was Asher.

Floppy as over-boiled spaghetti noodles, Sophie's legs completely betrayed her, and she worried as to whether they could continue to hold her up. A warm, fuzzy sensation coursed rapidly through her veins. All reasonable brain activity went caput like a fried hard drive, and she forgot her own name.

Before he noticed her, with her mouth gaping open from the next garage bay, he pulled his ratty cotton shirt over his head and used it as a makeshift grease-rag to wipe the black grime off his hands and face. Now that was just unfair. His abs defied reality; that was more than a six-pack. Was that even possible? Without her consent, a dreamy sigh escaped Sophie's mouth.

Dammit, he heard. Asher turned in the direction of the sound. If he was surprised to see a stranger standing there, he didn't let it show. "Hey. Want to give me a hand with something?"

What? She managed to pull her gaze from the ridiculously chiseled abs in front of her and looked at his face.

Not helpful.

Warm, whiskey eyes surrounded by dark lashes brushed over her from head to toe and back again. His sharply angled jaw was accented by last Friday's five o'clock shadow. His brown hair, a few shades lighter than his stubbled beard, was a few weeks past needing a trim.

The corner of his mouth quirking into a devastatingly attractive smile, he asked, "I can't get the light at the right angle, mind holding the flashlight?"

She surprised herself with a docile nod of assent and ambled brainlessly over. May as well extend her arms out and start drooling, demanding brains for dinner.

He handed her a flashlight, which she accepted without thinking. As if talking to a clueless child, he showed her the location of the black hole that had swallowed the lost bolt.

Scowling, she remembered herself. She was an intelligent human being. Not a zombie-giggling-horny-groupie flashlight holder. "Actually, I just got in. Pippa's waiting for me so we can go unload the moving van."

With a nod and a heartbreaking sigh, he ran a wiped-clean grease-blackened hand through his already mussed hair. "Of course. Sorry. Never mind. I'm good." Eyes lingering on her lips for a fraction of a second, he shifted his focus to the flashlight.

Well, now she felt like a jerk. Refusing when he tried to take the flashlight back, Sophie moved closer towards the truck. "Sorry, it's been a really long drive. My brain turned to mush after being stuck on I-5 behind an accident for hours. What do you need?"

Asher's gaze flashed back to hers and stayed this time. His eyes softened, the whiskey warming to a gooey honey. "Thanks. I really appreciate it. I lost a fucking bolt." Gesturing at the engine compartment, he scowled at the beast that had so cruelly swallowed such a tiny, critical part. "If I could just get the light in the right spot to see what I'm doing, I think I can reach it."

Sophie walked closer to the truck and shined the light down into the engine, searching for the proverbial needle in a haystack.

"It's right down there." He gestured as he approached. Moving to her side, smelling deliciously masculine, all sweaty and half-naked after working in the garage all day, he pointed where he'd last seen the bolt.

Inhaling his mind-bogglingly rugged scent, an unexpectedly appealing mixture of engine oil and mountain air, she tried to focus on her task. "Here, you hold this," Sophie ordered as she handed him the flashlight.

Stepping up onto the rusty chrome bumper, placing her feet wide apart for stability, she rested one hand on the side of the truck and leaned down over the engine. With her free hand, she grimaced as she reached deeply into the narrow opening where the light shined on the troublesome bolt.

Stretching to her shoulder until she nearly fell headfirst into the engine, she was able to grasp it out from the crevice it had been lost in and hopped off the front bumper. *Got it*. She almost cheered but didn't want to sound too eager.

Holding the prize between two fingers, she rested the other hand on her cocked hip and raised an eyebrow. "Looking for this?"

Smiling with relief, he tried to grab the bolt from her hand.

Feeling uncharacteristically flirty, she pulled it away, hid it behind her back and demanded a thank you with a raised eyebrow and a taunting smile. It had been a painfully long time since she'd flirted with an attractive man... and meant it.

Clearly enjoying the challenge as much as she did, he closed the distance between them. Stopping inches away from her, he drove her mad as she ached with the need to get closer, nipples standing at attention. She could feel the heat radiating off his body, warming her down to the bone. Biting her lip, she managed to withhold the dreamy sigh that tried to escape, again.

His hands trailed down her arms, his fingers tracing every groove in her skin, until he reached her hands, his chest a breath away from pressing against hers.

Stunned by the electricity between them, she didn't have the wherewithal to maintain her tease and her grip loosened. Snatching the bolt from her hand, he stepped back and flipped it in the air like a coin. If she weren't so aroused by the playful smirk he wore proudly, she'd smack it right off his arrogant face.

Seeing her offence at his lack of politeness–well what was actually an expression of *oh-shit*, because she couldn't believe she'd reacted so strongly to him–he leaned toward her and placed a sadly fleeting kiss on her cheek. Hesitating a moment longer than needed, he whispered, "Thank you." His breath brushed across her ear, before he pulled away.

Before she knew what had happened, he was back under the truck. What the hell was that? Her cheek still burned where his lips had been, her hand still gripped the non-existent bolt in the foolish hope that he'd touch her again.

She'd really lost her marbles. Shaking off the moment, she grabbed her bags and headed for the house. Berating herself for falling into exactly the trap Pippa had warned her against, she tried to deny the desire he'd stirred in her.

Pippa was already inside. Lincoln and Grady had gone to unload the bulk of their belongings alone and head home for the evening. Sophie was glad for some peace and quiet. She really enjoyed Lincoln and knew she would hit it off with Grady as a friend, but his persistent attentions were getting exhausting.

Everyone expected them to get together, particularly now that they were best man and maid of honor, and living in the same town, but Sophie just didn't see it happening. Maybe once she was settled, she'd give it a try.

With her fresh new start, maybe a fresh new look at his handsome face would tempt her. Although, after her response to Asher, she wasn't so sure.

S ophie inhaled the familiar, fresh and homey scent of the Sutherland's house as she stepped inside. Dinner was nigh; Denise was clearly cooking up a storm to welcome the girls.

Home... good feeling. Not that it was actually her home, but it immediately felt that way, since her first trip, like a favorite aunt and uncle's home you visited every summer. Part of that was Denise, ensuring she had a welcoming hug as she entered, cheery conversation, and her own space when she needed quiet. What else could she call it, but home?

The open floor plan set the tone. To the right of the entry, the dining room flowed into the kitchen. To the left, a sunny great room was cozy and inviting with plush furniture, a huge fireplace, and family-style coffee table. Straight ahead, an understated staircase led to the large loft sitting room that was surrounded by four bedrooms.

Of the spectacular home, her favorite part was the massive wall of windows that displayed a broad mountain vista. The Cascades were glowing green as the sun was starting to lower in the sky. She could almost smell the breeze wafting through the fir, pine, and cedar trees in the evening sun.

Young kids would have been a terror in this house. Throwing stuff over the loft rail to the living room below. Blasting the tv loud so the whole house could hear. No wonder Denise and Paul had built their own master suite downstairs, under the open loft and behind thick walls.

Dropping her bags in her bedroom, Sophie freshened up in the connecting bathroom. Well, the Jack and Jill bathroom that attached to Pippa's bedroom. Of the four bedrooms upstairs, each pair shared a bathroom in between. Normally she shared with Pippa, but, judging by the men's toiletries scattered around the left-hand sink, and NAVY swim shorts hung over the shower, Denise must have moved Asher and Pippa around.

Another drawback to the loft-style bedrooms looking over the living room: she could hear everything that happened downstairs. Enough problems of her own, Sophie didn't care for eavesdropping. More secrets, more worries. She was just leaving her bedroom and about to head downstairs, when the conversation below stopped her.

"Go easy on him. He's had a rough time." Denise's voice was just above a loud whisper, the soft volume paled in contrast to the firmness in her tone.

She'd heard Pippa receive an earful more than a few times about her refusal to bring Sophie to visit when Asher was home, making it a rarity when Pippa actually saw her brother over the years. Certainly, she never spent holidays with him, as Asher typically offered up holiday vacations to others of his SEAL team with families of their own.

Pippa's voice was not so soft, not caring who heard her annoyance. "Why is he staying in my old room next to Sophie? She's no match for him. Why do you think I've never been here when I knew he was going to be here? I love my brother, but I'm sick of him leaving my friends brokenhearted."

Before she realized the gravity of what she'd done, Sophie found her fingertips in her mouth, her nails quickly wasting away to nothing. Dammit, she didn't want to bite her nails. Disgusting habit and a glaring sign of weakness.

Guilty, guilty, guilty. She'd been around Asher for a grand total of five minutes, and already was fantasizing about him taking her from behind while she was leaned over the hood of his truck. What was up with her rabidly horny imagination running on overdrive? Grady was just as attractive but didn't cause nearly the reaction.

Clanking pots and pans echoed across the house, as Denise shuffled through the cupboards more dramatically than necessary. "He's your brother. I put him in the quietest, most spacious bedroom since he'll be here the longest. And, you haven't seen him much these last few years; he needs to be able to escape when things get hectic. Knowing you and Lincoln might appreciate a little privacy when he stays the night, I put you in the complete opposite room."

Pippa's voice softened a bit. "I do appreciate your thoughtfulness. I love my brother, despite our differences during those awkward teenage years. I'm so proud of his accomplishments. But–"

Before Pippa could finish, Denise cut her off with now frank exasperation in her voice. "He's been home for a month. Guess how many times he's been out?" She didn't let Pippa answer. "Not once. I don't think Sophie is in any danger. He doesn't talk much, doesn't go out, nor has he during his last several trips home. If you had come to visit him more often, you might have noticed."

Her friend's guilt was almost palpable from clear across the house. Despite their differences, she did care about her brother. Even when they were at the worst of odds, Pippa still called him every month. "You're right. I'm sure I'm overreacting. Do you think he's going to be okay?"

Denise sighed. "I don't know. He won't say much, but he's seen some terrible things. It's been getting better. I think the therapy and R&R has been good for him. Just... go easy on him, okay?"

"I will. He's still okay with being in the wedding party, right? Because it's all about me, and he'll look very handsome alongside Lincoln and Grady up front." Pippa laughed at herself. She was not someone Sophie would consider selfish under normal circumstances, so joking about it reflected her self-awareness and guilt when her thoughts strayed toward self-centered.

Denise laughed with her. "Whether he's agreeable or not, it'll be good for him. He and Lincoln were always good friends anyway. Even before you two got together."

Sophie's poor imagination went wild, imagining she and Asher on a double date with Pippa and Lincoln, then later the roles reverse at her own white wedding with Asher. *Where had that come from?* Raw lust was one thing, but wedding bells was the last thing on her mind. Must be all the wedding talk rubbing off on her.

Chapter Three

"Don't you wear those filthy boots in the house, Asher Sutherland." Denise hollered at her son as he entered the house. Can't get away with anything around here.

Obediently, Asher pulled off his smelly old combat boots and socks, bundling them up with the greasy t-shirt he'd already peeled off. In front of Sophie. It really hadn't been intentional. Although, her reaction had been a nice boost to his self-esteem that had undergone too many hits the last six months.

Although unnecessary, Denise's worry was quite reasonable. As a considerate person, he wasn't about to leave the nasty shoes for the entire house to smell, not with the dinner table less than twenty feet from the front door. Wearing nothing but his ragged jeans, clutching his grubby work clothes, he dashed for the stairs.

In his hurry, he nearly bowled over Sophie. He hadn't exactly allowed for proper introductions earlier, but none had been needed. With the raving his family had done about her over the years and pictures around the house like she was one of their own, he knew exactly what Sophie looked like. Knew about her accomplishments in college, how Aunt Jane was hoping she'd join her soon-to-be two-person accounting firm.

Miss Perfect is what she was. An enlarged UCLA graduation photo of her wearing a sweet little white sundress was even framed over the mantle with the rest of the family photos. He'd developed a total crush on her from the moment he'd seen that photo.

None of the pictures or stories were even close to reflecting Sophie in person. Mysterious with those stormy gray eyes. Cute with her easy dimples. A fucking knockout with mile-long legs. Hair that was artfully neither blond nor brown but a rebellious mix that declared she couldn't, or wouldn't, be labeled.

Playing the ever-humiliating game of which way to move to let the other pass, they shared a clumsy smile as both were stuck on the wrong side of the landing. Her spontaneous, lyrical laugh resonated in his head, a pleasant surprise that no one had told him about. Genuine, sweet, feminine... with a hint of wicked.

Gripping his boots and shirt in one hand, he leaned against the wall and motioned her across gallantly. He caught her scent on the way by; so clean and soft. Something subtly floral and earthy but not overpowering, more like she'd been hiking through wildflowers rather than bathing in perfume like his late grandmother.

Dammit, not at all what he needed right now. Pippa had been smart to ensure they never met. Well, no good way to say it; he enjoyed women. A lot. And she tended to make friends with some very attractive women.

Not that he'd done anything like that in years. Too busy training, then too many floozies looking for the company of a Navy SEAL for the night. Easy access sort of cured his quickdraw dating habits.

One look at that sort of women and he pictured his dick rotting away from STDs. No thank you. Not that he'd ever even let a woman touch him unless there was a high-quality condom between any part of her and his dick.

Plus, he liked to think that he'd grown up a bit.

Sophie was different. She exuded an easy confidence and, well, she was downright capable without making a fuss about it. Without regard for her pristinely white t-shirt, she'd climbed right up onto his truck and pulled out the bolt he'd been trying to reach for hours. Given him a spectacular view of her ass in tight denim while she was at it.

He'd enjoyed her double take when he'd peeled off his grease-stained shirt. That hungry look on her face matched his own reaction. In an instant, his little crush had blown up into a colossal case of gut-wrenching lust.

But... more than anything, he needed to *not* make it with Pippa's best friend. Again. That relationship was tenuous enough.

Cringing, he vividly recalled the worst of all his conquests was on Pippa's prom night. He'd been visiting from college. Pippa and her good friend at the time had met at their house. Her friend... what was her name again? Dammit, he couldn't even remember her name. Whatever, she was nineteen and friendly and... experienced.

Unfortunately for Pippa, what's-her-name was a little offended he never called her back after and had silently blamed Pippa for his callousness. Pippa hadn't even known why her friend stopped talking to her for months. He'd gotten an earful when she found out.

Yeah, he should probably steer clear of Sophie. Based on his response to her today... fuck, he was still battling the threatening erection, it wasn't going to be easy to stay away from her. He'd been celibate for so long he was about to call Guinness. How tough could a few more weeks be?

After a quick shower, his second today, he wasn't quite so sweaty or coated with motor oil. Inevitably, some of the grease was still embedded in the creases of his hands. Throwing on his cleanest t-shirt and jeans, neatly folded in his drawer–thank you Mom–he dashed downstairs in time to join the family for dinner.

When he'd first gotten home, he'd tried to hole up in his room twenty-four-seven, even for meals. His dad had put a stop to that right away. He'd been right, which Asher wasn't pleased about. PTSD wasn't going to get any better if he isolated himself, so said his therapist.

His mom was just putting salmon, salad, and homemade baked fries on the table. That's what smelled so good, they were crispy and everything. Dousing the homemade fries in ketchup, he dove into his meal ravenously.

Wolfing down the delicious handful of fries, he glanced up to find the whole table was looking at him. Denise scowled at his abhorrent table manners. Paul gave him that look, the *Don't be a dumbass* look he'd earned many times in his life. Pippa eyed him anxiously, ensuring he wasn't looking at Sophie. Sophie, however, bit her cheek in a teasing smile before starting on her salmon.

Giving his mother a wink, he slowed down and tried to eat like a normal human being. His mom ought to dine with sailors on a sub or destroyer sometime. Not so keen on the manners.

Hating to cook for himself, Asher had spent most of his meals in the galley on base or eaten microwaveable meals in his closet apartment alone. A few times a month, he'd go out with his few pals, Zane and Jack. Despite his relief to leave the Navy, he missed his friends.

Granting him a reprieve, Denise opened the table to conversation. "Pippa, darling, is your appointment at Tracey's Apparel and Alterations tomorrow or the next day? I forgot to write it down."

Politely swallowing her mouthful, Pippa delicately wiped the corners of her mouth before speaking. Showoff. "Didn't you get the calendar I shared with you? It's tomorrow at two o'clock. You'll be there, right?"

"Of course, sweetie. I wouldn't miss your final dress fitting. Why was I thinking it was the day after? I can't seem to get your calendar to sync with mine." Denise looked into the air as if the answer was hovering above the table.

Pippa hopped up from the table and grabbed her organizer from her purse. "Then, the day after we meet the caterer and finalize the menu, then we confirm the cake order. Then on Monday we pick up place cards, Tuesday the party favors should arrive. The rehearsal rehearsal dinner is in ten days, the day after Freya gets in. Then the bridesmaid and tux fittings for the last-minute tailoring.

"Oh, and the bachelor and bachelorette parties, but we haven't nailed down dates for that yet since we hadn't decided what we're doing for those. Bridal shower will be after the rehearsal rehearsal dinner, and rehearsal dinner just two days before the wedding, a day to relax, then the Big Day." Breathless from the long litany, Pippa beamed at her organizational skills.

Seated next to her, Sophie pointed in the air with a fry and nudged her friend. "Did you really just say rehearsal rehearsal dinner? I've never been married, but I wasn't aware that was a thing." At least someone had their head on straight around here.

Rolling her eyes at her friend, Pippa nudged her back. "It's totally a thing. Just ask Pinterest. The rehearsal dinner is all of us, the wedding party, Lincoln's family. The rehearsal rehearsal dinner is just the wedding party so everyone can get to know each other."

Trying to make sense of what her friend had just said, Sophie considered for a moment. Asher liked watching her think. She wore her thoughts right on her sleeve. Nothing dishonest or shrouded. "That sounds fun. We can nail down bachelor and bachelorette parties and other to-do's together. And I'm looking forward to meeting Freya." She was too good to his crazy sister.

Pippa's eyes lit up. "Perfect, we can have it here. I'll whip up a tasty dinner and then we can relax in the hot tub."

Wedding planning banter bounced around the table until his head was spinning. No one seemed to notice that he didn't have a useful thing to say on the matter. He cared, of course, but he sort of planned to just show up where and when he was told.

Lincoln was a good guy and would take on her lovable crazy; he was glad Pippa had reconnected with him. Although, knowing Pippa, their reuniting in Seattle hadn't been a co-incidence. Nothing she did wasn't premeditated. Including the fact that he hadn't laid eyes on Sophie until it became unavoidable.

Despite his better judgment, his eyes kept straying across the table to Sophie. Catching him watching her, she bit her lower lip shyly. Devouring a cluster of fries, he nearly choked as he imagined those perfectly lush lips sliding over his cock so smoothly. *Knock it off,* he mentally kicked himself.

After dinner, Asher cleared his plate and was surprised to find Sophie right behind him, handing him her plate. He took her plate and rinsed it before putting it in the dishwasher. She was back with more. Kept coming back with more plates, pans, whatnot... until before he knew it the dishes were done. He'd dodged dishes from the day he'd gotten home, but some-how, he'd just done them all. Sneaky woman.

He refused to glance in his mother's direction. Without even looking, he could see the smug, if not shocked, expres-sion on her face as she relocated into the living room. Might as well go all in. He grabbed a bottle of red and the last of the white and topped off the wine glasses in the living room.

Settling in on the end of the well-cushioned, beige linen couch facing out the window, Asher crossed his feet on the coffee table and leaned back to enjoy his wine. Sophie sat in the seat opposite his, her crossed feet not quite touching his. Was it hot in here?

A few millimeters separated their feet, and he was toast. If even almost-footsy made his head rush with Sophie, he couldn't imagine the inferno of just touching her, his tongue running between her perfect breasts, his hands gripping her ass as he... Blinking, he brought himself back to the moment. Must be the long epoch without getting any, and he hadn't gotten much action in the few years before that.

The rest of the evening was actually relaxing, despite his overactive imagination. No one expected any input from him. As usual, Pippa carried the conversation quite well on her own, bouncing wedding ideas off her willing listeners.

Paul had a few comments, mostly involving money-saving alternatives. Sophie mostly sat back and smiled, enjoying her friend's enthusiasm, but her ideas clearly differed. Not that she would make Pippa feel any less for having big ideas.

The four of them had been a tight unit when he was a kid. Perhaps he'd blown it a bit his teenage years, but they'd still been a good team. Somehow, Sophie didn't feel like a guest in their midst. Like Lincoln always fit right in. He'd known then Lincoln was the guy for his sister. His parents must have felt it as well, having included pictures of Sophie and Lincoln mixed in with those of their own children.

Across the coffee table, Sophie pulled her feet in and curled up in her chair. Immediately, he felt cold at the distance between them. She sipped the last of her wine, her smile warm and her gray eyes sleepy. Even fatigued, he didn't miss the storm that still lingered behind them.

Like dark clouds that hinted at a dark past she masked with her easy smile, her eyes held a deep intensity. He'd never quite seen eyes that shade before. If it weren't for those eyes, he'd think she was a goodie-two-shoes like his sister. Those eyes had seen more than their fair share.

Sophie, Denise, and Paul turned in early. As soon as the bedroom doors were closed, Pippa's face changed from calm and collected to determined and nosy. Fast as a damn cheetah, she left her own seat and sat opposite him, leaned forward in full ready-to-pounce position.

"Don't even think about it." Her eyes drilled into him, like lasers blasting him into submission.

"Sorry?" He played innocent. He knew exactly what she was talking about.

Counting on her fingers, she made a rather embarrassing list. "Jenny, Alyssa, Fiona, Bethany. Oh, and don't forget Lyric."

Oh yeah. Lyric. That was her name. She wasn't very lyrical in her noises, a bit more of a hyena. Not that he'd spent more than ten minutes in her company. But she sure seemed to enjoy herself.

He lowered his feet to the carpet and set down his empty wine glass on the coffee table. Trying his very best to not crack a smile, knowing it would throw her over the deep end, Asher wiped his expression and faced his sister and her accusations. "I am really, truly sorry for... well, for ruining your friendships, and I won't let it happen again."

Not sure what to do about the lack of argument, Pippa leaned back and adjusted her posture. "Okay."

"In my defense, they really weren't very good friends if they judged you based on my failings–" She tried to interrupt. Understandable, this was not his best retort, but on all those occasions, it had taken two to tango.

Grimacing, he powered on before she could bowl over his poor defense. "-Pip, I haven't done anything like that in years." She gave an unladylike snort and rolled her eyes. "Really, sis. It's been nearly two years since I've even been with anyone."

Brow rumpled; disbelief threatened to take over her expression. "Two years?"

And he went on, when he probably shouldn't have. "Yeah. Two years. Back in the day, I was a stupid, albeit horny, kid. I grew up a while back. You just weren't around to notice."

The ability to think things through before speaking or acting had never quite come naturally for Asher. His foot ended up in his mouth more often than not. Or his dick where it shouldn't be. Well, at least he'd grown out of that poor impulse control issue.

"Besides, most of those were when I was on break from college or the navy. With the amount of credits I was taking to graduate early, then the brutal SEAL training... let's just say I was eager for a little release." Not that he needed to defend himself, but he felt defensive, dammit.

All had been old enough; always more than consensual. He never made any promises. They clearly hadn't been decent friends to Pippa if they'd blamed her for his not calling. Or to jump in her brother's bed so easily.

Her face dropped and her eye softened. "I'm really sorry. I admit that I avoided visiting when I knew you'd be home. Usually, I'd bring Sophie home as she didn't have any place else to go, and she's the best friend I've ever had, so I definitely didn't want to risk losing her. I certainly never brought her to San Diego with me the few times I came to visit; I learned that lesson with Jenny from freshman year at UCLA. I don't know how I would have gotten through finishing up at UCLA and finishing grad school without Sophie. And, quite frankly, she's hot and she doesn't date much."

He was a pretty decent judge of character and seriously doubted that Sophie was the innocent Pippa seemed to think. "She's gorgeous, but I'm not doing that to you again. Even if she begs, I'm not going to have sex with her." Well, maybe if she begged.

His poor imagination flashed to all kinds of erotic fantasies... of Sophie laying naked on the hood of his truck, begging him to lick her sweet pussy... *Cut it out.* Don't dig that hole any deeper.

"Really? Because at dinner you were looking at her an awful lot—"

"You're my baby sister; you are so much more important to me than a convenient lay. That's all those were in the past, my own ego. Trust me, my ego has quieted." Too quiet lately. That brief kiss on Sophie's cheek today had been the most action he'd gotten in forever, and her taste had left a permanent imprint on his lips.

Pippa rose from her chair and aimed for the stairs. Briefly, she paused and looked back over her shoulder at him. "Sorry, Ash. I wish I'd come around more. And I sort of miss that ego. You are different. Quieter."

Not quite sure how to respond, he gave a brief nod. He was different. Losing half your damn team on one really bad op did that to a person.

Chapter Four

T-Minus 20 Days

B right-eyed and bushytailed, Sophie's eyes popped open at five in the morning. Same time as they did every day. Creature of habit. Which, she wasn't ashamed to admit.

She'd started waking early as a teenager to get some alone time before Yvette started to stir. She still enjoyed those few minutes of peace before the rest of the world was awake. Had to if she wanted more than a three-minute shower, as it took Yvette half the damn day to primp, then gaze at her own reflection in the mirror.

Slipping on her running attire, she tiptoed down the stairs and out of the house. The sun was thinking of rising soon, casting a shadowy blue glow across the landscape, just enough to see where she was going. There was a path that ran along the edges of the property that was perfect for a run. She'd made a habit of running it every morning she was here visiting in the past. Someone else must enjoy it too, the path was so well worn.

Thighs on fire, lungs burning, she pushed on, adrenaline and sheer force of will driving her on. Glancing at her smartwatch, she kept going. Two miles. That ought to do it for today, but she was enjoying the fresh air so much she wasn't ready to stop.

Rounding a bend, she caught sight of the rugged mountain view glowing in the predawn across a sprawling valley. She had no idea how far she was from the house now; this place was truly magnificent. A perfect place to refresh.

Sadly, she shouldn't slow to enjoy the view today, or she might not be able to get her momentum going again. Keeping her pace, she moved on and planned to return to the spot another time. Maybe with a picnic.

Asher saw the collision coming before she did. Inevitably, painfully she barreled into him at full speed.

Having the extra half second to prepare, he managed to shift just far enough to the side to catch her and try to control the fall.

The momentum was too much, and they spun in a circle before they crashed to the ground. His arms wrapped around her to steady their rapid descent, spinning their bodies so she landed on him rather than the boulder she was otherwise headed for.

Groaning from the force of the landing, Asher gripped Sophie as she lay sprawled across him. Air barely moving through his crushed lungs, he managed to ask hoarsely, "You okay?"

As soon as she recovered from the force of the impact, she realized he was wearing nothing but Navy running shorts. Their bodies were rather indecently intertwined, sweaty and breathing heavily... her brain was useless. She managed to sit up and ease herself to a stand. "I'm okay. You?" she managed. That was the best she could come up with?

Rescuing him back, having been saved from the major force of the impact by his swift catch, she held out a hand to help him up. Finding a smile at her chivalry, he grabbed her hand and let her help pull him up. A thrill ran up her spine at his touch, the adrenaline blasting into overtime now.

"Fine. I'm good. See you back at the house." He stretched out the aches from the fall, turned and continued down the path. Sophie blinked a few times to remember what she was doing, then continued on her path.

Finishing a satisfying run, Sophie dashed upstairs for a quick shower. Feeling better than she had in weeks, she slipped on a denim skirt and t-shirt, a subtle splash of makeup and ran the brush through her hair. Coffee. Need caffeine.

Not yet six. The rest of the household was still asleep. Sophie tiptoed down the stairs, finding the other early riser in the kitchen already. Asher was just pouring himself a warmup.

Seeing her approach, he reached up into the cupboard above, grabbed an artisan ceramic mug and poured her a cup. Without a word, he gave her a friendly smile, handed her the freshly poured cup of coffee, and headed for the front porch with his own. Sophie looked out the window at his destination. Perfect timing. The sun was just coming up over the mountains.

Hands cradling her cup, she headed out the slider and sat on the Adirondack chair next to his. Not that she was trying to sit next to him, knowing it would bother Pippa, nor did she want to interrupt his peaceful reverie, but it was the only other chair with an uninterrupted view of the sunrise. The moment the sun rose above the mountains, she felt something in her chest awaken. When was the last time she enjoyed a moment so tranquilly?

Sitting side-by-side, they sipped their coffee in silence. The penetrating focus of the sun was about to crest over the faraway peaks. Purple and orange stretched across the endless sky.

"Why accounting?" Asher glanced at her, then back to the sunrise just as the sun peeked out over the mountains.

Why did he care if she was an accountant? She knew what people tended to think. Thick glasses, frumpy frocks, boring conversationalist. Pissed her off.

Sophie looked over at him, green circles dancing in her vision that the sun had imprinted. Feeling snarky, she snapped back, "Why the navy?"

He downed the last of his coffee in one big gulp, the corner of his mouth quirking up. "Touché."

Okay, maybe she was being a bit defensive. Too many had taken one look at her and couldn't figure out why she *chose* to be an accountant. Why she didn't want to do something more glamorous. An heiress, her mother had strayed from the expected path as well and never looked back. She liked to think the rebellious streak came from Colette.

Quickly distracted, his eyes straying to her thighs, he took a slow, deliberate breath. Realizing her skirt had hiked up dangerously high in the reclined chair, Sophie pulled it down a bit, although she was suddenly tempted to hike it up an inch just to see his reaction.

Shaking himself back to the present, he rose from his chair and headed back into the house. Somehow, despite the intellectual irritation with him, she enjoyed his eyes on her legs. *What was wrong with her?*

She probably should have just made friendly conversation, but his tone had been downright brusque. Judgy. Why accounting? She loved it. It was where she belonged.

Her aunt had blown through every penny she ever brought in. Blew through her own inheritance before Sophie was even born. Ever the struggling actress, she made her way with bit parts in commercials and an occasional soap opera. Rarely would she stoop to waitressing.

Any nonsense like that stopped when Sophie came into the picture. More importantly, when her income came into the picture. Well, what little of her income was available due to clever planning on her mother's part.

Unlike her aunt, Sophie made sure her inheritance stretched to pay for college, grad school, and left enough to give her a good start at life after. After watching her aunt, she was extraordinarily motivated to make it last. She wanted to buy a house one day, vacations with the family she hoped to have, never worry about living paycheck to paycheck.

Clearly, Asher had more trouble talking about his decisions than hers. According to Pippa, he was planning to join Paul at the family hardware store. But he'd just gotten home and needed time to settle in. She understood that more than she could say.

From what she heard about him from Pippa, he was an overconfident thrill-seeking rogue that tended to leap before he looked. As quick to jump in the sack as he was to dive out of a plane. Seeing his brutal pace on his run, then his tranquil moment watching the sunrise, she could see a glimpse of what he had been, followed by the serenity that he valued now.

Later that evening, stretching every aching limb in her body, Sophie took up half the booth at her new favorite restaurant. "I'm ordering everything on the menu. Who knew wedding errands were so exhausting? Especially the dang dress fitting? And I didn't even have to try anything on."

Perusing the menu, Pippa nodded blankly. "Agreed. I suddenly see why women go on a crazy diet beforehand. That was a close one when she almost couldn't get the zipper up, and I didn't gain a pound." Pouting pitifully, she held the menu closer to her face. "I can't even read the menu, and it's written in gigantic Times New Roman font."

An adorable, sunny server, maybe twenty-one at best, dressed in black jeans and a black polo shirt with a black apron, glided over to take their orders. "You ladies look like you could use a drink."

Sophie wanted to argue, but Jillian, as her nametag read, had a point. "God, yes. I'll have a glass of your house white."

From across the booth, Denise and Pippa added an order of the same. Denise's phone chirped like friendly little birds tweeting in her purse. Reading the message, she nabbed Jillian before she left the table. "Wait, add an IPA to that. My son will be here in a few minutes."

Feigning a smile Sophie knew to be fake, Pippa nodded. "I'm glad Asher's getting out. He didn't want to have to fend for himself tonight, huh?"

Rolling her eyes, Denise sat up in the booth and gulped half her water in one sitting. "I think he's more afraid of dinner alone with your father." Denise ignored the forced pleasantries. She knew her children and their headbutting well enough by now.

Sophie, however, wasn't comfortable with the rivalry. With no siblings of her own, nor any cousins, uncles, grandparents, or even a mom or dad anymore... just the one horrible aunt, she really didn't comprehend the stubbornness. It was hard to see why Pippa couldn't just suck it up and make amends with her brother. Or why Asher would go out of his way to avoid his father. Regardless, she didn't say anything. She supposed one had to have family to understand.

Sitting quietly, engrossed in the menu, Sophie kept silent. Macaroni and cheese or fish and chips? Even a cheeseburger sounded good right now. Hell no on the salad; as much as she loved a spring mix with fresh fruit, she needed carbs and grease today.

Before long, Asher strolled up to the table looking outrageously sexy, as usual. He'd clearly just showered after a day working on his truck; his hair still damp, crisp white t-shirt clinging to his very nicely sculpted chest and broad shoulders, with low slung faded, but clean, jeans and pristine black running shoes. Sophie tried not to sigh, but he was a freaking work of art.

Pippa hadn't been wrong in preventing their meeting, that was for sure. How her best friend hadn't noticed the blazing hot chemistry already, she'd never understand. Although, with the incredible hyperfocus Pippa had, often to excess, she may not notice anything but the wedding for the next few weeks. When studying for her GREs, she hadn't even noticed Sophie had chopped off her hair into a regrettable pixie. She envied women that could pull off a short, spunky do.

"You ladies look wiped out. Dresses chasing and attacking you all afternoon?" Flashing an amused smirk at the heavy-lidded table of women, he slid in the empty seat next to Sophie. Under normal circumstances, she might have scooted to the far end of the booth to make room. Like a moth to the flame, she couldn't seem to move away from him.

Jillian appeared with drinks a moment later. "Alright, drinks plus some more water for the table. What are we hungry for this evening?"

Swimming in chaos, the words on the menu made no sense to Sophie's exhausted eyes. "I need comfort food," she pouted.

Quite helpfully, Jillian took charge. "Macaroni and cheese with an added layer of cheddar and tomatoes."

Lightbulb shining over her head, Sophie added, "Brilliant. Plus jalapenos. Lots of them."

"You got it." Jillian made the rest of the rounds before walking away with a swing in her hips. Sophie envied that sort of energy right now.

Asher nudged her with his knee. "Jalapenos on macaroni? That sounds just plain weird." Rather than pulling away after the friendly nudge, his knee stayed, their legs melting and fusing together.

Taking a slow sip of her wine, Sophie licked away a stray drip from her upper lip and looked up to find his eyes on her mouth. Maybe she ran her tongue over the crease of her lips deliberately, knowing he was watching, or maybe not. It couldn't be helped. Turning slightly, the distance between them closing as a result of the motion, she flashed him a sly grin. "Jalapenos make everything better. Adds a little heat."

His eyes managed to leave her lips and reach her eyes, but he was no less flirty, the corner of his mouth turned up mischievously. "What about on ice cream? Apple pie?"

"Amazing combination." Briefly, she allowed her gaze to get lost in his warm, whiskey eyes. With a flipflop in her chest, her heart took a moment to remember how to beat, as if it had been getting it wrong all these years.

A timely interruption from Pippa brought her back to the moment. "Sophie adds spice wherever possible. I'm actually not sure she willingly puts anything in her mouth that doesn't set her on fire."

Choking on his poorly timed sip of beer, Asher caught his breath and muttered a few expletives under his breath. Sophie couldn't hide the blush at the visual, biting her lip to keep from saying anything. Quickly changing the subject, Asher managed to speak without coughing. "Did your dress fit okay?"

Good subject change. Pippa beamed, ready to talk wedding again. Sophie didn't know how she did it; she was weddinged out. "Just barely. I'm having them adjust the bust a little, add some lace to the—"

"Okay, going to stop you there. I'm thrilled for you, but descriptions of lace are a bit beyond my pay grade." Asher looked befuddled as the topic turned to lace. Sophie flashed to Mr. Bennet of Pride and Prejudice and his rather disgusted thoughts on lace conversations. She held back the giggle, thinking he wasn't likely to appreciate the reference. Later, Pippa might enjoy it.

Asher, uninterested as he was, managed to show support for his sister. Despite their avoidance of each other, they really seemed to get along well. Teasing and referencing good times from their past, they clearly had a happy history. It hadn't been all tense, and they had a number of mutual friends, male and female, over the years. Like Lincoln.

Denise was a hoot. Sophie had been so young when her mom died, so she hadn't realized moms weren't just parental units. She'd always adored Denise, but it was good to see her joking around with her children. "Pippa, stop worrying, your butt looked great in the dress."

"That's not what I meant. I like my butt. I just mean that before she removed that extra strip of lace, it almost made me look like I was wearing a bustle or something." Oh boy, Pippa was getting downright giggly. And after only one glass of wine.

Quite timely, Jillian brought around their entrees. Piping hot, Sophie's bowl of cheesy, spicy goodness made her mouth water. As requested, it was almost more cheese and tomato and jalapeno than pasta.

Before she could taste the melty, gooey goodness, Asher's fork dove in and scooped up a massive bite with a little of everything on it. "Wow, that's amazing. Ouch." Gulping the last of his beer, he tried to cool his mouth.

Snagging a cluster of fries off his plate, Sophie dipped in the special sauce and shoved the bite in her mouth. He flashed her a teasing accusatory glare, but spun his plate so she had easier access to the fries. Pippa and Denise were lost in their respective entrees, fortunately not noticing the easy camaraderie that was developing across the table.

After devouring the entire bowl, with Asher's help, Sophie groaned with a full belly. Leaning back in the booth, Sophie extended her legs, nudging Pippa's out of the way so there was room for her. "I'm so full. Maybe I should have ordered that salad."

Asher shook his head. "Nah. That was fantastic. Mom, you want to make that sometime?" He leaned back in the booth next to Sophie, the back of his hand grazing hers out of sight under the table.

The connection was light but shockingly arousing. She should pull her hand away, but the contact was like an unbreakable conduit joining her practicality and her fantasy world. It couldn't possibly be intentional.

With still a feather-light touch, he swept his index finger across her knuckles in a silent and inviting, *Hello*.

Offering her credit card to Jillian before the bill even arrived, Denise nodded. "Sure thing. But I'll have to put some of those jalapenos on the side or your dad will have to chase it with a whole bottle of Tums."

"I can pay for mine, Denise. You don't have to–" Sophie hated others covering any expenses for her. Freeloading, even if happily offered, was a painful reminder of her aunt.

Denise winked at her. "I wanted to. It's because you argue that I want to treat now and again."

After all was paid up, the four meandered out to the parking lot. "Hope you don't mind, Mom, but I borrowed your car. Truck still wouldn't start today."

Denise nodded. "That's just fine. I was thinking of bringing my box of leftovers to your dad anyway, so why don't you hop in with the girls and I'll take my car. He just texted me; he'll be working late tonight. Inventory tomorrow and their early counts aren't adding up."

Sophie didn't quite know Asher well enough to read his expression, but he was clearly not impressed. His expression turned grim in uneasy acceptance. He handed his mother her keys and climbed in the backseat of Sophie's CR-V.

As soon as the engine started and they were moving, Pippa immediately started back in on wedding talk. Surprisingly, she'd made it through a good part of dinner without talking about it. Understandable; it was a big deal and she'd had too much to worry about with exams, graduating on time, job interviews. She hadn't been able to focus on the wedding much before now.

"I can't wait to see us all in our formalwear. The bridesmaid dresses with their old-fashioned silk will complement the old-fashioned lace of mine so well." Pippa babbled a mile a minute, overjoyed by the day's accomplishments and the next steps on her calendar.

Rolling her eyes adoringly, Sophie glanced in the rearview mirror. Asher held a similar expression, fond of his sister but not at all on her same page. Sophie savored in the stolen glance at him, his chiseled features softened with love and amusement. Until his eyes met Sophie's in the mirror.

Briefly, they shared a silly smile and eyebrow raise over Pippa's animated descriptions of her vision. Sophie felt a bubble of heat forming low in her belly as his gaze locked with hers. Focusing on the road, Sophie couldn't help but glance back again a few moments later. Big mistake.

Taking advantage of her concentration elsewhere, Asher had been watching her. His expression was no longer jovial. Something darker, penetrating, hungry. Forcing breath in and out, Sophie had to remind herself how to get home.

Chapter Five

T-Minus 12 Days

Asher doubled his normal run this morning. After yet another night of fucking erotic dreams, he awoke writhing and imagining Sophie doing some dirty, possibly illegal deeds with his body. Hopefully some extra distance on his run this morning would tame that raging erection that just wouldn't quit.

Every morning since she'd arrived, he'd passed Sophie on the trail, then quietly sipped coffee with her while watching the sunrise. Again, he passed her this morning as they ran the trail in their normal opposite directions. A glutton for punishment, he ensured he timed it right to pass her on the run every day. She ran like Wonder Woman, agile and determined.

He was starting to get hooked on their morning routine. She didn't push like his family. Instead, she was content to sit quietly with him and enjoy the moment.

Sometimes they'd make casual conversation. Comments on Pippa's wedding plans. About the weather. How that last hill on the trail to return to the house was downright murder. She was easy to talk to. Never made him feel judged or foolish. Easy to look at, too.

He'd left early in the hopes that the extra distance wouldn't make him miss sunrise. Normally, he was running to escape the damn demons that haunted him each night. Not the last few nights; those dreams were painful in a very different, very pleasant way.

The nightmares really weren't as bad lately. He slept well most of the time, but now and again, one would wake him and leave him sobbing. Getting back to sleep after one of those was damn near impossible. Thoughts of Sophie were a welcome diversion.

Wiped out, about gasping for breath, he slipped off his running shoes and padded across the house in his socks. Huh, maybe she was already done with her run, as they hadn't passed on the trail. She wasn't on the patio yet, nor was she in the kitchen. Perfect; he hadn't missed her. *Sunrise*, it was sunrise he got up for every morning, *not Sophie*.

The house was still dim, save for the kitchen and stairwell nightlights to light his way. The predawn gray glow was starting to morph into a deep orange that saved him from a bruised knee as he nearly crashed into the table at the top of the stairs.

Shutting himself in his bedroom, he flicked on the excessively bright overhead light and peeled off his running shorts. Studying his shoes, he scowled. Damn, these were wearing out already. He may not invest much in his wardrobe, but good running shoes were critical. Wear something uncomfortable or broken, and he was off his feet for a week or more.

Rushing so he could catch Sophie *and* the sunrise, he opened the lever door to the bathroom and realized his mistake almost immediately. She wasn't downstairs or outside or still running because she was in the shower. Getting out, actually.

Sophie stepped out of the shower, her skin pinked from the heat, her wet body slick and toned. He instantly went rock hard. The blood all rushing south, he stood like a moron, his feet glued in place.

"Asher." She looked as shocked and sounded as breathless as he felt.

Both stood awkwardly in place, staring at each other's naked, wet body. He tried not to stare. Well, maybe not. The opportunity was too good to pass up.

She was so fit, but those breasts were so pert and would be a perfect handful. Her confused, lush lower lip was red from the steamy shower, just waiting to be sucked on.

Stop it. Not going there.

Although, she looked equally pleased with what she saw. Until her eyes landed on his rock-hard erection. The corner of her mouth quirked up in amusement. Feeling suddenly shy, he tried to cover himself. No towels on the shelf, he looked like a moron with his hands covering his raging hard-on.

"I'm so sorry." He slowly started to back out of the room.

"Not to worry, my fault. I thought I locked it." She searched the empty shelf for a towel, making do with the hand towel next to the sink. What was she planning to cover with it?

Trying to be helpful, to distract himself, and maybe stay an extra few seconds to enjoy the view, he nodded towards the switches on the wall. "It's, uh, there's a button to lock both doors."

Not covering, just drying. She was a cruel, mean-spirited, outrageously sexy woman. Did she have to linger, caressing each breast with the towel as she dried it? Run the towel leisurely down each long leg? She pretended to pay attention to his instructions, glancing at the switches he'd pointed to.

Trying to maintain a shred of modesty, he kept one hand over the goods, well, as effectively as he could, as there was a fine line between covering a full hard on and just plain holding it. Regardless, he showed her the locking mechanism with his free hand. Not that she was shy in the least, apparently, not bothering to hide anything with the hand towel.

"See, there's one button to lock just your door, but this other button locks both electronically."

She smiled sheepishly. Who knew sheepish was so damn sexy? Well, it was on her anyway.

"I'll just leave you to finish up." He slowly backed out of the bathroom.

"I'll be just a moment. By the way, there aren't any towels." She winked at him as he closed the door.

Keeping his hands off of her was going to be damn near impossible. He was already having a hard enough time. *Dammit, don't say hard.*

He was having a *difficult* enough time before but didn't see her more than their morning routine, and then again at dinner with his family, so it was all aboveboard. Otherwise, he spent most of his time in the garage just avoiding her, so he didn't get too close.

Now, her lithe, naked body was going to take up permanent residence in his head. He didn't know many accountants, but doubted many others looked quite like she did. Or reacted so nonchalantly in a situation that totally floored him, and he didn't blush easily.

Sophie's heart was about to beat right out of her chest. The thundering was downright deafening. She'd about lost it, especially when she'd seen he was rock hard. Just looking at her? Kinda flattering really.

Surely, she should be horrified. But she just couldn't make herself *not* replay the moment over and over in her head. It hadn't been easy to stay so calm; she had to build a spreadsheet in her mind and try to solve the national deficit to keep her mind off of his spectacular body. He was not just built, he was... built. Damn, she was overheating just thinking about it.

She'd seriously dated a few times. Had been intimate with a number of no-commitment partners in her brief wild period. None had made her feel anything even close to what she'd felt just now.

The way he looked at her. No one had ever looked at her so lustfully. Had made her feel so desired.

Cracking open the door to his bedroom, she let him know she was done and dashed into her room before he could see her bare ass as she fled the bathroom. Typical, no towels, today of all days.

Not a problem, Sophie would jump in and move things along. Never wanting to wear out her welcome, Sophie always helped with chores. And she liked staying busy.

Throwing on a sundress as bright and breezy as her mood, she floated down the stairs. Her attitude was unbeatably light this morning. Despite consciously knowing she should be feeling guilty for her very dirty thoughts, she couldn't help but feel she was floating on a white puffy cloud of imagination.

Pouring two cups of coffee, she brought Asher's cup outside and set it on his chair next to hers. Sunrise was still a few minutes out. Hopefully he wouldn't dawdle and miss it. Although, after his reaction to her a few moments ago, she'd know why he was delayed in the shower.

He didn't disappoint. She was almost afraid he'd avoid her now that they both had each other's wet, naked bodies permanently tattooed in their memories. Dressed in tan cargo shorts and a snug t-shirt with NAVY written across it, he joined her directly outside and picked up his coffee as he slid into his chair just in time.

Taking a sip of the hot coffee, he broke the silence before it became awkward. "So. That was interesting."

Coffee cup hovering at her lips, she poorly hid her almost-maybe-embarrassed grin and licked her lips before taking a sip. "*Interesting*. Good word for it."

"Nice body. By the way." He avoided eye contact, instead staring ahead at the impending sunrise. His cheeks were tight, fighting the corners of his mouth turning up in amusement.

"Thanks, I work out. And ditto." Might as well be honest. She usually didn't get to be honest in relationships. *That's okay, I like pepperoni on my pizza... Your mother didn't hurt my feelings at all... Of course I orgasmed, you're a stallion.*

Not that this was a relationship. It wasn't. Couldn't be. If for no other reason, and there must be good reasons, Pippa would kill them both. She couldn't do that to her best friend.

"I like your tattoo, what's it of?" Amused grin gone, he looked like he actually was interested. Few had cared before, more aroused by its location.

Even fewer actually got to see her tattoo. Sophie blushed. Dumb idea for when she has children someday, but she hadn't been thinking of that when she requested it placed on her right low abdomen just above her hairline. It could be seen if she wore a skimpy bikini, but otherwise it was her little secret. Which was part of why she'd chosen the location.

"It's a Scandinavian compass. I went a little nuts when I turned eighteen and lived on my own. Since my mom died, I've never really had a home. Somewhere in my youthful logic, I figured it might help me to find my way home one day, guiding my choices along the way, as the myth behind it tells. Besides, it looked good with the belly button ring I had around the same time."

"It must be working. You seem pretty set on the whole home and direction part of life." He sipped his coffee slowly, watching the sky in the distance. Not pushing, but supporting. "Why did you get rid of the belly button ring? Bet you looked fucking hot in it."

She grinned, enjoying his compliments. As the proper accountant she'd become, her last few boyfriends would never have used phrases like *fucking hot* to describe her. More like, *lovely.*

Lovely was nice to hear. But there was nothing like having a *fucking hot* Navy SEAL be unable to describe her attractiveness without expletives. And, for him to get a spontaneous erection just looking at her naked body.

"How did you get out of the military without any tattoos?" None that she'd seen, anyway. And she'd seen more than she'd bargained for.

"Can't make up my mind. Everything seems too trite or fleeting or excessive. Maybe someday. Once I figure out what I want." He was very matter of fact. Didn't seem bothered by his indecision. Or he was accepting of it anyway.

"Makes sense."

They sat in silence again. Not awkwardly, more of an understanding sort of quiet.

"Why accounting?" He glanced her way, not seeming to care that he was missing the moment the sun was coming over the mountains. His expression was curious, genuine.

"It may sound boring, but I like numbers. Making sense of a budget, making it last."

"It doesn't sound boring. It sounds like it makes you happy." He looked back to the sunrise, but it was too late, the sun was too bright to look at.

He didn't seem to notice he'd missed anything, glancing back to her. Answering her question before she had a chance to ask, he shared a bit of himself with her... the gooey center, not the drool-worthy outside this time. "Everyone thinks I joined because I needed the adrenaline rush. They're not entirely wrong, but I knew I was going to end up high on something, get some girl pregnant, or just plain wasting my life away doing nothing relevant. Honestly, despite my stupidity, I wasn't a complete moron. I never did any heavy drugs. I never committed any felonies, nor have I been arrested. A few speeding tickets over the years, but nothing major. And, I have never *not* used a condom, contracted any STDs, or gotten anyone pregnant."

He was serious. Must have scared himself with his prior juvenile path of self-destruction.

"They don't let just anyone be a SEAL."

He laughed at that, the wood of his chair squeaking under his weight as he turned in his chair to face her, his knee resting against the arm of the chair. "No, they don't."

"I don't think Pippa has had a rebellious day in her life. Where did you get your roguish streak?" She shifted towards him as well, their bodies only separated by the arms of their chairs.

Shrugging, he contemplated for a moment. "I didn't want to work at Sutherland's Hardware Store, so I did just about everything I could come up with to convince Dad it wasn't for me. When drugs and sex didn't work, I went to college. When that didn't work, I joined the Navy and bought myself eight more years."

Stretching his legs in front of him before resting his arms behind his head and melting into the chair, he sighed before continuing. "I didn't have a clue what I wanted out of life; I just knew it wasn't the same things he wanted for me. Pippa wasn't interested either. She got out of it by expressing her interest in being a sweet little elementary school teacher, which, we all know Pippa, and you don't question her plans."

"None of your impressive, very respectable endeavors seemed to appease him?" Sophie curled up as unconsciously close to him as she could get without actually touching him, or that would cross a line that shouldn't be crossed.

"It was easier to have a little fun and let him cringe at the fallout of my dastardly deeds." Finally rising from his chair, he held out a hand. Sophie let him help her out of the deep chair.

Standing toe to toe, she realized just how much taller he was. And she wasn't short. "And now he expects you to step up?"

"Even if I wanted to, I'm still working on fixing me after the shit that I went through." Leaning down, he paused before their lips met, then let his lips brush across hers before pulling away. Yearning stirred low in her belly, burning from deeper in her core.

Releasing her hands, he added, "Pippa would kill me if I even hinted that I was interested in you." He stepped backwards, rubbing the back of his neck. "Just want you to know. I'm more than interested, but I can't."

Sophie picked up her coffee cup from the arm of the chair. She walked past Asher and stopped at the sliding glass door. Turning back, she smiled sorrowfully. "Ditto."

Lincoln was over for dinner and he and Pippa glowed talking about their day. They had spent hours planning the table layout, centerpieces, music playlist, other odds and ends Sophie never knew were a thing.

Sophie was overwhelmed by the whole thing. Who knew even the color of tablecloth was such an ordeal? She just might have to elope.

After dinner, everyone pitched in with dishes so they were done in a flash. Even Asher. She'd created a monster; a helpful one. Judging by his pink-hued socks, he was even trying his hand at laundry. Apparently, he'd hired it done while living alone, not having had a machine in his apartment.

After dinner, Lincoln said his farewells and headed back to his and Grady's place. While the others puttered for the evening, Pippa invited Sophie to join her on the front deck. Just the two of them, perfect. Maybe she could lay some groundwork. They sat in cushioned chairs around the propane fireplace and settled in around the fire to relax.

Pippa sighed, looking out at the glow of the setting sun creating a soft luminosity on the mountains. "Am I too neurotic?"

Trap! Don't go walking into that. Why couldn't she have studied psychology? "In what way do you feel neurotic?"

Eyes filling quickly with unshed tears that were rapidly threatening to spill over, the dam ready to burst at the slightest tremor, Pippa pouted, "With all of the wedding business. I don't give a crap if I carry a two-hundred-dollar bouquet of white lilacs and roses. I'm good with a handful of daisies."

"It's easy to get caught up. There are just too many expectations for weddings. And big price tags." She hoped she was helping rather than making it worse. Holding her breath as she anticipated Pippa's potentially explosive response, she pulled her legs in and reclined in the cushy chair.

"Maybe I should just call the whole thing off and get hitched at the courthouse. With a small party here after." Flood level met but not quite exceeded, a single tear trickled down her cheek.

"Do you trust me?" She could talk her out of this, she had to. That's what friends were for, right? Talking each other out of a crisis? Wasn't it an official maid of honor duty?

"Of course." Pippa looked her in the eye as if it was the dumbest question she could ever ask.

"I have to ask, how far is the wedding over budget?"

Pippa sniffled and swallowed the impending sob. With a small but persistent nod, unable to speak lest the dam burst, she hinted the answer was significant.

"Want me to run the numbers?"

Again, she nodded pitifully. Whispering through a wet voice, Pippa said, "Thank you."

In the minutes it took for Sophie to grab her laptop and poor a glass of wine for each of them, she found Pippa already looking frazzled, her normally tame hair wild and frizzy. Surrounded by loose sheets of paper, hair knotted and standing on end, Pippa sat at the dining room table, poorly organizing the receipts and invoices she had for Sophie to review.

Recognizing a financial emergency when she saw one, she rolled up her imaginary sleeves and took charge. "Let's get started. We can fix this."

Handing her friend the wine, Sophie nudged Pippa out of the way and started to organize the scattered papers. She let a soft hum pass her lips now and again, a subtle smile crossing her lips as she worked. Not intentional, but she knew it let Pippa know all was going to be okay, so she didn't try to prevent her oddities.

"You can go take a break while I work on this. Go for a swim or go relax on the patio." Sophie didn't mind her friend's hovering but wanted to give her a break. She clearly needed it.

Pippa shook her head, too tense to even consider a break. "You and Asher are the only freaks I know that exercise for relaxation."

Eyes on the spreadsheet she was efficiently building, Sophie sighed. "Don't knock it 'til you try it."

Relaxing a bit, Pippa sat back in her chair and sipped her drink while Sophie sifted through stacks of receipts and invoices. It reminded her of all the times they'd sat elbow-to-elbow at their dining room table just like this, doing homework instead.

"It seems like you and Asher have been making friends."

Shit. "I guess so."

Smoothing her crazy stress-hair, Pippa was starting to visibly relax. "I'm glad. He needs friends. I don't think he's socialized at all since he got back."

As much as she hated the line of conversation for fear of revealing something, she was glad Pippa was no longer quite so frantic. "Have you told him you're worried he's not getting out much?" Good thing Sophie could multitask with the best of them.

Pippa scowled and pulled her hair into a messy ponytail. "He wouldn't want to hear that from me. Maybe Lincoln or Grady. Or you."

"Why not his own sister? It's clear he values your opinion." She glanced over at Pippa's surprised reaction, then returned her eyes to the screen. Pippa really had no idea how much her brother desired her good opinion.

"He's always done his own thing. I'm actually shocked he is considering working at Sutherland's." Rolling the stress out of her shoulders, Pippa sipped her wine.

"Why don't you have a talk with him? Tell him you worry about him. He may seem tough, but everyone wants to know someone cares about them." Sophie had always longed for a sibling. Thus, she didn't understand why they couldn't just talk it out; why they didn't realize how lucky they were to have each other.

Downing the last of her wine in a hasty gulp, Pippa stood and restlessly started to tidy the kitchen that had already been cleaned after dinner. "I should. We'll see. It's complicated; he's never exactly sought my advice, or heeded it when it was given."

Creating a few summary tables, totals, Sophie had a completed budget analysis, ready for review. It had only taken two hours of distracting her friend to power through. If only she'd offered sooner. If she'd realized it was such an issue, she could have saved Pippa a lot of worry. "Okay, I found some of your issues."

"Already? I've been at it all week." Pippa set down the pan she had found to dry and dove next to Sophie at the table. She studied the spreadsheet blankly.

Poor thing was too overwhelmed to even make sense of it. She pointed out where costs were possibly higher than necessary. "I'm not any expert in what things should cost for a wedding, but I see room for improvement. I agree, daisies would be much more practical, and just as pretty. The forecast calls for nice weather, so we shouldn't need the propane heaters. And the covered space at the venue is big enough for most everyone, so you won't need this big of a tent, if at all."

Pippa responded really well. A little organization went a long way. Reviewing the numbers line by line, she could see some of the unnecessary expenses and how everything added up so quickly. "I really would rather carry daisies. And we don't need anything special in the aisles. Heck, Christmas lights would be cheaper than the paper lanterns I was looking at."

"To be sure. Of course, let's not lose money on anything you have already purchased or cannot return. Or anything that you've paid a substantial down payment for." Sophie turned to Pippa to gauge her reaction. She was taking it really well.

Sighing a deep, relieving breath, Pippa nodded. "We should be good on that. I can call the caterer too and ask her where we can cut last minute corners without losing quality."

"See? You're good at this." Sophie nudged her friend playfully.

"Thanks. I owe you bigtime."

Sophie knew exactly when she was going to call in this favor but feared the price for what she had in mind was much, much steeper.

Chapter Six

T-Minus 11 Days

R ising from the table she'd commandeered as her temporary desk, Sophie stretched her aching neck and shoulders as wide as her limbs would extend. Although it had been concise yet informative to begin with, Sophie wanted her resumé perfect before she met with Jane. Jane was a bundle of pure sweetness in a tiny package topped with a gray mop of hair. Energetic, brainy, downright likeable.

Still, Sophie didn't want to be a pity hire. Not that Jane would hire her out of pity. She was generous, but she wasn't the type to hire her just to be nice. Foothills Accounting was a successful local business, which wasn't by coincidence. Jane was as shrewd as she was kind.

Argh. Nails getting increasingly short, Sophie tore her fingers from her mouth and paced the dining room. She was going to drive herself nuts. This was the perfect job in the cutest little town where she already had friends.

Family, really. At least the closest thing she'd known to family in fifteen years. Blowing this would mean she'd have to start over.

Stop fretting. Her resumé looked awesome. That internship with Meckel and Jones had been a great learning experience. With the knowledge she had gained, she could comfortably manage the typical tax prep, as well as personal and small business accounting at Foothills Accounting and offer more extensive budget financing for local businesses as a new service, if Jane was agreeable.

Pink Floyd's *Money* blasted from her phone. Dammit, not now. Not ever, really.

"Hello, Yvette." Even the name grated on her nerves. She was not allowed to call her Aunt. Nor was she to ever even hint to anyone that Yvette was a totally made-up name. Born Bernadette, she'd found Yvette suited her better as a stage name.

"Sophie, dear. How have you been? You must be done with school by now." Voice dripping with honey, she was all politeness.

Cringing, Sophie made a concerted effort to not bite her nails through the call. Yvette had hated the little habit, so of course Sophie had done it as often as possible in front of her in her own silent protest. Until, of course, Yvette started taking them out for manicures together, talking nonstop while draining their rationed funds. "Yes. Did that graduation gift you promised finally get returned undeliverable?" Blank pause. "Because you forgot to put postage on it? Remember? That's what you told me two weeks ago."

She hadn't believed the story then, and certainly didn't believe now that Yvette had even considered sending her a graduation gift. However, she did enjoy calling her on her fibs and embellishments wherever possible. In the nicest possible way.

"Of course. It must be lost in the mail system. Anyway." She giggled in a lilting falsetto she'd rehearsed for hours on end when Sophie was fourteen and had discovered having friends over was never going to work. "Your twenty-seventh birthday is what, next week?" Greed oozed like slimy green ectoplasm, clogging the airwaves between them.

"Gosh, is that coming up so soon? I'd forgotten." The trust fund from her mother and grandparents would be fully in her control on her twenty-seventh birthday.

Colette, her mother, had known she would get stuck with her only living relative, money-grubbing Yvette. Having lived just the two of them since her last grandparent had passed away the year before Colette, there hadn't been anyone else. It was Yvette or foster care. Sophie didn't envy that her mother had been forced to make such a tough decision for her young daughter.

Shrill laughter pierced through the line. More of her natural laugh than the other, it was somehow more grating and ingenuine. "How silly of me. I was so afraid I'd missed sending your birthday present. Can you send me your address so I can mail you a present?"

Very fishy. She'd never sent her a present before, despite many fictitious tales of the extravagant gifts she'd sent in the past that never seemed to pass post office muster. Why would she start now? Buttering Sophie up wasn't likely to entice her to share her fortune. "I actually don't know my address offhand, and it's temporary anyway."

"You are staying with Pippa's family then? Foothills, right?" Uh-oh.

Sighing, sinking into the nearest chair, Sophie couldn't find the energy to invent a decent story to buy her more time. "For now."

"I know you aren't working yet, but if you have anything set aside from the allowance your dear mother left to support us, her only remaining family... I have an audition coming up for a Netflix pilot. My landlord is breathing down my neck for rent, but I won't have it for another few weeks." Sophie was almost surprised Yvette didn't get more roles. She was an awfully talented actress when it came to asking for money.

Dreaming of refusing, as she so desperately wanted to, she feared the repercussions if she did. Now and again, she actually pulled off a decent rejection. Learning from her aunt, she would spin a tall tale that at least bought her some time. However, she'd learned that it never worked out in her favor, as delays led to devious repercussions.

Unintelligible, deafening sobs lanced through the phone, jarring the thin membrane of Sophie's eardrum. "My landlord. He'll evict me if I don't come up with the funds, or else he'll... I don't even want to say it."

And Sophie didn't want her to say it either.

"He's threatened to get his money's worth, 'one way or another.' Oh Sophie, I'm so scared."

Oh boy. This was even better than last time. Yvette wasn't stupid. She didn't ask every month, only when Sophie had had just enough time to recover from the berating herself for sending money the last time.

Time to end it. End the manipulation. Break off all ties. Her knuckles paled to a ghostly white as she clutched the phone, desperately trying to find the courage to stand up for herself. Chewed to the nub, her poor fingertips of her non-phone hand were raw.

"Your dear mother, my sister, was such a generous soul, Sophie. You're just like her. Generous, kind. Always taking pity on your dear Auntie Yvette. If you sent enough for rent and a minor procedure, like Botox, I'll nail the pilot and will be able to start sending you money. Just like I always wanted." Sophie may not be allowed to call her Aunt, but Yvette sure liked adding it when it benefited her.

Last time she'd landed a decent part, a minor, but recurrent, role as a hooker on an HBO drama, she hadn't asked for money for a year. A Netflix series would set her up nicely, leaving Sophie undisturbed when her birthday came around. "Fine. I'll send it to your PayPal account."

Yvette's bubbling gratitude chafed against her ear. "You're such a dear. With that pretty face, maybe I could get you a part as an extra on the show? As my cousin?"

Clamping her jaw shut, she refused the offer and ended the call before she exploded. Dammit. Why couldn't she just refuse? It was never going to end. Even if Yvette got the role, it would always be one more thing.

Why couldn't she just leave her alone? This was how Sophie realized she had a knack for accounting. At the ripe age of fifteen, she discovered that she wouldn't eat dinner unless someone other than Yvette managed the bills. At that, food was still often scarce and minimally nutritive as Yvette was usually "dieting" for her next role.

When she found she actually enjoyed making sense of finances, she decided she wanted to help others with her skills. By the time she was sixteen, she had them on a very strict budget and did all the shopping, paid all the bills. It had only taken threatening Yvette that she would call CPS for her to agree to the negotiated budget.

"Everything okay?"

Sophie spun around in a fury at the sound before she remembered she was in a safe place. Telephone disconnected. Denise stood a few feet away, eyes heavy with concern.

"Yeah. Sort of. It's my aunt asking for money. Again."

Denise reminded her so much of her mother. Not in appearance. Denise was soft as a pillow and always available for a hug. Her own mother had been slender like she was, a champion triathlete herself, but was equally available for a hug.

"Sophie, dear. I'm so sorry. That woman is a real piece of work. Gave me the creeps on the HBO show." She added, although Sophie already knew it wasn't a Denise sort of show, "I checked it out after you mentioned it to me."

Mischief brewing in her honey eyes, Denise meant it. With her got-your-back attitude, topped with salt and pepper hair slicked back in a fiercely tight braid, Denise was a force to be reckoned with. A lot like Colette had been.

Not uptight or high-strung like Pippa. No, Pippa was her father through and through. My way or no way. Denise had the finesse to make others do what she wanted and be glad they did.

Why couldn't Sophie emulate either approach? Open a can of metaphorical whoop-ass on her aunt. Or somehow convince her she didn't *want* Sophie's money?

"I say no as often as I can, but she just keeps calling. Manipulates me with a sob story or a thinly veiled threat that she won't hesitate to act on." She managed to hold back tears, but barely. Moments like this made her miss her mother more than anything.

With a fighting sneer, Denise put on her angry eyes. "Next time, you hand the phone to me. I'd love to tell her a thing or two."

And that's where Asher got it. The take-no-prisoners, strike-first-and-ask-questions-later that he was known for. They even shared the warm, whiskey glow to their eyes.

Letting Denise pull her into a hug, her limbs went limp, and she sunk into the older woman's arms. "Thanks. For everything. You make me miss my mom. In a good way," she amended.

Emotion filtered through Denise's kind voice. "Now that is a woman I would like to have met." Pulling back, she gently tapped Sophie's nose with the knuckle of her finger. "For being raised by that witch through your adolescence, your mother must have been an amazing woman for you to have turned out as wonderful as you have."

Turning to head for the kitchen, Denise started to toss together a restorative lunch. Returning to the table, Sophie accepted that her resumé was as good as she could make it. Jane would take her or leave her, and she'd be okay.

Colette had been a truly amazing woman. A trust fund baby herself, she'd never acted the privileged debutante like her sister had. At age nineteen, she'd met Nate Jones and fallen head-over-heels in love. Within a few months, she was pregnant with Sophie.

Although Sophie hardly knew her father, she knew he was a decent sort of man. She remembered him reading to her, telling her exciting stories of his excursions in the army, about his growing up years in Oregon fishing and hunting and camping. Colette's parents hadn't exactly blessed the quick marriage initially, but they came around when Sophie was born and had been exactly the doting grandparents every kid should have.

By the age of twelve, Sophie had lost a mother, a father, and four grandparents. Nail-biting was one of many coping strategies she had adopted, some better, some worse than that.

As the daughter of a single mom, she'd learned self-reliance from an early age. It wasn't until she was left to Yvette's inattention that she learned the real meaning of responsibility. Yvette had blown through her own trust fund years prior, and always had her eyes on Sophie's. Once Sophie learned to balance the checking account, they could eat regular meals and didn't worry about eviction, but it had required sacrifice. Not for Yvette, of course.

After turning eighteen, within a few days of her high school graduation, she'd gone a little nuts. Subconsciously, she'd known she was trying to convince Yvette to leave her alone. Consciously, she'd known she needed to stretch her wings.

Reliable to a fault despite her boundary-pushing, she'd gone straight to UCLA after high school and earned decent grades. But she experimented a bit. Knew just how many beers it took to reach hangoverville. Learned it was an incredibly stupid idea to smoke weed before an exam. Tried out a number of partners, male and female both, until she better understood herself.

By junior year of college, she was done screwing around. Buckling down, she worked to graduate on time. Pippa had been one of the best things to happen to her. A family girl from a small town and likeably decent, she embodied the fun, girl-next-door sort that Sophie was at heart... but a bit more extreme.

They'd met at a highly anticipated basketball game. Set to be ranked well in March Madness, UCLA had been on fire that year. Sophie had needed a little break from cramming for exams and went to a big game with a miserably dull date. Pippa had made a similar mistake and was there with the guy's good friend. Hitting it off right away, the two chatted through the game and moved in together the next year.

Turning the key, he heard the slightest tease of the engine trying to wake. Poor, tired old truck had quit right about the time he got back from the mission that wiped out too many of his team. A record-breakingly horrific op.

What glowing luck, to have his truck die the day he got back. He couldn't bring back his friends in one piece, but dammit, the pickup was a piece of machinery. He'd managed to patch it up again and again, but the days it actually ran were becoming fewer and farther in between. His copy of the Chilton's repair manual he'd inherited with the old clunker was so worn he could hardly make out the words anymore. Even YouTube was out of ideas.

His therapist had asked if maybe it was time to let the truck go. Ha. The metaphor was painfully obvious; he wasn't dumb enough to miss the message. Nor was he giving up.

Laying on his back, he rolled under the chassis and stared blankly at the antiquated parts, looking for hints at what might be ailing the old rig. Kicked up by a warm gust of summer breeze, a mouthful of dust swept across his face, grit sticking in his teeth.

Vision obscured with thick dust, the explosion echoed again and again in his ears. He turned sharply, mid-stride, and sprinted back to the explosion, Zane close at his heels. Another blast knocked them both to the ground, dropping him to his hands and knees. Grabbing Zane in the dusty commotion, he pulled him into the cover of the alley. Incensed, Zane tried to pull away to run into the fire after the others.

"They're gone. We need to get out of here," he'd shouted over the ringing of his ears.

"Not all; they can't be." Zane's voice was as hollow as his own, his eyes crazed with uncertainty. Gritty debris and ash caked onto to the thick sweat on his face.

Fuck. They couldn't just leave them.

Taking aim, they covered each other as they re-entered the street. Dead quiet, there was no sign of anyone left to defend against. Not that anyone could see through the pervasive airborne debris to shoot them anyway.

"Anyone there?" Pulling himself out from the crumbling doorway on his elbows, Jack hacked up whatever particles had lodged into his lungs. Sticky, bloody sputum clung to his chin.

Ignoring the possible danger, Zane was at their friend in an instant. Covering the pair, Asher remained vigilant, keeping his back to his friends and watching the street, the nearby buildings. It was too murky, zero fucking visibility.

Muted by the ringing in his ears and the echoes of broken concrete still breaking off of the rubble, he could just make out the crunching of boots approaching. Rotating his head at the sound, he faintly made out a wounded enemy rounding the corner, on his way to check for others, as they were.

Fearing his own end, the enemy didn't hesitate. Neither did Asher. He wasn't losing another friend today.

Silencing the scream that filled his chest, Asher whacked a loose part with the flat side of his wrench. Trembling, he slid out from under the truck. Wiping away the dust-coated sweat and tears from his face, he hopped back into the cab.

Turning the key again, he elicited a tired, but steady response. Shutting off the weak rumble of the engine, he dragged his own creaky joints out of the truck. The hood was still open, as it was so often these days. Standing in front of the cool motor, he checked the connections. He was almost there. Had already replaced half the damn parts, rebuilt what he could alone.

"Even your grandpa knew that truck wasn't going to live forever." His mom came out of nowhere, ice water and a sandwich in hand.

"What time is it?" He glanced around, remembering his phone was plugged into the stereo across the room. Silent now, his playlist must have run out. How long had he been lost in the flashback?

Shaking her head, she cleared some tools from the table and set down the lunch she'd prepared. "It's two o'clock."

No wonder his stomach hurt. Even small children were known to figure out that belly ache meant mealtime. "Thanks." He wiped his hands on the shop rag he'd remembered to keep handy this time.

Tearing into the sandwich, he about moaned at the gooey grilled cheese with its perfectly crispy outside and a heap of cheese and chipotle mayo oozing out the side. Studying the sandwich, he attempted to solve the mystery as he swallowed the huge bite. Was it really that good or was he this hungry? "This is brilliant. Why have you never made this before?"

Denise smiled proudly. "Sophie's favorite. She had a rough day, so I called Pippa to find out what I might be able to convince her to eat. I made a spare, realizing you hadn't eaten either."

He swallowed a mouthful of the cheesy goodness. Chuckling from deep in his belly at his mother as he downed the rest in a few massive bites, he teased, "Food doesn't solve everything."

Considering what she'd said, he worried after Sophie. She seemed to have everything figured out, so what could have spoiled her appetite? "What's up with Sophie?"

Steam blasting out of his mother's ears, he could see her getting fired up on Sophie's behalf. She'd already burrowed her way into the hearts of his sister and parents, and he suspected she was heading right for his, too. "Have you heard anything about her upbringing?"

He shook his head. His Sophie knowledge was pretty limited by design.

"Her dad was in the army, killed in action when she was no more than five. I'd love to have met her mother; she sounds like she was an incredible woman. So tragic though. Her mother died when Sophie was twelve." Denise leaned back against the workbench, ignoring the grease and oils that were deeply embedded in the woodwork around here.

Asher gulped down his water. "I had no idea. That's terrible. What happened to Sophie?"

Denise shrugged as she fought back the rage that boiled just under the surface. "Her Aunt Yvette, a chronically struggling actress in Los Angeles, took her in. Her parents and her grandparents set her up well. But her mother must have known what a greedy monster her aunt was, and arranged for a pretty stringent allowance from her trust fund. I don't know the details, but I do know that Yvette still calls her for money."

"She calls Sophie for money?" What kind of aunt asked her niece for money? If his stomach weren't so happy from the delicious lunch, it would be roiling on her behalf.

"Poor Sophie just got off the phone with her, manipulated into sending her more money." Denise stood tall again, stretching her neck and rolling her shoulders as if preparing for a knockout punch. Instead, she picked up his empty glass and plate. "If I could get my hands on her aunt... I'd show her a thing or two about human decency."

Fuming, Asher wasn't sure the term human decency was the wording he would have chosen. "Sophie doing okay?"

Denise nodded. "She'll be alright. She's a tough one. Anyway, thanks for listening to me vent. I almost had violent thoughts."

He chuckled and rose his hands in the air in feigned surrender. "Heaven forbid. If you're considering violence, everyone better flee. You've got a lot of pent-up aggression in there."

His mother rolled her eyes and motioned at him with the empty dishes. "You'd better watch yourself mister. You don't want to be in the way when I get angry."

A true pacifist, he couldn't picture her going Hulk-crazy. Might be fun, though. She was full of fire. Yet, she managed to be very effective without throwing punches.

Chapter Seven

Sophie needed a break. From everything. Yvette had ruled so much of her life. Faintly, she remembered the few times her own mother had taken Yvette's call when Sophie was a kid. Occasionally she'd sent money to keep her sister out of prostitution and life on the streets. Or that's what Sophie figured out much, much later.

Strolling out to the garage, hair on fire despite an hour of useless meditation, followed by therapeutic spreadsheet design, she decided to take a drive into town. Or something, anyway, to clear her mind.

She needed to get started with work. Soon. Maybe find a place to live. Keep herself occupied.

A familiar screech of mechanic tools rang out from the third garage bay. Asher's legs stuck out from under the truck. Silence. Another screech. Silence again.

In a flash, Asher appeared from under the truck and popped up to stand, distracted by his current automotive repair mission. From afar, still standing in the huge doorway of the open garage bay, Sophie watched. He hadn't noticed her yet. He hopped in the driver's seat and tried the engine.

Started right up with a rumble then a purr. A whoop of satisfaction echoed out of the truck cab. He revved the engine, noting it responding appropriately. Jumping out as quickly as he'd hopped in, Asher checked under the hood.

No squeals or rattles. Better than when he'd tried a few days ago when Sophie had left with Pippa and Denise for yet another round of wedding errands, followed by a lady's lunch. The grinding sound it made that day had been terrible. Sophie moved closer, not quite sure if she was heading to her car or to Asher.

Something tugged and pulled in her gut the moment he laid eyes on her, creating a gnawing, craving sensation like she hadn't eaten in days and his touch was the only food that could bring her back from the brink of starvation. His expression heated, her breath caught in response. He dropped the hood and stalked toward her like a predator moving in for the kill.

Stopping a few feet from her, he was careful not to get too close. Not that it cooled anything down. If anything, it made her tense in anticipation of the final strike.

Seeing she held her car keys and purse, the fading redness of her eyes from her self-pitying crying jag, his posture opened. "Where're you headed?"

"Nowhere, actually. I just need some fresh air." She looked back to the mountains, hearing them call her name.

"Want to hop in? I need to take her for a test drive." He gestured toward the smoothly running truck with a shrug and a smile.

Biting her lip, she nodded. "Sure." Finding herself suddenly the shy one, she climbed in as he held the door open for her with subtle finesse.

They were quite the pair today, she noted as he climbed in the driver's side. She wore a pink cotton sundress, her hair neatly straightened and styled in an effort to perk herself up. As usual, he wore a low-slung pair of jeans with a fitted, ragged t-shirt; this one had SEAL printed across it and had clearly seen better days, as the jersey fabric was faded with a few rips scattered around the stiff white letters.

Backing out of the garage, his hand rested on the seat behind her. He wasn't even touching her, wasn't even trying to make a move, and her skin prickled, longing for a physical connection. He shifted into drive and the truck rumbled down the driveway. Her shoulder suddenly felt cold at the loss of the almost-contact.

Turning up the hill, he tested the engine's muster up the hill, it's rumbling engine complaining, but cooperating.

"Don't you think we ought to stay within cell phone range in case the truck breaks down?" Despite the recent improvement in the truck's functionality, she had her doubts it would make it up the mountain roads. After all, this was the first she'd ever seen it leave the driveway.

Scoffing, Asher shook his head in feigned disbelief. "This baby will do fine. Besides, I brought my toolbox just in case. And I brought this great long, skinny arm that can reach into awkward places in the engine to retrieve things for me."

"That's a brilliant plan. Unless we need a tow."

Glancing over at her, he looked a little defensive with his jaw set firmly. "Hey, Grandpa bought this truck right off the lot in the early 1970's; over three hundred thousand useful miles on it. It's a worthy truck."

Sophie could hear the fondness for the rusted piece of machinery. "It's a classic; I'm not questioning that. You must be a decent mechanic to have kept it running all this time. Did you learn that from your grandpa?"

"Yeah," he answered wistfully, his head tilting and his eyes steady on the road.

"Denise or Paul's dad?" She'd met Denise's dad twice before he passed away. He was a jovial man with a rubrous complexion and a smattering of wiry gray hairs on the top of his head, but he hadn't quite seemed like he'd ever been the handy sort.

"Paul's. The second Sutherland of Sutherland's Hardware, but a much better grandpa and mechanic than shop owner." His tone was pure pride.

"You were close?"

Asher kept one hand on the shifter and the other loosely on the wheel as they crossed a long bridge over a rocky river, continuing to climb in altitude. "Yeah. Grandpa retired early, as my dad was more than ready to take over. Plus, Grandpa preferred to play. So, while Dad worked seventy-hour weeks—mind you, that he didn't have to work—Grandpa would come over and take me fishing, hiking, camping."

"Pippa was fond of him, too. He and your grandma. He passed away, what, five, six years ago?" The truck wound round the bends of the hillside as they gradually increased altitude.

"Yeah. I was deployed, deep cover op, and didn't find out for two months. He and grandma were on a cruise in Alaska. He got sick while they were there and died of pneumonia a few weeks later. Refused to admit it was more than a simple virus. Pissed Grandma off so much, she followed him to the grave a few months later. Stubborn ass." The words sounded harsh, but the tone was regretful, affectionate.

"I'm so sorry." Sophie didn't know how to respond. She'd lost so many, she ached to think of others going through that same pain.

Before reality sunk in too deeply and irrevocably, in the form of Yvette's disinterest and manipulation, she used to imagine what it would be like if she'd had a grandparent that could have taken her in when her mom died. Chocolate chip cookies after school, trips to the park or the movies, learning to sew, knit, fish, and camp. Life doesn't always work out the way it should.

He patted her knee and gave her leg a sympathetic squeeze before moving his hand back to downshift for the next turn. Slowing the truck, they pulled into an overgrown road Sophie wouldn't have otherwise noticed. Not seeming to care that not much was left of the road, Asher drove them over the grassy ruts, breaking branches of the shrubs and low hanging trees along the way.

"Are we allowed to be down here?"

"Not exactly. It's an old logging road, but it sold hands three or four times within a few months' time, years ago, so no one realized they never locked the gate. Those of us who noticed didn't exactly advertise it."

After a quarter mile of bucking and bumping in the springy old seats, they came to a small clearing with scattered stumps and patches of tall grass. No concerns about traffic, they parked in the middle of the path. Looking her up and down, taking in her attire, he hesitated. "It's a bit of walk; you okay in that?"

Sophie glanced at her outfit. The dress was one of her favorites, pretty but practical. She'd worn light tennis shoes with it. "All good. We should have brought a picnic."

They climbed out of the truck. Asher came around to meet her and led the way. "Didn't you just have lunch?"

"Yes. But now we're out in nature so I feel like I need to bring supplies." She grinned up at him. Hiking hadn't exactly been Yvette's thing, of course, but her mom had loved to hike and would always bring a backpack full of snacks, even for brief jaunts in the park.

"Hang on." Asher disappeared for a moment, returning with a branch of leaves and berries. He popped one of the orangey red berries in his mouth and handed her the tasty looking bundle.

"I didn't know raspberries grew wild around here." She took the offered branch and studied one of the berries.

"Salmonberries. They're everywhere around here this time of year. Try one."

Popping one in her mouth, she was surprised at the pleasant taste. A bit seedier and tarter than a raspberry, but very refreshing. "Thanks." She munched a few more as they walked.

Before long, they reached a babbling brook bathed in shade from the surrounding maples and alder. The place was a surprising oasis, something one might find in a fairyland. Linking his hand with hers, Asher led her over and under a few fallen trees until he found just the right one.

They stepped up onto a massive tree trunk that had fallen across the creek. Maybe a foot and a half wide, it was wide enough that she didn't have to worry much about watching her balance. The bark was already stripped off by time and weather, so she had no trouble walking across it. Asher stopped halfway across and sat down, his feet dangling over the side. Sophie sat next to him on the log, her feet facing upstream while his faced down, a few inches of space between them. They watched the stream pass below them, the surface of the water a good three feet beneath their shoes.

At first, they took in their surroundings, listening to the summer birds chattering away around them. Eventually, they commented about the scenery, the weather, growing into more personal topics. They visited comfortably until Sophie's cheeks hurt from smiling and chatting. Later, she couldn't have recalled what they talked about. Something, nothing, anything.

For someone his family didn't think talked much, he was surprisingly easy to visit with. Even more so out here than he was over their morning coffee. She didn't want to pry, but from some of the things he said, it was more than the distance and friendships that had widened the distance between he and Pippa.

Such polar opposites, Pippa and Asher may not have understood each other as kids, but there was hope for them to figure it out now. She didn't bring it up today; they were having too nice of a time. Knowing them both well, she could see they just needed to break down a few walls to be good friends again.

Paul was a good dad; he just didn't see Asher for who he was. Maybe never had. Although, it sounded like Asher hadn't made any effort to show him anything worth seeing, in his youth or lately. Which, Sophie regretted, was unfortunate, as she was getting to see so many of his good traits.

Rays of sunlight filtered through the leafy canopy above, dancing across the babbling creek below. A maple leaf floated downstream, under the log, then continued on its merry way. Sophie leaned her head on Asher's shoulder, more relaxed than she'd been in ages. He'd definitely picked the right spot for her to decompress.

"Hang on. Don't look as I try to stand up; there's no discreet way to do this in a dress." Swinging her legs up onto the log, Sophie tried to maintain her decency as she stood.

"No promises." He didn't promise, but she noted he did try to avert his eyes from any potential underwear showage. For a pair trying to avoid anything beyond friendship, flashing him intentionally wouldn't be prudent. Didn't stop her from considering it.

Returning with an armful of sticks and leaves, Sophie sat down on the log, straddling it this time, facing Asher. The dress was a bit high on the thighs in this position, but she managed to keep it PG.

Laughing with total confusion, Asher flipped his leg across their fallen tree, so he straddled the log facing her. "Did I miss something? Are you part beaver? Bird? Other forest animal building a home?"

Chuckling, she shook her head. "Didn't you ever read Winnie the Pooh? It's a favorite pastime in the Hundred Acre Wood." She handed him a stick. "On the count of three, drop your stick."

Holding their sticks as far upstream as they could reach, they let go on three. Watching the sticks pass beneath them, Sophie cried out with a whoop of delight, "My stick won."

"I think that was my stick. Yours was bent more than that." Laughing at himself, or the silliness of the situation, he was getting into the game.

Flipping her hair out of the way, she was in full competitive mode now. "Nice try. I totally won that round." Holding her stick up, he caught her drift and raised his up for comparison so there would be no argument this time.

The game went on until the last of the sticks, some broken in half to make it last longer, had been tossed in the stream. "You're going to make some beaver or salmon very happy downstream."

Both giggled like silly children as the last of their sticks drifted out of sight. Asher glanced down, suddenly a hotblooded adult, noting that her skirt had hiked up a little further in the excitement of the game. She was just barely covering the important stuff.

Looking back up, his eyes locked onto hers. Slowly, he grazed his hand up her thigh, teasing the edge of her skirt with his thumbs. Eyes hungry, melting her with the heat behind them, he asked, "This okay?"

Brain turned to mush, entirely distracted by the feather light contact, Sophie nodded, biting her lower lip as she struggled to steady her breathing. "Yes."

He shifted closer to her along the fallen tree, pulling her legs over his to link them together. Both hands now stroking the smooth skin of her legs, teasing along the edge of her dress, he leaned in and lightly touched his lips to hers.

Pulling back no more than a breath away, his eyes didn't stray from her lips. "This okay?"

Sophie reached her hand up and ran her fingers through his tousled hair as she gripped the back of his head to pull him closer. Lips touching in a light kiss, both smiling playfully, she whispered, "Yes."

Running her tongue along the crease of his lip, she urged him on. He groaned in response and moved his hands up to her waist, pulling her closer against him. Deeper, more intense, they moved together as the creek murmured beneath them. Hands splayed around her waist, he held her steady as he kissed her, exploring, tasting, experiencing.

She felt herself slipping irretrievably into uncharted territory. Sensation rocketed through her; her heart thundered like an avalanche in her chest.

Pulling away before she was ready, equally breathless, he leaned his forehead against hers, his hand moving to her cheek in a soft caress. "The sun's starting to set. We should probably get back."

Hating to see the moment end, but knowing he was right, she agreed. Both rose cautiously on the log, a little less steady than they had been a few moments ago. Sophie held his hand to steady herself, more emotionally than physically.

Continuing hand-in-hand to the truck, they didn't say a word. They climbed into the ancient pickup and Asher fired up the engine. Tried, anyway. It didn't move. He turned the key again. Nothing.

"Shit. Hang on." Groaning in frustration, Asher climbed out of the truck.

Sophie glanced at her phone. Nothing. Out of range. Refusing to sit helplessly, despite having no idea how to fix a car, she joined him and stared cluelessly under the hood.

Dashing to the truck bed, he grabbed a few tools and started tightening bolts, checking connections. Sophie didn't know much about engines, but she did know batteries well enough. "Is this supposed to be loose like that?"

Asher stepped over to her and looked at the wire that should have been attached to the battery she was looking at. He laughed out loud. "Yep, that's the one. Must have come loose on the bumpy road. I'm a little embarrassed I didn't think to check the damn battery first. Let's just blame my wandering imagination." He flashed her a dashing wink.

He quickly connected the detached wire and hopped back into the truck. Sophie strolled cheerfully back into the truck. His self-effacing attitude, the pure appreciation without criticism or chauvinistic undermining, was incredibly refreshing. Not that she'd dated too many jerks, but there were enough out there that that she was wary.

The engine fired right up this time. "Nice one." He leaned across and pulled Sophie in for a brief, but heated kiss. As he pulled away, he plucked a twig from her hair. "Let's get back before anyone notices we left together."

Sophie sighed, wishing they had more time. "I hate secrets."

"Me too. Let's feel things out and see how it goes? I don't want to stress Pippa out before the wedding. Let's not provoke the wasp's nest of pre-wedding psychosis she's developed. What she doesn't know won't hurt her." He paused, considering. "I only promised to not have sex with you, and I haven't broken her trust on that one. Yet." He flashed a tempting glance her way before turning the truck around in the clearing and getting them back on the road.

"For now, we can see where this goes, up to but not including sex, so neither of us breaks that promise. Feels like a lie of omission, but I'm willing fudge it a bit." Whew. Sophie rolled down the window even further to cool her raging sex drive.

How had this happened so quickly? It had been forever since she'd been so caught up in someone. Never, actually, that had she felt the fire in her belly with a simple look from someone. One easy glance from those whiskey eyes, and her limbs went weak and burned like she'd taken a shot of the smoothest whiskey in the bar.

They pulled up to the house a short while later. Pippa was just heading into the house with grocery bags full of food and flowers and wine bottles. She briefly took note of the truck pulling in the driveway, but thankfully didn't stick around to chat.

Sophie knew her friend's fear came from losing more than one good friend due to the heartache Asher could cause if things went poorly with Asher. As long as she protected her heart and didn't ditch Pippa, she was good to go. Right?

Asher parked quickly and checked Sophie one more time. He pulled another twig from her hair. Running her hands through her hair, she made sure it was the last. "That could make this afternoon look way worse than it was."

He grinned smugly and soothed her with a warm chuckle. "Agreed."

Sophie reached across and smoothed out his hair where she had dug her hands into it. After climbing out of the truck and making sure it didn't look like anything had happened, they grabbed the final grocery bags from Pippa's car and headed into the house. She bit her lip to hide the happy smile that was rapidly becoming uncontainable.

Chapter Eight

The front door wide open, Pippa was frantically unload-
ing the groceries she'd just brought in. "Great timing,
helpers, you're here. Now get out of my hair while I make
dinner." Oh boy. Pippa was in full pre-wedding panic, and they
still had more than a week to go.

"Pippa, it's the rehearsal rehearsal dinner. Remember, the
one that's supposed the be fun and relaxing? Just your closest
friends? You get to delegate and tell us all what to do to
make the wedding happen without a hitch. Well, there will
be people getting hitched... you know what I mean." Sophie
tried not to laugh at her own joke. Pippa was too far gone to
appreciate the humor.

Pippa's lip extended in full pout, only pausing before diving
back into the grocery bags. Yikes, she loved a silly play on
words normally. Poor thing was so overwhelmed. "I know. I
think I scheduled too much. Too many events and too many
details." Her speech rapid and high pitched, she rambled. "I've
been planning this wedding since I was fourteen."

Standing in front of Pippa so she might stop, or at least
slow the frantic pacing, Sophie put her hands on her friend's
shoulders to stop the manic movements. "As a teacher, you
know that part of planning is knowing when to schedule in

breaks and when to delegate. No one will be arriving for another half hour. Why don't you get started on dinner while I take care of the flowers and get the wine chilling? Then, we can relax while dinner is in the oven."

Nodding with the pouty lip still out, Pippa did as she was told. When she disappeared into the pantry to grab a vase for Sophie, Asher issued a quick sigh of relief and a wink. Avoiding any unnecessary risk for getting caught now that the situation was momentarily diffused, he disappeared upstairs.

Asher stood back and watched his sister frantically setting and resetting the table. Shifting the flowers between the center of the dining room table to the entry table then back again. He was dizzy just watching. "Pip, it's just the rehearsal rehearsal dinner. You've been working nonstop for an hour."

"I know. I can't help it. Freya just flew in last night and will be jetlagged, so I need to be sure there's plenty of coffee. Lincoln and Grady have been working long hours to get their law office up and running. You hate crowds. Sophie has been so sweet to put up with me and be at my beck and call. I just... I want everyone to have fun and really get to know each other."

He risked stepping closer and took the flowers from her hands. "They looked nice on the table. Everyone will have a great time. You love everyone coming, so why won't they like each other?"

"What if someone forgets their swimsuit? I told them we're hitting the hot tub after dinner." Having forgotten about the flowers, she was now removing plates from around the table and stacking them back up for a buffet style dinner.

A single chime echoed from the doorbell and Lincoln popped his head in, with Grady coming in right behind him. Asher gestured a *thank god you're here* at Lincoln. Turning back to his sister, he jumped on the opportunity to run away. "Lincoln can help you with the plates, I'm sure."

As directed, Lincoln and Grady had stepped up their game a bit and were wearing slacks and button-up shirts. Apparently, this was a "casual" affair. He took the stack of plates from Pippa before she dropped them and handed the stack to Lincoln.

Whispering discreetly in the ear of his future brother-in-law, he pleaded, "If she's this crazy for the rehearsal rehearsal dinner, what's she going to be like at the wedding?"

Lincoln laughed and took the plates Asher was forcing on him. "I got this." Lincoln set the plates back around the table and walked over to Pippa. Taking her hands in his, he kissed each and then her forehead. "Love you, Pip. It's just us." He dragged her to the kitchen and poured her a tall glass of chardonnay.

Grateful he was off the hook, Asher turned to the stairs to grab his button-up shirt he'd been strong-armed into wearing tonight. As it was eighty-six degrees out today, he'd changed into khakis but had left the button-up shirt until the last minute. He stopped in his tracks before he made much progress towards the stairs.

Sophie was coming down wearing a pale blue satin slip dress. In the heels and short dress, her legs somehow looked even longer. The dress hugged every subtle curve brilliantly. The satin looked as slick and smooth as her skin that morning coming out of the shower. Draping in the front, it accented those marvelous breasts.

She gave him a secret wink as she passed, leaving him with his jaw hanging open. Turning to watch that fine ass as she headed for the dining room, he noticed he wasn't the only one enjoying the view. Grady looked at her downright licentiously.

Asher had never even thought that word before, but it fit. Jackass wasn't subtle about his perusal either. Grady walked right up to Sophie and placed his hand on the small of her back to escort her to the dining room.

He should have known. She and Grady were perfect for each other. Grady had his shit together, was a decent guy, would treat her well. Asher shook off the jealousy and dashed up to change into the stupid shirt.

Sophie couldn't remember the last time she'd laughed so hard. "Freya, I'm so glad you're moving back to town. As much as I adore Pippa," she said, winking at her best friend, "I could use someone with decent taste in movies around here."

Raising her nearly drained second glass of wine, Pippa glared at Sophie playfully. "I like a good cry now and again. Not every movie needs a happy ending."

Freya, Sophie's declared new friend and Pippa's closest cousin raised her glass in a toast. "Sophie, I promise to watch Captain America movies with you as often as you need me. Pippa, you're on your own with the tearjerkers."

Yeah, she definitely liked Freya already. Taller than she was, wild waves of black hair, piercing blue eyes, and a sharp intellect... but clearly good taste in movies as well. Freya had been studying art throughout Europe for the last few years, so Sophie hadn't been able to meet her yet. Close in age to Pippa and Asher, the cousins had always been good friends.

Rising from the table, Pippa managed to hold her laughter long enough to be the boss again. "I really appreciate you guys putting up with my bridezillaness. I had no idea I would have such tendencies–"

Lincoln coughed into his fist, discreetly muttering, "Bull-shit."

"Remember that thing you wanted to try on our wedding night? Not going to happen if you keep that attitude." Pippa winked at her fiancé. "On with my bossiness. Let's head to the hot tub. We have spare suits if you need them."

Grady teased this time as he rose from his chair. "Pippa, you scare me too much for me to ever forget one of your commands."

In her bedroom, Sophie quickly put on her favorite one-piece suit, glad she'd remembered to shave her legs and bikini line this morning. She hadn't been in the pool yet and couldn't wait to slide in. Despite the fans, the house was just plain hot on days like today.

Wrapping herself in her towel, she hoped she'd beat the others. No such luck. Grady waited just outside the back door.

"I was hoping to get one of the good spots in the hot tub before everyone else got out here. I haven't been here in years, but the times I was over in high school, I discovered the best spot in the tub." Grady made casual conversation as he put his hand on her back again.

He kept doing that. It was so possessive, and she didn't particularly want to be possessed. She supposed it was actually a sweet gesture; it just struck her wrong tonight. Maybe because she wished it was someone else's hand.

"Go for it. I'm taking a quick dip in the pool first." She crossed her fingers he wouldn't change his mind and decide to join her for a swim. Without waiting for his response, she silently declared her independence and walked right up to the pool and dove in, swimming half the length of the pool before surfacing again, then swam the rest of the length leisurely.

When her mother had been alive, she'd been part fish in the local swim club. In high school she'd joined the swim team and had kept up with it through college as well. Yvette couldn't argue with no-cost school sports, and she appreciated when Sophie wasn't underfoot.

Reaching for the far wall, she turned around, debating whether to swim a few laps or just float for a while. Asher strutted out of the house in black board shorts that hung just low enough she could see the narrowing of his low abs. Strutted was the wrong word. His walk was confident, but it lacked the cockiness of a strut.

He didn't even pause as he reached the edge of the pool and dove in sleekly, with hardly a splash. Swimming the length of the pool, he surfaced inches in front of her. Grinning with the rush of sensation, he was clearly as at home in the water as she was.

Rolling her eyes playfully, she swam around him and stopped in the middle of the pool to float and look up at the stars. She could just hear the others in the hot tub, laughing and enjoying themselves. She'd join them in a few, but she couldn't resist stretching her body in the bathwater-warm pool first.

Why hadn't she gotten out here before tonight? It had been too long since she'd loosened up like this. Listening to the Darth Vader sound of her own breathing with her ears just under the surface, she lay perfectly still and stared up at the night sky. A shooting star passed the length of the horizon before burning out, no sign it had ever existed.

She should have been startled by the body that came up from under her like a surfacing submarine. Hands circling her waist, cheek pressing against her own, Asher lifted his head from the water, an otter snuggling with its mate. Did otters mate like that? Relaxing into him, she succumbed to the deep yearning for the skin-to-skin contact.

Then she was more afraid Pippa would see. What was he thinking? Shifting, she rolled so she was facing him. He was still only inches away.

"Don't scare your sister like this. I am actually a little terrified of her right now," Sophie joked. Mostly joked. Undeniably a little bit serious.

Asher slicked his hand through his hair and brushed out a thick spray of water. He whispered back, "She can't see us." He nodded his head toward the hot tub.

Huh, fancy that. The sides of the hot tub and waterfall pouring out of it were high enough that the hot tub residents were rather clueless about the pool happenings. Unless they were trying to see over the side.

"We still shouldn't." Sophie searched Asher's eyes, seeking his refute.

Ignoring her thinly veiled protest, Asher leaned in and pressed his cool, damp lips against hers. Testing, teasing, he kissed the corners of her mouth, her lower lip. Fire stirred low in her belly at his feather light touch. Relying on him to keep them afloat, she wrapped her arms around him and deepened the kiss, letting the embers ignite into a full wildfire.

Clinging to him, she devoured him, and he kissed her back with equal fervor. Forgetting to tread water, they slipped carelessly underwater and perpetuated the kiss until they ran out of air.

Surfacing again, both were breathing rapidly, from the lack of oxygen, the kiss, or both. Asher looked to the hot tub, realizing the risk they'd taken if anyone had made the effort to check on them. "I'm sorry. I shouldn't have... we shouldn't have. She's going to kill me."

Sophie swam a few feet away, needing the distance or she'd dive right back into his arms. "Agreed. We're not a couple of horny teenagers. We can be more discreet."

Feeling absurdly sad, her heart shattering a little bit, Sophie swam to the steps. Looking back, she saw Asher watching her distance herself, his face drawn, his misery mirroring her own. She'd never betray her friend, but she wished she could tell her friend what she was feeling, and how much pushing this aside sucked.

Whatever it was brewing between her and Asher, chemistry or something, it was stronger than any crush she'd ever felt. It's not like she was the type to jump in some guy's bed because he had a reputation and an incredible body. Concealing her feelings from her friend was downright painful. Foreign.

Pasting on her cheeriest face, Sophie knew she couldn't go pout alone like she'd wanted, and instead joined the others in the hot tub. She didn't look back at Asher again, knowing he would be avoiding the crowded hot tub. The four in the tub scooched a bit to make room for her.

Grady made sure there was an open seat right next to him. He was perfect for her; maybe she could muster up an attraction. His interest was clear. "Have a nice swim?"

"Yes, that pool is amazing. Swimming has always been a favorite outlet of mine." She tried to ignore his arm stretching out on the edge of the tub behind her, his hand grazing the edge of her shoulder. Why didn't that create any tingles like even a simple glance from Asher? Maybe Pippa was right; her brother was a lady killer and would dump her as fast as he had the rest, once he'd gotten her into his bed.

Pippa nudged her with her foot. "I was surprised you hadn't been in yet. Asher practically lived in the pool growing up. He's part fish like you are." For someone so against them being together, she certainly wasn't helping by pointing out everything they had in common.

Attempting to give Grady a chance, she politely turned towards him. "You swim much?" Please say yes. It might make him more appealing.

Distracted, his eyes poorly tried to stay on her face, but unmistakably glanced down her top. He hesitated before responding. "Huh? Oh. No, not really. I can, but I prefer relaxing in the hot tub. Horseback riding, or even golf or hockey are more my outlets."

Great. She hated all three. Not only that, for a decent guy, he sure didn't seem to realize a woman could tell when he was checking out her boobs. She could tell he was trying to be subtle; he just was failing at it. Didn't help she was nipping through her swimsuit, transitioning from the refreshingly cold pool to the sweltering tub. And she couldn't deny the fact that she'd worn her top that hinted she may slip out of it with a deep breath to torture Asher.

She nodded politely, having no idea what more to say. Her eyes wandered in the direction of the pool stairs, where Asher was just coming out and drying off. He looked as miserable as she felt, his movements dragging and lethargic.

P ippa hollered to her brother, "You coming in? We've got room. I think these boys have the bachelor party planned without you."

Throwing the towel over his shoulder, he walked over, but didn't get in. Standing awkwardly at the side, he put his non-towel hand on his hip. "I'm tired, think I'll hit the rack." Looking to Lincoln, he managed to smile and a wink. "We hiring a stripper or flying to Vegas?"

Lincoln pulled Pippa closer and kissed her loudly on the cheek. "Hell no. A round of golf at the club—as lawyers we are mandatory members. Then, thought we'd join the ladies at Ahab's, as neither of us really have any friends outside of you losers."

Asher spared a glance for Sophie, clearly noting her keeping the maximum distance from Grady, yet Grady's hand lightly brushed her shoulder. He just barely managed to hide his wince as he restrained himself from hauling Grady's ass out of the tub and kicking it.

He gritted his teeth to hide the vivid, violent picture form-ing in his head. So, this is what jealously felt like. A very new sensation when it came to women. He didn't really care for it.

Poor cavemen were judged rather harshly; not their fault they dragged their women off to where other cavemen couldn't see them... And drove them wild with pleasure after peeling off their little cavewoman skimpy scrap of leather clothes... hour after hour. *Down boy.* "Sounds great. I'm a terrible golfer, if it helps. Will there be beer involved?"

Hand now fully on Sophie's shoulder, Grady pretended he wasn't doing it on purpose. Asher watched as Sophie struggled to find a polite way to let Grady know she wasn't interested. She was too dang nice, never wanting someone to feel bad. Of course, she didn't realize she was torturing the poor guy by not telling him outrightly how she felt.

Lincoln chuckled. "Is there another way to play golf?"

Sophie slowly inched away, but clearly couldn't figure out how to do it without making it look like a very public rejection. "Why don't you boys go finish planning in the pool or inside while we girls plan in here?"

Eyebrows scrunched together, Pippa looked at her like she was nuts. Thankfully, she seemed to finally catch Sophie's dilemma and agreed. "Good call. We'd hate for you to hear about our plans for the stripper we've hired for our party before we join you at Ahab's."

Lincoln kissed his fiancée sweetly before climbing out. Grady gave Sophie a friendly wink and followed the other guys out. Freya eyed the interaction with curiosity.

Watching the boys dry off and wander back into the house, Pippa waited until the door was closed before she drilled Sophie. "What gives?"

Chest rising out of the hot water as she took a deep breath, Sophie didn't want to completely lie to the best friend she'd ever had. "I'm just not sure I'm interested in Grady."

Shifting across the tub, Pippa put her hand on Sophie's forehead. "No fever. You're not any paler than usual." She shifted back into her own seat. "What's wrong with you? You and Grady would be great together. I thought you were into him."

Sophie pouted pitifully. "He's gorgeous and funny and decent... if perhaps a bit forward. I'm working on being into him but it's just not happening."

Finally, Freya piped in, floating just above the jets at her back, her eyes closed peacefully. "You can't force these things. If the pheromones aren't there, it just isn't going to happen."

Pippa splashed across the tub, almost reaching Freya. Magically, the spray stopped a few inches before her relaxed, jetlagged face. "Don't encourage her. Sophie will stew and procrastinate and overanalyze every little detail and wind up eternally single."

Smug grin on her face, Freya didn't bother opening her eyes or even looking at her cousin. "Maybe it takes an outsider to see, but Sophie doesn't need any help in the romance department. She's picky because she's not settling for anything less than remarkable."

Pippa rolled her eyes. "You're a hopeless romantic. You haven't heard about the many, many broken hearts Sophie left in her wake. All very attractive, good guys that she wouldn't give the time of day."

Sophie liked Freya's description better. "Thank you, Freya. You may be my new best friend. See Pip? I'm selective, not a settler."

Pippa shrugged. "Fine. As you sent the boys away, now you have to plan the bachelorette party."

Sophie considered for a moment. "Do you want a bachelorette party before we meet up with the guys? Won't it just be the three of us?"

"You were kidding about the stripper, right?" Pippa's distaste was clear.

She considered teasing but was running out of steam. "Yes, totally kidding. How about we just head to Ahab's after the bridal shower, be silly just the three of us until the boys join us?"

"Perfect. But you still have to wear the hokey wedding party tank tops I bought you."

Sophie grumbled. Freya scowled but didn't move from her comfy spot.

"Hey, I got caught up in the moment at that bridal fair. They're purchased so you're stuck with them." This time, Freya sent a halfhearted splash at Pippa.

Chapter Nine

T-Minus 10 Days

Sophie hated bridal showers. Pippa's Aunt Tammy had required full participation in every ridiculous game. As the maid of honor, it wouldn't have looked good if she'd bowed out. She made the mandatory toilet paper bridal gown (which she lost), completed the timeline about Pippa and Lincoln's relationship (which she won), and endured a polite sampling of those nasty pastel mints that don't quite fully dissolve in your mouth then get stuck in your teeth for hours.

Flashing before her eyes, her future terrified her. "Pip, please don't let Tammy throw your baby shower when the day comes. I'm not smelling melted candy bars in baby diapers." Buckling into her CR-V, she ensured Pippa and Freya were settled before she started the engine and shifted into gear.

Groaning, Pippa pouted audibly in agreement. "If you dibs it now, we can hopefully avoid the otherwise inevitable shower games."

From the backseat, Freya laughed. "They weren't that bad. We all giggled and got to know Pippa and Lincoln's magical love life better."

Turning around in her seat, Pippa shot eye-daggers at her cousin. "You didn't plan any bachelorette party games, did you? You're not like your mother with party games, right?"

"Just a few. Not to worry, they're fun and will help us get to know each other in a less PG way. I did buy you a penis crown as well." Freya leaned into her purse and withdrew said crown.

Pippa laughed out loud and put on her special crown of phalluses. "This alleviates any guilt I have about the brides-maid tank tops I'm making you wear." She gestured to their skintight black tank tops with pink sparkly writing indicating their roles, Sophie as the Maid of Honor and Freya as Brides-maid. Pippa had worn her own white with gold sparkly letters indicating that she was the Bride.

"These rather announce to the world, look at my sparkly breasts that are trying to bust out of this thin jersey cotton, don't they?" Freya looked down and admired the sparkles. "Think the boys have similar shirts?"

Rolling her eyes, Pippa snorted indelicately. "Hell no. Lincoln considered it, Grady would have gone along with it if he had to, but Asher refused outright."

Freya leaned forward and nudged Pippa. "Think Asher's bummed no stripper? Didn't he sleep with the stripper at Mark's bachelor party? What was it, like his first trip home from the navy?"

Pippa groaned, "Why did you have to remind me of that? Mark had a fit. The stripper charged double when she realized Asher had no interest in actually dating her."

Sophie neatly avoided the conversation. She knew Asher had a history, and she knew it was bad. Had he been some sort of sex addict? Or just a slut?

Still leaning between them from the backseat, Freya whispered, even though it was still just the three of them and Asher wasn't around to hear. "Is he okay? Mom says he hasn't been leaving the house much since he got home, what, a month or two ago? Although, consider the source. You know what a gossip Mom is."

Pippa sighed, her worry unmistakable. "I don't know. He goes to the VA weekly for therapy; it was twice weekly at first. He tried some of the meds they prescribed but didn't like the side effects.

"I actually don't think he's dated in a really long time. When I threatened him about Sophie, he mentioned he hadn't even been with a woman in two years." Pippa shifted to pleasantly disappointed, trademarking a whole new emotion that was uniquely Pippa.

Freya looked shocked. "Two years? Poor guy. I haven't made it that long since I lost my virginity."

Snorting, Sophie rolled her eyes. "Perhaps if you two get stuck in a dating rut like I've been in, two years might not sound so bad."

"That is one of the many perks of being engaged. On-demand sex." Pippa waggled her eyebrows and admired her engagement ring comically.

"My vibrator is on demand anytime and doesn't get tired." Sophie couldn't help but throw that one out. Hard to resist when her best friend was crowned with penises.

Nodding in agreement, Freya added, "Excellent point, if not quite as satisfying." Turning to Pippa, she asked, back to Asher, "Do you think he's grown up or lost interest?"

Pippa shrugged. "I couldn't say. The last few years, really since he joined the SEALs, he hasn't gone out partying or acted promiscuous. He doesn't even drink more than one or two drinks in a night anymore, and even that's a rarity."

Sophie couldn't stand it anymore. Did they not know him at all? She knew he had a history, but since she'd met him, what, eleven days ago, he hardly drank, he had a strict daily exercise regimen, ate well, worked on his truck, and was trying to make sense of his future. He didn't verbalize it, but likely make sense of his past as well.

And very regrettably was not having sex with her. She couldn't help but defend him. "He is nearly thirty and has lived away from you all for almost twelve years. A lot can happen in twelve years."

Keeping her eyes on the road, Sophie tried not to fluster when Pippa stared at her suspiciously. "You and he haven't..."

"Of course not." She hoped she didn't overdo the denial. They hadn't slept together, that was true. Nor did they intend to. Well, not yet anyway.

"He keeps to his room or the garage most of the time, what makes you think you know my brother so well?"

Oh boy, this was getting ugly. Pippa had some serious issues when it came to her brother. Normally she mostly spoke pretty well of her brother, but Sophie suspected the wedding stress was thinning the filter and letting the negative feelings surface.

"You're right. You know him way better than I do. I share a bathroom with the guy. As they say, you can learn a lot about a person based on their bathroom." Sophie confidently bullshitted her friend as she pulled into Ahab's.

"True that." Freya nodded from the back seat, finally leaning back as they pulled into the parking lot.

Pausing, Sophie added one last defense before getting out of the car, as subtly as possible. Turning toward her friend, she brought her knee up to the center console. "Pip, just nine years ago I was a freshman in college. I told you about those first few years, before I met you, right?"

Pippa softened. "I know about the tattoo."

Sophie gestured loosely. "I did a lot of things you wouldn't dream of trying. The tattoo is a drop in the bucket. I had my share of one-nighters and drinking and smoking. Am I at all like that anymore?"

She hadn't been stupid though. Experimented with weed and alcohol, but didn't get into anything heavy. Had a little random sex, but always used protection and only with guys and girls she knew from the dorms, never some random hit from the bar.

Patting her friend on the arm, Pippa pursed her lips in sympathy. "Not at all. You're ridiculously responsible. I get it. I'll give him a break."

Hand on Sophie's shoulder, Freya halted their progress out the door. "Tattoo? I have several, but the way she said it, yours sounds quite mysterious."

With an impish wink, Sophie shrugged and got out of the car.

Ahab's was packed with hiking boots and IPAs. A local favorite, from what she had heard. Clearly the tourists loved it too, judging by the sheer number of outdoorsy types mingling, their bikes and kayaks strapped onto mud-encrusted Subarus in the parking lot.

It was clear why it was named Ahab's when they walked in. Fishing nets, and even the hull of a massive wooden ship, covered most of the ceiling. Model whales and fish, seafaring quirkiness in general, dominated the décor. The far wall of the bar was a huge mural of an old-style maritime scene.

Sophie had to shout to the server that greeted them to be heard over the swarm of summer adventurers scattered around the pool tables, seated at high-top tables, and more crowded several rows deep around the bar itself. "Were you able to save us the table for six? Sutherland?" She'd given Pippa's surname, hoping it would carry a little weight.

Perky and not an inch over five feet tall, the server was so animated that she danced as she talked. "Sure did, come on back." Following the bouncy black curls through the crowd, they arrived at the only open table, tucked away in the back corner. Two round, high-top tables were pushed together and decorated with white balloons.

As they sat at the table, Sophie expected the chipper woman to take their orders. Apparently, that wasn't as important as catching up, so to speak. She'd have to get used to small town friendliness and the fact that everyone knew each other. "Hey Pippa, congratulations on the wedding coming up. I heard Asher is back in town. Is he coming tonight?"

Aha, that's why the name Sutherland carried weight here. Not the pillar-of-the-community reputation from the senior Sutherlands, rather a devoted member of the Asher fan club. Pippa masked her groan with an overly perky smile. "Thanks. And yes, yes he is."

Perky server with the big boobs nearly forgot to take their order, then remembered why they were here. "What can I get you ladies while you wait for the rest of your party?"

Freya ordered them a pair of pitchers, one of the hoppiest on the menu and a fruitier seasonal ale for variety, plus glasses for six. She added an order of nachos and wings and pretzels with cheese dip. And waters all around.

Scoping out the food at nearby tables, Sophie observed nothing more than ordinary tavern food. Nothing special. Music blasted from a modern electronic low-profile jukebox, currently playing Halsey. There were pool tables, darts, a few arcade games. All was as expected, standard tavern amenities, aside from the over-the-top hokey whaling décor... in the middle of a mountain town.

Nothing about Ahab's made sense. "Why is this place so popular? I'm honestly not seeing anything extraordinary about it."

Looking around, Pippa took in the scene as if for the first time. "It's a little weird, I'll give you that. There was a crazy article about it in *The Stranger* about twenty years back. A feature on Captain Ahab himself; how he settled here after his whaling days were done. Nearly as creative of a marketing scheme as the Bavarian themed tourist town of Leavenworth northeast of here, the article put us on the map and Ahab's has become a bit of a cult-classic."

Freya waved down their boys that were making their way through the crowd. "You can't head up to the slopes without stopping here on your way home. There's a curse to those who don't pay their respects and toast the captain, or so goes the legend."

Throwing his arms around an unsuspecting Pippa, Lincoln growled playfully as he embraced his fiancée. She squealed before she realized it was him and smacked him in the chest. She nearly fell out of her chair laughing.

Sophie felt Asher's eyes on her as he approached. Silently, he pulled up a stool to sit in the corner next to her. Publicly, he acknowledged her with little more than a look and maybe a polite greeting, but, under the table, his leg pressed against hers like a magma-hot magnet. Even the small amount of denim-to-denim contact set her on fire, words and coherent thought flying right out the window.

Distracted, she didn't notice Grady settling in opposite. He stretched his foot across and rested it on her stool footrest. Subtly, she kicked it as if she hadn't noticed his foot was there. He politely apologized for the intrusion, and she politely apologized for not realizing his foot was there.

Perky-big-breasted-ex-lover of Asher's suddenly appeared out of nowhere with the pitchers and glasses. She poured Asher's until the glass overflowed, her eyes batting as she vied for his attention. "Hey Asher." She gratuitously flirted as she leaned forward to give him a little extra attention with her impressive cleavage.

Lips tight in a forced polite smile, he acknowledged her. "Irene. Hey."

Irene looked for a way around the table to get closer, but he was boxed in the corner. Tapping her foot as frustration overtook the poor thing, she finally gave up and walked away. Pippa rolled her eyes and poured beers for the rest of them.

Moments later, Irene reappeared with the snacks. And her phone number on a napkin. With a lipstick kiss under her number. She slid it across the table to Asher before waggling her curvy ass as she walked away.

With a curse under his breath, he stood from his stool, taking the napkin with him. Approaching Irene at the bar, he handed her back the napkin and whispered something in her ear. Irene's face dropped and she looked so dejected.

He whispered again, and she hugged him and gave him a big, toothy grin before she let him walk away. Irene's sudden change of heart made Sophie wonder what on Earth he'd said to her.

Staring at her brother like he was a total alien stranger, Lincoln manually closed Pippa's gaping jaw. Sophie could just hear Lincoln telling Pippa, "Told you so."

"Told her what?" Freya nabbed the cheesiest chip from the stack, loaded it with guacamole, and shoveled it in her mouth, leaning forward for a bit of juicy gossip.

Lincoln looked around, ensuring Asher wasn't yet within earshot yet. "I think he's seeing someone. Like, off the market."

Grady shook his head, looking puzzled. "I thought he never left the house, who could he possibly be seeing?"

Freya bit her lip to hide her smile.

Pippa rolled her eyes and gestured none-too-subtly at Sophie. "Who cares, as long as he's getting out and isn't making moves on–"

As Asher approached, Pippa cleared her throat and changed course. "Starting work for Dad soon, right Asher?"

Sliding in the corner next to Sophie again, he returned to his stool. "That's the plan," he admitted as he cautiously sipped his full-to-the-brim beer, discreetly wiping the overflow off the saturated cardboard coaster.

Conversation strayed to varying topics, from the bizarre to the mundane. Freya came stocked with bachelor party games, but fortunately was easier to tame than her mother. "Okay, so no one wants to play Truth or Dare and a fat *no* on the Scavenger Hunt. Too bad, I had some pretty awesome clues planned."

A combination of eyerolls and polite smiles aimed at Freya and her determination to play one of her well-researched party games. "Okay. Tough crowd. It was a long flight." She sighed deeply in dramatic disappointment, but smiled and shrugged with an unshakable positivity. "How about *Never Have I Ever*? The version where you win if you've Never'ed the most. You know, whoever is the most innocent and gets to all ten fingers-of-innocence first is the winner. Not the drinking version; we're too old for that nonsense."

Pippa giggled. "But we're not too old to compare inappropriate things we've done."

Asher finally was able to take a full sip of his beer now that he'd drained off some of the excess head Irene had generously given him. Stomach acids churning, Sophie felt nauseous at the image that provoked. He swallowed the bubbly brew and raised his eyebrows at his cousin. "What are we, still in high school and trying to figure out who's still a virgin and who has experimented with drugs?"

Pointing with his index finger around his own nearly drained seasonal brew rather haughtily at Asher, Grady looked a bit… irritated. "Afraid you'll lose, frogman?"

Stiffening, Asher downed half his beer with a chug worthy of the most seasoned sailors. "I *know* I'm going to lose. More to the point, you afraid you'll win, boy scout?"

"Sorry, that was the one activity my dear parents didn't enroll me in. Try again." Grady shrugged and set down his beer.

Topping off glasses for the table, Freya admonished the bickering pair before it escalated. "If you're going to compare dick sizes, let's do it properly. Sophie, you're the only female unrelated to both contestants, care to be the judge? Let's go boys."

Sophie choked on her beer. "As appealing as that sounds, why don't we just try a different game?"

Apparently, Grady was in full jackass mode. Sophie had never seen him act like this before. Nor Asher; he was sitting eerily still, but he looked like a bull ready to charge.

Grady extended a finger, heatedly watching Asher for his reaction. "I've never killed anyone."

Growling, Asher puffed steam out of his nostrils. His jawbone was flexing a mile a minute, his arms tensing as he held back a well-deserved punch.

Sophie subtly reached down and put her hand on his vibrating knee. He wasn't wrong; you didn't push a veteran on something like that. Especially as she suspected there was a little misplaced guilt embedded in his PTSD.

Wanting to avoid a fight, Lincoln quickly tried to tame things. "I've never smoked pot." He extended a finger and smiled at his excellent life choice.

Most of the table now had one to two fingers extended. Not Asher.

Freya went next, considering, then nodded reflectively. "I've never sixty-nined. I may have to rectify that, but I just don't understand the appeal. Why not take turns? Much more satisfying for everyone. But I'm not much of a multitasker."

"Excellent point. It sounds like patting your head while rubbing your tummy." Pippa considered for a moment, considering her Never. "I've never stolen anything."

Knowing she had to participate, Sophie tried to come up with something. She wasn't doing very well, only one finger extended. After being the grownup for six years with her aunt, she'd made the most of her brain-not-done-developing adolescent rebellion when she got to college.

This had been before she'd met Pippa, of course. A truly good-natured, cautious person, Pippa understood Sophie's past but would never have been close with her during her tough years.

Trying to think of something Asher might be able to Never, she was stumped. "I... I've never done it outside." She shrugged, hoping it would work.

Nope, still nothing. They went around a few more times. Asher refused to offer his own Nevers. Freya shook one of her many extended fingers at him. "Ash, Grady and Pippa here are about to win. You've got to come up with a Never of your own, cuz; you're getting your ass royally kicked."

He shrugged. "Fine. I've never been in love." It almost looked like he'd been stewing on that one for a while but hadn't wanted to share that personal little tidbit until he was forced.

A very short while later, game over. Asher lost hands down, no pun intended. Sophie didn't feel so bad; she was only a few fingers behind him in the losing status.

Pippa tried to kick her under the table but didn't realize they were so far apart and nearly tumbled off her stool. "Sophie, I can't believe you failed so miserably at that. You were a naughty girl before I met you." Not actually judgmental, she flashed a wicked smile at Sophie.

"I had to explore many of life's offerings, good and bad, out of the clutches of my evil aunt, before I knew what I wanted for myself." She raised the frosty glass in the air to toast a fond farewell to her past and drained the amber liquid, until she was down to nearly half what she'd started with. Was that like saying it was half full? She was so much more the optimist now than she'd been before meeting Pippa.

Without a change in expression, as he sipped his beer, Asher's free hand joined Sophie's under the table. With impressive subtlety, he slid his hand into hers so no one would notice. Her long fingers slid between his like they belonged there. The heat the simple gesture stirred was still such a new sensation, setting every nerve in her body on fire with arousal and comfort in an unexpected, cohesive combination.

Freya topped off the non-driver's beers. "We should have had this at home, then we could play beer pong and I could watch you all get loose and tell me all your secrets."

Asher snorted, a dark, thunderous veil covering his gaze. "Not sure you want all of them, cuz."

Letting out a rich belly laugh, Lincoln teased, "And, I'm officially done with party games. I'm going to see where we're at on the billiards waiting list."

After a short wait, one of the requested pool tables freed up. Leaving it to teams of two, Sophie declined, knowing her skills would be rather pathetic compared to the others as they smack-talked about their impressive strategies. Never having much talent at billiards, she was more than happy to hang back. Asher had stayed pretty quiet after *I Never* and offered to wait for the next table.

Watching the others settle in at billiards, Asher scanned the room. Looking above them, he smiled when he saw the dart board over their heads. "Wanna play?"

Sophie glanced up, noticing the dart board for the first time. "You're on."

Releasing her hand, he rose from the table. Rubbing her fingers together reflexively, she felt cold at the loss of contact. He disappeared to the bar for a moment and returned with two sets of darts while she moved to claim the dartboard.

Hands gripping Sophie's hips, looking helpful from afar, his thumbs caressed under the hem of her top as he backed her up to the line to start the game. Stepping out of the way with a wink and a devastating smile, he let Sophie go first. She let the dart fly.

Nailed it. The board anyway. The bullseye was a long way off. Or anything that carried any point value. Of her three darts, one of them actually scored a few points.

Not that they were playing competitively. Asher took her spot at the line and nailed a cluster right in the bullseye. Scowling at his perfect throws, she wasn't quite sure she wanted to play darts anymore.

With a shrug, he pulled the darts from the board and handed hers back. "We won't keep score." He grinned.

They neither kept score, nor kept much conversation for a few rounds. Not awkward or anything, more companionable silence. He showed her a few pointers, and she actually made a few decent throws. Hand-eye coordination had never been her thing.

"Did you work at the hardware store with your dad growing up?" For the first time, Asher missed the dart board entirely.

Stalking to the dropped dart, he picked it up without a word and walked back over. "As little as possible. Wasn't really my thing, and I was in a hurry to graduate from high school, getting ahead by taking classes at the community college, so I didn't have much time to work." Trying again, he nailed the next round of shots.

She knew she shouldn't pry. It wasn't polite. He just... he exhibited absolutely no enthusiasm for working in the hardware store. She hadn't seen it yet but had heard it was pretty well-stocked with practical and high-end goods. "Is it your thing now?"

He shrugged again and scratched at a non-existent itch in his thick five o'clock shadow. "It's a job. Sitting around the house is less my thing."

Sophie nudged him and laughed. "I don't think I've ever seen you sit still at home. What would you do, if you could pick any job in town, what would it be? Mayor? Beautician? Mailman? Go back to school?"

As she wasn't actively playing anymore, he stole her darts and threw them too, with a bit more fierceness than before. "I have no idea."

Staring at him a moment, she tried to come up with a good occupation for him. "You'd make a good cop. Or an EMT."

Asher pulled the darts from the board and went at it again. "I've thought about it. Not the EMT thing. The cop thing. But there's no way in hell Old Chief Larson would even let me in the door. Unless I was in cuffs."

A riotous laugh echoed from their friends at billiards. Somehow, drunk Pippa had hit her ball off the table and was crawling around on the disgusting floor looking for it.

"Oh boy, time to get these folks home. Who drove you guys?" She noted Lincoln was as red in the face with laughter as much as his fiancée. Freya looked to be a little less drunk, but only marginally.

"Grady drove. He's only had one." Together, they watched the scene unfold before attempting to clear their friends out... before any damage or irretrievable embarrassment occurred. Without taking his eyes away from the comical Three Stooges scene, Asher asked, "You want to round them up and figure out who's sleeping where tonight?"

Standing side-by-side, both stalled before moving on the plan. This could prove interesting if any one of the group wasn't ready to leave just yet. "I can do that." She nodded.

Pippa popped up with the ball and let out a boisterous. "Woohoo."

"And... that's my cue." Sophie mobilized to round up the inebriated troops.

Asher headed for the bar and gave his credit card to Irene. Sophie couldn't help but like him even more, knowing he was paying for the whole night without asking for reimbursement or even letting anyone else know who settled the bill.

Although it turned out to be more difficult than herding cats, she finally rounded up the drunks. Not normally drinkers, they'd gone all out for the party and were total lightweights. Surprisingly, they were all pleasant when she announced it was time to go home.

She liked how they decided to spend the drunk part of the evening together. That's how Lincoln and Pippa operated anyway. They tended to find the whole girls' vs boys' night out a bit weird.

Lincoln planned to come home with Pippa to hold back her hair when she inevitably puked, but it was going to be quite a contest to see who puked first. Grady offered to drive Freya home since they were the only ones not going to the Sutherland residence, but Sophie suspected it was also to avoid vomit in his car. No choice in the matter, Sophie rounded up the others to hop in her car.

A long, giggling drive later, fortunately without any up-chucking from the tipsy peanut gallery of two in the backseat, they pulled up to the house. Lincoln treated Pippa to a wobbly piggyback ride into the house.

Without the same enthusiastic pomp and circumstance, Sophie headed to bed, feeling suddenly very much alone. The drive home had been rough. Fortunately, the oblivious, twittering bachelor and bachelorette in the back seat didn't catch the raging sexual tension of silence in the front seat.

Sophie sighed, considering the odd turn her heart had taken. She wanted to talk to Pippa, to tell her what she was feeling. So physically close to Asher these last few weeks, yet so far, it was becoming physically painful to not be able to touch him when they were near. Sophie was regrettably, agonizingly stuck without being able to act on that overwhelming yearning.

Judging by Asher's tightly clenched fists and rapid pulsing of his jaw, he was suffering from similar affliction, struggling to abstain from acting on the powerful compulsion. He'd headed straight for the dimly lit pool to burn off the tension as the rest headed for bed.

S ound asleep, in the midst of weird dreams about poison dart frogs, Sophie awoke to the sound of... what was that? The sound was coming from Asher's room. She'd left the bathroom door open a crack, too tired to realize she hadn't closed it all the way. Or, perhaps, on some level, left it open in case he decided to sneak into her room during the night.

Tossing off the covers, she tiptoed cautiously into the bathroom. He hadn't closed his door either, whether it was subconsciously or intentionally, she'd never know. Sophie peeked into his bedroom and saw him thrashing in the bed, hollering someone's name.

She knew he had PTSD and that waking him in the midst of a nightmare could be dangerous for them both. It was torture watching him so terrified. In the glow from the moonlight shining through the window, she could see a glisten of tears on his cheek as he opened his eyes and lay still on the bed.

From the bathroom doorway, not wanting to get too close until she knew he was fully awake, Sophie whispered his name. Nothing. She whispered again.

Sitting up with a jolt, Asher rubbed the sleep and moisture from his eyes and searched the room for the sound. When he saw her, his face softened. "Sorry, did I wake you?"

With a sympathetic smile, Sophie responded, "Yeah, but that's okay. Who's Jack?"

Swinging his legs over the side of the bed, he took a sip of water from the glass by the bed. "One of my team. Good buddy. We lost three guys that day. Jack never walked again. Zane and I found him, barely a scraped knee between us. It was my last fucking op before my discharge went through."

Sophie walked softly across the bedroom and sat next to him, shoulder-to-shoulder. "I'm so sorry. Pippa mentioned you were going to the VA for therapy?"

He nodded somberly, lips pursed tight. "Yep. It's helping. I'm a lot better off than I was. I don't get as many nightmares anymore. Only a few flashbacks in all."

"That must have felt awful, to return unharmed while others weren't so fortunate." She tested the waters and slid her hand into his for the second time tonight. The connection made the world look a little less bleak.

His body relaxed against her, his focus shifting from the ceiling to their joined hands. "That pretty much sums it up. Checking out a fucking noise we should have just left alone; Zane and I were across the street when the building blew. I got a stupid scuff on my knee. I've got this tiny little scar still, a neat reminder, tattoo, of how I dodged a bomb and left others to die."

He flicked the small white line on his knee before continuing. "Fucking thing is, why me? Why Zane? Of the six of us close enough to feel the blast, we were the only two without a damn thing to lose. The only ones who made it out okay. Other guys had families. Shit, Jack was about the happy-go-luckiest guy you could know. Now, he's a morose lump in his wheelchair."

"I'd love to say something about destiny or a greater purpose, but I have no idea about any of that. Everyone I've ever loved, before I met Pippa, died before I even finished growing. Life doesn't make much sense sometimes." Exhaling her sadness wearily, she hoped she wasn't making things worse.

She'd questioned the same thing so many times. After years of searching, unable to find any deeper meaning in pain, she no longer let it stop her from thriving. Squeezing his hand, she leaned against his shoulder. "But we're both here. I'm glad you're here."

"Yeah. Not much more to it than that. Life fucking sucks sometimes. Other times, like right now, it's pretty great. I'm glad you're here, too." He pulled her hand up and softly pressed his warm lips to her knuckles. "I've felt much less alone since you got here. Whatever that means."

Sliding her legs up, she crawled into his bed and stole one of his pillows. Fluffing the pillow dramatically, she rested her head and pulled the blankets up, snuggling in at his side.

Watching, he chuckled, a confused smile crossing his face. "Forget where you are?"

"Nope." She curled up on her side closed her eyes. Without argument, he laid back in the bed and enveloped her in his arms. Within seconds, Sophie felt his breathing slow, his body relax. She was out a few seconds later.

Chapter Ten

T-Minus 9 Days

A sher woke with a mass of hair spread across his face. One arm pinned, he found himself wrapped around the octopus that was wrapped around him. An unexpected smile crossed his face. He'd slept great.

Sophie was nuzzled close, her head on his shoulder. Daylight streamed in through the open window, casting a warm glow on her smooth skin. She was gorgeous when she slept, her features soft, lips slightly parted. He'd never actually sleeping-slept with a woman before and found it remarkably arousing to wake up with one in his arms. Well, this one anyway.

Wow, that would have been a good Never for last night's game.

Although he hated to ruin the moment, he knew it was late morning already. He tried to gently wake her with a kiss. Eyebrows scrunching in adorable confusion, she wasn't quite awake yet.

He kissed her again, lingering a little longer this time. Her lips formed a satisfied smile before her eyes opened. Hand moving up to stroke his rough-bearded cheek, her lips, still warm from sleep, locked onto his. Immersed in the moment, she wrapped her legs around his waist and her fingers gripped in his hair.

Rolling her underneath him, Asher deepened the kiss, exploring her waiting mouth. Sliding his hand under her shirt, he grasped her breast, his calloused hand rough against her satin skin.

A sigh escaped her lips, her hands wandered down his sides and clutched his bare ass. Already hard, Asher instinctually moved against her. Glad she'd worn underwear to bed; the thin cotton was the only thing separating them before he did something stupid.

Fully awake now, she shifted her hands around front and ran her fingers along his iron-hard erection. Holy shit she wasn't shy. After a delicate caress, about torturing him with the feather light touch, she gripped the base of his cock firmly. Fuck, he about lost it.

A gentle knock thundered at the door, shattering the incredible moment.

"Dammit," he muttered as he leaped off of her. Sophie's eyes widened in panic and she bolted out of bed.

"Asher, can I come in?" His sister's soft voice carried through the door, jarring him like a damn IED exploding.

Frantically searching for pants, Asher pulled on his discarded jeans from last night. "Hang on."

Still in her camisole and panties, Sophie ran for the bathroom, only to find the door locked. The door handle wasn't budging. Shit. Apparently, she hadn't figured out the lock after the naked lesson the other morning.

Diving under the bed, Sophie disappeared from sight. Asher had never seen her move so fast, and when she ran, the wind followed her lead. At the last second, he grabbed a sweatshirt so he had something to hide the erection that just wouldn't fade. It had been way too long; poor guy wasn't calming down.

Holding the sweatshirt crumpled in front of him as if he meant to wear it, but really to maintain his dignity, he made it to the door just in time. Pippa was opening the door a crack to check on him.

"Were you still asleep? It's after seven. I don't think I've ever seen you sleep in this late. Or Sophie, for that matter; we must have stayed out later than I thought." She yawned, noting the daylight streaming in through his open window.

Asher turned it around on her. "Considering we had to drive a few drunks home at an ungodly late hour, give us sober few a break. How are you up so early?" She did look a little pasty this morning. Maybe a little green.

"We moronically scheduled the meeting with the minister the morning after the bachelor and bachelorette party." Her voice crackled as she spoke. Miraculously, she didn't try to push past his hand on the door.

Well, for a moment. "Wait, why are you blocking me? Is... You didn't have sex with Sophie, did you? After what happened at Mark's bachelor party?"

Pippa pushed past him, her angry eyes searching the room. She did a quick barrel through the room. Glaring at him, not quite satisfied, she went to the bathroom and tried to get in. Finding the door locked, miracle of miracles, she assumed Sophie was in the shared bathroom.

"Don't trust me?" He shrugged innocently.

"No." She completed her visual sweep of the room.

Asher gritted his teeth. He knew why she was so paranoid. She had plenty of friends growing up, but once they were... well... matured... although he regretted it, many came over to take a ride on the Asher train. He'd dug his own grave.

"Pip, really. I'm not that guy anymore. And I don't think Sophie's one of those girls." Shoving her out the door, he tried to close it in her face. Nicely, of course, but he was a little irritated.

She stuck her foot in the door so he couldn't lock her out yet. "I'm sure that's true. Just... not Sophie. I couldn't bear it if you broke her heart."

He knew what she meant. As much as she cared for her friend, she couldn't handle the heartbreak of losing another friend to his recklessness. "I know, Pip. I'd never do anything to hurt you." He amended, "Not intentionally anyway."

"I know." Downtrodden, not relieved by his reassurances, she started to leave. "Breakfast is keeping warm in the oven when you're hungry. We're off to see the minister."

Finally, she unwedged her foot from the door. Immediately, but quietly to avoid arousing suspicion, he closed and locked the door. Never to leave it unlocked ever again. Walking around to the far side of the bed, he watched as Sophie wiggled her way out from under the bed.

"You need to vacuum under there more often." She brushed a few dust bunnies out of her hair, looking incredibly adorable.

Smoothing her wild hair, he caught himself and pulled his hand back and left it to hang uselessly at his side. "I can't do this to Pippa. Shit, this sucks. But, I... I like you. A lot."

Biting her lip, Sophie looked away. Her eyes were moist from the dust or from the moment. He dared to hope it was the moment. Where was that coming from? He'd never wanted a woman to get emotional over him before.

"I like you, too. Maybe we can try the friend thing out for now? At least until after the wedding?"

Hating it, but knowing it was a good idea, Asher nodded. "Yeah."

She looked up at him, her arms crossed protectively across her chest. "I have a meeting with your Aunt Jane today about the business. Sort of an interview, but she refused to call it that, as she says she's hiring me anyway."

Shoving his hands in his pockets so he wouldn't touch her, his body clearly not on board with the friends-only thing, Asher nodded. "That's great. She'll be a good business partner. You know where the office is? I have a few errands to run, so we could head in together." He quickly corrected, "As friends, of course."

"Sounds good. You know how to pick locks?"

Scowling at the bathroom door, Asher shook his head. "I usually just kick them down. If I have to kick it down, you have to explain to Dad why the door is off its hinges."

Sophie wasn't wearing anything but her lace-trimmed tank top and flimsy little cotton panties. Coming out of his bedroom wearing next to nothing, or even his clothes, would really not be helpful at this point.

Pulling on a t-shirt, erection finally at ease, Asher offered, "I'll unlock it from your end. If there's anyone out there, it may take me a bit." Sophie nodded and hid behind the bedroom door while he ventured into the open loft area.

Coast clear, he casually strolled to her room, then dashed in before anyone saw. How the hell the door had locked itself, he'd never know. Stupid electronic locks. It was one of the finest on the market when they'd built the house. His dad had been so excited to stock it at the shop.

Standing in the middle of his bedroom, hip cocked out to the side in pure attitude, Sophie stood waiting for him. He tried not to let his gaze linger on those long legs. Tried not to notice her soft, handful-sized breasts were perky and braless under her tank. Tried not to notice how sexy she looked, all rumpled from sleeping curled up next to him last night.

When Pippa got back from her honeymoon, he was going to have to have a serious talk with her. He wasn't letting Sophie go.

He'd been a dumbass back in the day, which he knew. He'd always had a bit of trouble controlling his impulses. That was why he rushed his way through high school, then majored in the fastest program he could find; he knew he would flounder for years otherwise. Then joined the navy without a fucking clue what he'd been getting into.

There was this little box on a form to request his preferred unit, and he thought, SEALs are awesome, why not? His impulsivity got his in trouble more often than not, so he'd worked hard to be sure he was constantly on the move before it bit him in the ass.

After a quick shower, he dashed downstairs. Thank goodness most of the house appeared to be gone. Pippa and Lincoln must have left for their appointment already.

Coffee. Sleeping in so late, the caffeine headache was kicking in already. The pot nearly empty, he poured the last of the dregs into his cup. Measuring the fragrant grounds, he made a full pot, anticipating the need for a little extra kick this morning.

Sophie would be down soon and be looking for her morning caffeine fix, too. And, as he was, she'd be a bit twitchy from missing their run this morning.

Smirking with what he knew was a dumbass grin on his face, he imagined what might have happened if they hadn't been so rudely interrupted. She was definitely not the innocent everyone seemed to think. After that stupid game last night, then this morning...

The way she'd tormented him with that feather-light touch until he forgot his own name, then squeezed him so tight... he about came in her hand. He'd been right about those perfect breasts of hers, too. It was going to be a fucking long wait to have her.

Again, rudely interrupted. What was with his family? Paul lumbered around the corner and joined him in the kitchen.

Thank god he'd worn thick, snug jeans to keep things subdued this morning. He needed to get his own place. Fast.

"Morning, Asher. Don't usually see you sleep in so late. Exciting bachelor party last night?" Paul stood next to him, also waiting for the fresh pot of coffee to finish brewing.

He knew his dad was just making conversation, but he couldn't help but feel defensive. Yeah, he'd nailed Mark's stripper that night, but it hadn't exactly been planned or anything. Everyone else had passed out drunk before she finished her routine. With a sailor's tolerance, he'd been just fine, all systems in full operation. She'd been looking for a little after party action, and he was happy to accommodate.

Crossing his arms and leaning against the kitchen counter, Asher nodded. "It was fun. Not too crazy. I don't usually stay up so late. Guess I'm getting old."

Snorting, Paul nodded. "Wait until you're my age. If you're usually up so early, maybe you want to take an opening shift at Sutherland's?"

Nodding, Asher silently agreed with the proposal. Every fucking opportunity and Paul brought it up. Not even much of a segue this time.

Shit, he didn't want to work at Sutherland's, but what else was he going to do? He didn't want to live with his parents forever. It had been long enough already. He'd built a decent savings, but he wanted to save up for a house one day, not blow it on daily expenses just to escape his father while he was unemployed and clueless about his future.

"Great. Are you still thinking early to mid-July? That old truck that seems to occupy your every waking hour will be fixed or in the junk yard by then." Paul looked at him skeptically.

Why was the coffee taking so damn long? "Sure."

Paul sighed like a tired old dog, leaning against the kitchen cabinets, his arms folded and legs extended. Looking up from the tile floor, he looked at his son. "Asher, if you're not up to it yet, just say so."

That wasn't it. "I'm sick of sitting around the house. I just... I don't know. I don't know what I want long term." He was a grownup. Why couldn't he explain to his own father what the problem was?

Shaking his head in disgust, Paul started his characteristic pacing around the room, his already ruddy complexion flushing to beet red. Might as well start kicking dirt like the bull ready to charge that he was.

"You've been putting it off for years, jumping around from a useless political science degree to a futureless career in the navy, now you're hanging out in my garage every day working on a truck that's never going to run again."

Paul threw his arms in the air before starting the next lap of the kitchen. "Sutherland's won't be right without a Sutherland running it. I'm not going to be there forever. It's time to get your head on straight and come to work."

"My head is on straight." He felt the bull snorting inside himself. Pushing away from the counter, he fired back, louder and fiercer than he normally would have. "I have a fucking college degree. Graduated early, Magna Cum-fucking-Laude. Worked my ass off for the damn navy, one of the most elite units in the world, protecting my country from some truly nightmarish threats. If you want to see my hard-earned medals, that seemed to matter to some of the highest-ranking people in the nation, just let me know."

Arms folding across his chest, he stood his ground. "You're not wrong; neither of those were permanent, but they were respectable pursuits according to the rest of society. Not my own dad, though. Not the future you had planned for me, was it? Give me a fucking break."

The coffee pot sputtered as the last trickle of coffee streamed into the full carafe. Fuming, Asher topped off his cup, barely managing to avoid spilling over the top in his angry dudgeon. He grabbed another mug from the cupboard to fill for Sophie, knowing she must be waiting around the corner. She was too polite to interrupt, but he knew she would be working on a blistering caffeine headache like he was.

Brushing past his father with both mugs, Asher didn't wait for a response. Paul stood and watched, looking torn between tearing him a new one and leaving him alone. Thankfully, he didn't follow.

Asher could picture his father's indecision, a little devil on one shoulder and a tiny white angel on the other, both demanding he go after his son in some way or another. As usual, Paul stood in between–when the little devil wasn't taking over–neither finishing the fight nor making peace.

No Sophie around the corner, so he looked up the stairs and saw her waiting at the top, leaning on the rail. As he approached, the angry pit of fire in his gut rapidly morphed into an unusual combination of relief and arousal at seeing her waiting for him.

Dressed as the professional accountant, hair neatly pulled back into a stylish knot, he could picture her wearing cute little reading glasses. Whether she needed them or not, maybe she would be willing to try it out? Pull that mass of mixed, dirty blond hair out of its binding with a sexy hair flip. Yeah, this friend thing wasn't going to happen.

"You heard?" He handed her a mug and stood next to her at the rail.

Gratefully, she accepted the cup and took a savoring sip of the steaming coffee. Leaning against each other, shoulder to shoulder, they gazed out the large windows. The glowing morning sun lit up the room, the amber light almost blinding.

"I heard. He is proud of you; he just doesn't know how to say it." Her fingers sent a tingling reassurance up his arm and lodged in his throat as she caressed the back of his hand with the back of hers.

"Maybe." He glared at the fresh, steaming cup of joe, taking a cautious, testing sip before deciding it was safe to consume without risk of a singed tongue.

"He is. He just doesn't know what to do with you. He always knew what he wanted out of life, so he doesn't understand that you don't. You're brainier than he knows what to do with, yet at the same time you're indecisive and impulsive. You'll figure out what you want. Give it time."

Exhaling deeply, he tried to believe her. How had she figured him out so quickly? He still didn't have himself figured out, nor did his family appear to. "You seem awfully confident about that."

"I had a damn compass tattooed on me; I was so determined to find my own path. Had to map it out so I didn't get lost. You don't need a map or compass. Whatever the terrain, you find a way. Not everyone can do that. Certainly not so smoothly." She smiled up at him, her expression kind, knowing.

Paul ambled awkwardly out of the kitchen, glanced up at the pair, and stalked out of the house.

Despite her confidence, Asher hadn't found his flaws as beneficial as she seemed to think them. "Most find that my impulsivity gets me, and others, into trouble more often than not."

"Are you sure it's *most* that feel that way? It seems to me it kept you alive in the navy. You may have a case of survivor's guilt, but you're alive and well. Instinct, luck, whatever... you escaped some nasty scrapes. Got you through college too, pretty well, actually. I'm not so sure about that Magna Cum Laude, graduating early nonsense, but to each his own," she teased with a generous grin. "You go with your gut, roll with the punches. Not everyone has the keen instincts or the mental and physical dexterity that you do."

Considering, Asher liked the way she said it better. He was so used to being told to stop and think before acting.

If he'd done that, he'd be as dead as his team, or his legs as nonfunctional as Jack's. And wouldn't be here with Sophie.

"Don't you have that meeting soon? I can fix breakfast."

"Toast?" She looked suddenly panicked and gulped the last of her coffee.

Leading the way, he motioned for her to follow him down the stairs. Her nerves had kicked back in again. He had no idea why she was so nervous to meet with Aunt Jane; the woman was fierce but seemed to adore Sophie as much as the rest of his family and was as loyal and good-natured as they come. "You're in luck, I don't actually know how to make anything else. However, Mom made scrambled eggs, and I can dish it up for you."

"Maybe a little. That toast actually sounds better. I don't think the butterflies in my stomach left much room for anything else." She managed a weak smile and put her hand over said butterflies.

"Nervous about Jane? She's a total softy." Reaching the kitchen, he pulled out their finest loaf of sourdough and popped two slices into the toaster. Leaning back against the counter, he raised his eyebrow at Sophie mischievously.

Sophie stomped her feet and whined pitifully. "That's the problem. I don't want her to go easy on me. I want to be a fair partner, not a pity hire. What if she just hires me because she's a softy? Then I'll be a total drain to the business, and she'll be too nice to fire me."

Sighing, Asher realized this wasn't an easy battle. As much as he berated himself for his faults, Sophie clearly wasn't any more immune to self-criticism than he was. "Jane wouldn't pick just anyone to make her one-woman operation a two-women firm. Trust me. If she didn't truly think you were capable, she'd have told you about local businesses looking for an accountant."

Nodding bravely, Sophie was trying to believe his assurances. "Fair point."

He hooked his fingers in her belt and pulled her between his legs. Resting his mouth on the top of her forehead, he placed a gentle kiss before remembering they were just friends. Friends stood this way, right?

He didn't have many female friends, or friends in general, really. Surely some friends must stand this way and kiss each other platonically. Or was it only platonic if it didn't affect them?

"Didn't you have some amazing internship in Seattle? Work with some impressive accounting firm while you finished school?" He could feel her loosening in his grip, calming down a little. "Oh yeah, that's right smarty-pants, you have a master's degree, an accounting certification, and four years of experience in the field. And you've got a level head. Total pity hire. I have no idea what Aunt Jane is thinking."

She pulled back, looked up, and gave him a mocking glare. "I'll take that toast now."

"**L**et's take my truck."

"Is it behaving today? I don't want to risk a breakdown on my way to meet Jane. Doesn't look good to show up late for a not-interview."

Sophie looked so damn gorgeous, her confidence starting to blossom, strutting her stuff and dressed the part in a pair of slim black slacks paired with a feminine, yet outdoorsy floral top. Perfect for the local business scene.

Even with the heeled boots, she was still shorter than he was. He tried not to imagine how perfectly she'd fit against him in her bare feet. How her legs might wrap around him as he took her against the wall. On her knees in front of him with those lush, pink lips taking him in... *dammit, cool your jets.*

"Don't trust my mechanic skills? We made it back home last time." He raised an eyebrow in challenge.

Looking from his truck to her CR-V and back again, she shook her head. "If we're late, I'm blaming you."

With a casual salute, he dashed ahead and opened the creaky, yet functional, passenger door for her. "At the rate we're going, you'll be twenty minutes early as it is."

He fired up the engine. It wheezed and whined, but finally it turned over. "See? No problem." Hopefully. Easing it into gear, he held his breath. So far so good, shifting smoothly, clutch good, brakes working. What more could he replace on the damn thing?

The drive went smoothly, despite the lack of air conditioning. Her hair had been straightened and pulled into a neat bun so nicely, but now she wore a cute beachy, messy bun look after the wind got to it. Much more fun this way anyway.

They made casual conversation on the drive. It was nice being friends. When was the last time he'd been just friends with a woman? Ever? Although, he supposed it wasn't really friendship when he kept picturing her naked. Riding him like Lady Godiva. Calling out his name in triumph as she straddled him in an epic orgasm.

"I forgot to mention, I have an appointment at the bank after I'm done with Jane. I have some documents to sign so my trust fund can be deposited straight into my account."

Her mother sounded to be great person, and Sophie a well-loved kid. Her aunt must be a nightmare. He couldn't picture Sophie clothed in the too short but too wide Hollywood-wannabe clothes her aunt had passed along to her that she told him about. "Mom mentioned something about that. Your mom set it up to protect the money from your aunt?"

A look of disgust, Sophie nodded. "Thank goodness. I got a decent chunk at eighteen to help pay for college expenses, another at twenty-four, now I get full control of the rest on my twenty-seventh birthday."

"When's your birthday?" Rounding the bend, the truck lurched a bit, refusing to downshift, but finally managed to lock into gear without it stalling.

"Tomorrow," she answered nonchalantly, her gaze following the passing trees out the window.

"Tomorrow? Why didn't you say anything?" He tried not to act astonished, but it wasn't like his family to not start fussing already. Birthdays were a big deal in the Sutherland house.

Picking at a nonexistent fuzzy on her pants, Sophie shrugged. "I don't want to be a burden. Everyone's so busy with the wedding, I thought I might be able to slide under the radar this year. I hate the attention anyway."

"But do you hate cake?" He eyed her meaningfully, trying to get a smile out of her.

Grinning, she looked to be much more at ease with the joking than she had been with the talk of her birthday celebration. "Cake's okay. I'd rather have pie."

"Then pie you shall have." How many birthdays had no one even noticed? Or maybe known about but not cared? He knew Pippa wouldn't have missed a one, but how could his family be dropping the ball like this?

"I may want to sit and eat the whole damn thing alone, far from cell service anyway." And her mood was plummeting again.

Fearing why, he couldn't help but ask. "Lovely Yvette's going to start asking for more, isn't she?" Reaching the edge of Foothills proper, he slowed the truck for the first stop light.

Again, finding the most minute strings and fuzzies to pull off her black pants, Sophie shook her head. "Without a doubt. I'm debating giving her a final chunk with some sort of binding agreement so she can never ask for anything more. Wishful thinking, but I'm hoping that will satisfy her for all eternity."

"You don't owe her a damn thing. She abused your trust fund and did the least amount of parenting she could for you."

Asher found himself steaming, his fists clenching, ready to lash out at the injustice.

The old pickup was still alive and well as they pulled up in front of Foothills Accounting. Good thing too; she was upset enough, and missing this meeting would have wrecked her. His truck radio hadn't worked in years, so he glanced at his watch. "See, you're here precisely fifteen minutes early."

Grinning, Sophie grabbed her purse. "Meet you at the bank in... two hours? Maybe we can go for an afternoon hike after? As friends, of course," she quickly corrected.

Watching her enthusiasm quickly building, he couldn't help but smile with her. "Sure thing. I'll pick up some supplies in case we get lost in the wilderness," he teased, remembering her fondness for picnics.

She leaned across and pressed her lips to his for a quick peck on the lips. Friendly, almost platonic. Sort of. She must be having as much trouble with the friend-thing as he was.

Watching her walk in the building, he ran his tongue over his lips to savor her taste. It was going to be a long damn wait. He'd never really waited before, just dove right into the sex part.

Maybe he would have stuck around longer if he'd had to wait before... nah. None of them were Sophie. None were even close to worth waiting for like she was.

Chapter Eleven

A fter correcting the truck into the parking spot, he banged his forehead against the steering wheel. *Ouch*. It didn't help. He put some coins in the meter and strolled down the block to the diner, focusing on every little detail that wasn't Sophie.

As usual, Foothills wasn't overcrowded, but there was a constant murmuring of activity. Being mid-week, most folks were at work. Those that weren't were taking the kids to the small grassy park across the street or perusing the shops in search of the latest treasures. A small handful, like Asher, were headed into Larissa's Diner for a late breakfast, or a place to rest and consider their plans for the day over a cup of coffee or hot chocolate.

"Well, I'll be. Asher Sutherland. You get on over here and give old Larissa a hug." Straight out of Alabama, Larissa hadn't shaved off a trace of her accent in the thirty years she'd run Larissa's Diner in Foothills. She set down the menus she'd been holding and sashayed toward him.

Glad for the warm welcome, Asher met her halfway and pulled her in for a big bear hug, lifting her sturdy frame a few inches off the ground. Before he could step out of reach, she whacked him on the shoulder with the plaid hand towel she chronically kept draped over her shoulder. "Always the flirt. Although, not for long from what Irene tells me."

Shit. In trying to let Irene off easy, he told her he'd met someone. It was true, becoming truer by the day, but nothing he could actually let anyone know about. "Keep your voice down, I've got a reputation to uphold," he teased back, unable to hide the grin, hoping one day to shout from the rooftops that he had taken the fall.

"What can I get for you? You eat breakfast already?" She waggled back to her post behind the counter.

He gestured to a booth by the window. It was still a few minutes to ten. "Just passing the time. Cup of coffee?"

"Are you going to order a cup of coffee and not have a slice of pie to go with that? I've got my famous strawberry-rhubarb just finished cooling." She grabbed the carafe of coffee from behind the bar and followed him to his choice of booth and flipped a waiting coffee cup right-side up, setting it gently on the paper doily coaster and filled it with piping hot coffee.

Asher grinned, "How could I possibly turn down a slice of your strawberry-rhubarb pie?"

Leaving him to enjoy his coffee, she disappeared to grab the pie. He didn't have much of a sweet tooth, but he couldn't let her down by not trying the pie. And eating every last bite. Maybe it was her feelings, or maybe a clever sales tactic, but he couldn't say no either way.

After devouring every last gooey morsel of the pie and raving over it, two cups of coffee, and an hour of letting his brain wander to stranger and more confusing places, like what he was going to do with the rest of his life, he was beyond restless. One could only play so many games on his phone and stare out the window for so long.

Heading up to the counter, he cashed out. "Thanks Larissa. Can you have a whole one of your excellent strawberry rhubarb pies ready for me about this time tomorrow? Maybe another one, something seasonal you can recommend?"

She beamed at the praise. "For you, anything. I can whip up a fine blueberry pie to go with it. What's the occasion?"

"Birthday party."

A sly expression crossed her face, her eyes curious. "For your lady friend?"

Looking around the diner, he ensured no one could hear them. No one he knew, anyway. "That's right. Not a word now, okay?"

"Secrets don't help anyone, you know." Serious now, she held the full lecture he knew she could deliver. In spades. As the not-angry, or even bitter, mother of an ex-lover of his, he knew she was openminded and understanding. He also knew she was a hopeless romantic.

Her husband owned Ahab's and, although the two worked essentially opposite shifts, the pair was obviously as in love today as the day they met. Maybe more. Asher had made his preference for no-commitment very clear to Irene from day one, which she had preferred as well.

Which was probably why they still got along well. She'd been on the lookout for true love, and he'd had no idea what he wanted. So, they had just messed around with no strings attached.

Asher hated the secret more than he could say. Even if he and Sophie were *just friends* for now. Despite their efforts to cool down, they wouldn't be *just friends* if he didn't believe it and neither did Sophie. "I know. Trust me, it wasn't my idea, and I won't have to keep mum for long. No choice in this case."

One hand on her hip, the other waggled at him like the second mother she designated herself as. "She'd better be worth it."

"She is." He couldn't contain the smile as he imagined when he could bring Sophie in here and show her off. With a wave, he strolled out the door and caught the friendly air kiss Larissa blew in his direction. A friendly jingling announced his departure as he opened the diner door, warm air wafting across his skin as he entered the balmy street.

As morning had passed into afternoon, town was now bustling with locals and tourists alike, more than he remembered from his childhood, but somehow still pleasantly peaceful. Having another hour to kill, he tried to find something to keep him occupied. Sutherland's Hardware was a block and a half away.

Nope, not going there. Not today. Today was too nice of a day to stress himself out that way.

Not that he was practicing avoidance behaviors, as he now could identify this tendency in himself thanks to therapy. Cringing, he pictured himself selling plywood and light fixtures for the rest of his life. It was great work, and he wouldn't hate it. His dad sure liked it. It just wasn't for him.

He could picture himself still working for Sutherlands thirty years from now, simply because he hadn't found something better. It would be fine. He just wasn't eager to get stuck in a long-term career that didn't interest him in the least.

Instead, he headed into the next shop down. Sporty's was having a sale. He could always use new running shoes, maybe stock up on camping gear. His tent should be fine, but his sleeping bag hadn't been used in ages and was likely dust laden and moth eaten from storage in the garage.

The sale was pretty fantastic. Two-for-one sleeping bags. A nice, extra-long navy blue one with a green zipper in Seahawks colors had his name written on it. As luck would have it, right next to it was a lighter blue one with a black zipper that could zip right up to it to make a big sleeping bag for two.

Getting ahead of yourself? Yeah, probably. For a city girl, Sophie seemed to love the outdoors. Had she ever been camping? Not wanting to miss the sale, he picked up the pair of sleeping bags. Camping gear was a thoughtful birthday present, wasn't it?

On his way to the checkout, he accidently picked up a pink flashlight and gunmetal gray multipurpose tool for her. And that was it. And a gift card. She'd want some decent hiking boots. By the time he left, he had a nice amount of rewards points accumulated. Good investment, really.

Tossing the massive load of gear into the backseat of the pickup, he tossed his jacket over the top to cover the pile of booty. Pleased with his purchases, hoping Sophie would be as thrilled with the gifts as he was, he checked his watch. Nice timing. Sophie should be finishing up at the bank soon.

Sophie's knee rattled at high speed as the banker finalized the last of the documents. Each click of his fingers on the keyboard hammered into her skull, a thundering doomsday countdown. Outside the cubicle walls, she could hear the chipper greeting of a teller to a customer depositing her paycheck. At the self-service counter, two other customers were clearly good friends, ragging each other about last week's bingo tournament. All were happy and enjoying the marvelous afternoon. None were counting down the seconds until they were struck with a full-scale blackmail attack.

When would Yvette start the harassment? Would she wait until morning? She'd never remembered Sophie's birthday before, but something told Sophie she wouldn't miss this one.

"Miss Jones, your funds will be deposited directly into your savings account at 0800 tomorrow morning. If you choose to transfer any of it into a CD or mutual fund, I'll be more than happy to help." Around her age, maybe a year or two older, Kai Higgins, banker extraordinaire, extended his hand and shook hers in an easy handshake. He was incredibly handsome, with his rich olive skin, thick ebony hair, and dashing smile. Obviously feeling her out for a transition to a social conversation once their business was concluded.

"Thanks, Kai. I'll see you around." She grinned back at him, hiding her anxiety about the whole funds transfer. Maybe if she automatically put a large chunk into a CD, she couldn't get to it when Yvette asked, and she wouldn't be able to give her anything, even if she wanted to.

Smoothing his sapphire blue tie, he warmly added, "I'm sure we'll have more than a few mutual customers. Don't hesitate to call me if you need anything."

Sliding back in the chair, Sophie just rose to stand, her butt barely off the chair, when a deafening crack sliced through the air. The subsequent crash of debris from the ceiling left little doubt as to the cause of the noise.

Instinctively ducking down, she and Kai both hit the ground in an instant.

"Alright everybody, faces on the floor and hands behind your heads." A hoarse voice bellowed over the whimpers and screams from the four other bank customers and the handful of employees.

Subtly watching through the open cubicle doorway, Sophie did as she was told and stilled as four armed, masked figures spread out swiftly across the room. Each with a pistol in hand and another at the hip, they didn't seem to be locals looking for drug money.

Asher would be here any minute. Keeping her head low to the ground, not wanting to attract attention, she was only able to make out the bright sun shining into the tops of the windows. The cubicle wall blocked her from being able to see outside, and certainly there was no way to warn Asher to stay away.

From his spot on the floor a few feet away, Kai inched toward her. Subtly, sternly, Sophie shook her head, not wanting to attract attention. He stilled and responded with a glimmer of a nod, recognizing she was right. With a subtle eyebrow raise, he angled his head and silently asked if she was okay.

Nodding, she indicated that she was fine, appreciating the concern, even though he could clearly see she was unharmed and exhibiting no more panic than the others. Offering him a small, reassuring smile, she turned her head back to watch the chaos unfold.

Two of the bandits walked behind the teller counter, demanding to be taken to the vault. A third announced as he watched the few customers and bank employees on the floor. "We're thirty seconds behind already. Let's move it along. I won't hesitate to shoot anyone who slows us down."

The fourth watched the door, standing over the downed security guard. His gun drawn, eyes constantly on the move, the sentinel didn't miss anything.

Studying the guard through the wide cubicle doorway, Sophie searched for signs of blood or awkward positioning of his body. He looked to be okay. Yeah, he was okay. His chest was rising and falling slowly under the bandit's foot.

Whistling a cheery tune, Asher almost missed the unmistakable sound of a single gunshot echoing from the bank. Years of training and instincts flowed through him like a rapid rush of stimulants. The few pedestrians nearby looked around for the backfire of an engine and otherwise went about their day.

Sprinting along the wall until he reached the bank door, Asher listened intently without getting close enough to the window that he might be seen. A few whimpers and squeals, but otherwise the bank had gone silent.

Lacking a mirror, Asher turned on the camera on his phone and angled it so he could see in the glass bank door without giving away his position. One just inside the door, a security guard at his feet. In the distance, another one near the tellers, filling a bag with cash from their drawers. Where was Sophie?

Through the front door, open only a slight crack, he heard a disdainful voice announce, "We're thirty seconds behind already. Let's move it along. I won't hesitate to shoot anyone who slows us down." Judging by the matching uniforms and discreet, but very effective, twenty-twos, one in the holster and one in hand, they weren't amateurs.

If he were to try to make a move, someone would get hurt, maybe killed. They likely didn't want to add murder to their list of crimes. An organized unit, you'd think they'd hit bigger banks in bigger cities. Unless this was part of the gig; hit the unsuspecting small-town banks where they'd meet less resistance.

Sophie was in there somewhere. She was smart; she wouldn't do anything to put herself in danger. Unless it was to protect others. Anxiously, he scanned the room to find her.

"Asher, how the hell are you?" Jonah Larson, a few years ahead of him in school, stood at his side. Dressed in a black police uniform, shiny badge and all.

Crisply, succinctly, Asher whispered, "Bank robbery. I see two, but likely at least one or two more at the vault from what I can tell."

Larson immediately backed against the wall next to him. "It's payday. Armored truck would have been by an hour ago. I can get in the back door."

"If we interrupt, someone's much more likely to get killed."

"Fair point. I'm good with holding here."

From inside, a scream echoed. Panning his camera, he saw a woman being dragged by her hair across the room. "Never mind. Guess we're not that lucky. It's getting ugly, hostage. Why don't you head to the back? I'll take these two in front."

Larson didn't hesitate. Despite this being his territory, he didn't seem to question words of experience. Asher appreciated his lack of ego; ego usually ended up getting everyone else killed.

"Ninety fucking seconds. You're all slow." The asshole holding the woman by the hair shouted at the crowd. Trying to frighten? Play with them? Or would he kill her just for fun?

Asher didn't have time to wait for Larson to take position. The gunmen aimed his weapon at the hostage he'd taken.

As if a normal, happy customer, Asher strolled right in through the front door. Surprised, the gunman at the door spun to aim at him, but Asher closed the distance between them in a blink.

Interrupting the momentum, moving swiftly and methodically, Asher grabbed the gun with his far hand, pointing the barrel at the floor as he took control, and with his opposite elbow, he clocked the guy in the Adam's apple.

Coughing, clutching his throat, the door guard was temporarily out of commission. The asshole in the middle of the room turned and hesitated, assessing the sudden southward turn in the situation.

Big mistake. Asher took advantage of the pause and fired a single shot with the borrowed gun and nailed the guy in the shoulder.

Risky move with a weapon he'd never fired himself, but the shot was clear and no one behind in case he missed. Not that he ever missed. If he'd waited another second, the hostage would have been between him and the robber.

With breathing now calming but not yet stable, the front door man struggled to stand and threw a desperate punch at Asher's jaw.

Ducking, Asher used the guy's momentum against him and threw him onto the ground, his own feet rock steady.

With a swift jab to the head, he clocked the guy's skull against the tile floor and knocked him out.

Out of the corner of his eye, Asher could see movement from the back.

"Status?" One of the robber's demanded as she peered into the main area.

A quick rapport of two shots could be heard from the back room. Front area secure, Asher sprinted across the floor and leaped over the teller counter, sliding over the faux granite on his hip.

One of the robbers limped on a bleeding thigh towards him. Way to go Larson. Still armed, however.

Aiming at Asher with a shaking hand, the asshole tried to steady himself, furious and barely walking. Not a very good plan, adding murder to one's charge of armed robbery.

Easily containable, Asher ducked and rolled, swiping his leg and grabbing the gun from the flailing arm before it could fire.

Larson appeared from the back room, weapon drawn as he scanned the scene. Whipping his head around, Asher checked the room again to ensure any threats were still neutralized.

Sirens blared as backup arrived. Two more cops came rushing in and secured the scene. Pretty well trained for a small town.

Customers and employees of the bank started to rise, most speechless and taking in the chaos. It had taken less than a minute for Asher and Larson to come in and take down the robbers. His eyes wandered the crowd, searching out the reason he was here.

Stepping out from the far cubicle, Sophie's frazzled but smiling face melted him immediately. Closing the distance between them in an instant, he pulled her against him and held on until he was convinced she was safe.

Nuzzling against his neck, her breathing was calm and steady. Unlike his. In the moment, he'd been the machine he'd been trained to be.

Now, holding her, realizing how close he'd come to losing her, he knew she was never going to be just a friend. If she'd been hurt...

"Asher?" Larson interrupted, voice calm, steady, and barely above a whisper.

Tucking Sophie at his side, he turned towards Larson. Realizing he was still clutching the robber's gun, he double checked the safety and handed it to the officer next to Larson for processing. "All good?"

Larson nodded. "Nice work. You have some time to come over to the station to chat for a bit?"

Shit. Never good when a cop asks you that. His eyes strayed downward to the badge, noting that Larson wasn't just a cop, he was the chief. "Of course."

Turning to Sophie, he raised his eyebrows in question. "You want to see if Jane can give you a lift home?"

She shook her head. "I can wait. I'll come with you. I could use some time to cool down before heading home anyway."

Larson nodded. "Why don't I meet you both at the station? The others will be taking statements from everyone in the bank anyway, and it's going to take a while for everyone here to be cleared. Might actually be faster this way."

"Thanks, Chief Larson. We'll head right over." Sophie leaned against Asher as she gave the chief a tired smile.

"Chief Larson was my father. It's Jonah. See you in a few." He winked and left to check in with the cops on scene that had already started their questioning.

Heading out the front door, Asher couldn't seem to let go of Sophie. Not caring who they ran into or what anyone thought, he clutched her hand and wasn't letting go.

Jane stood outside the bank with a small crowd, anxiously wringing her hands until she saw the two of them come out. "Are you okay? I heard the shots and came out as soon as I saw the police arrive." Checking her nephew and her new partner for any sign of injury, she looked them up and down. Satisfied neither were hurt, she threw her arms around the pair.

Not one to be rattled easily, Jane stepped back, took a steadying breath, and put her hands on her hips. "Well. I'm just glad you're both okay." Noting they were holding hands, she added with a smile, gesturing, "I was going to hint to Denise that you two would make a nice couple. I see you beat me to the punch."

Shit. Sophie didn't deny it. Very matter-of-factly, she agreed, "I'm really glad you think so. We like each other."

Wincing, Asher pleaded, "Mind not saying anything just yet? Pippa would kill us both."

Laughing uproariously, pleasantly shattering the doom and gloom that hung over the crowd, Jane nodded in agreement. "I won't say a thing. I nearly forgot about... you know. All that fuss she threw. As much as I love my niece, sort of serves her right. Her first friend worth keeping around happens to be such a good match for you."

Neither knew quite what to say. What did she mean by 'her first friend worth keeping around?' Well, Asher supposed she really hadn't had a genuinely good friend since they were in grade school. What kind of friend snuck into her friend's brother's bedroom in the middle of the night? Ouch, Pippa was going to kill them both.

Jane watched his struggle to understand her comments and winked. "You'll figure it out. Just take good care of each other. I'm glad you're okay." Flitting back into Foothills Accounting, Jane laughed the entire way.

Adrenaline crashing, Asher leaned gently on Sophie, absorbing some of her strength.

Larson had been talking to him for an hour now. It had taken about thirty seconds to get her statement, then she'd been politely kicked out. She knew she could call Jane or even Pippa to come get her, but she didn't want to. This must have added to his stress level. She needed to stay, in case he needed anything.

The Foothills police station was actually pretty nice. From the plaque she read above the set of chairs she was planted in, it had been built over a hundred years ago and was one of the first in the area. Classically constructed with woodwork everywhere, wooden stairs and railing to a mysterious upper story, creaky hardwood floors, thick wooden doors. She could almost smell the timber under the scent of the receptionist's spaghetti.

Leaning back in the minimally cushioned waiting chair, she tried to stimulate circulation to her low back again. After her butt had formed a likely permanent indent in the flimsy foam and fake leather, she'd given up the effort to attempt to find a comfortable position. The receptionist gave her another sweet smile, but still had no updates for her.

Her knee was going a mile a minute. Glancing at her phone, she remembered she'd run the battery down to about nothing. Tempted to bite her nails, she sat on her hands to prevent a relapse. Well, another relapse. There wasn't much left to chew anyway.

Finally, the door at the far end of the office opened, and she could see Chief Larson standing in the open doorway. Jonah. He couldn't be more than four or five years older than Asher. A bit shorter, hair neatly trimmed, full beard. Fit but stalky. Gentle eyes; that was a nice thing to see in a police chief.

He shook Asher's hand firmly. Both men smiled. "Think about it. I'll look forward to your email."

In a typical military-efficient walk, Asher motioned for her to follow him out of the building, but didn't pause until they reached the passenger door to his truck. He was quiet, biting his lip to hide a smile as he opened her door for her, then dashed around the front of the truck and hopped in the driver's side. The suspense was driving her crazy.

"Well? What was that all about?" She demanded as she buckled her seatbelt, bouncing slightly on the spring-loaded seat.

Finally, he fired up the engine. After three tries, it cooperated. "He offered me a job. Well, sort of. I have to formally apply and send him my resumé, then he'll check references and cover all the official bases."

"That's fantastic. I guess Old Chief Larson retired, huh?"

"About three years back. Young Larson, Jonah, took his place. Good guy. Nothing like his father. He was a few years older than me in school. We got along well." He put his hand on the gear shifter to get them moving towards home, but he paused, considering for a moment.

Pulling his hand back, he turned to Sophie. Leaning across the truck, the chest strap of her seatbelt following, she met him halfway. Cradling her face with his hands, he kissed her deeply, intensely, packed with emotion. He rested his forehead against hers, ran his tongue over the crease of his lips, enjoying the taste of her on his lips.

Satisfied grin pasted to his face, he sat back up and shifted into first gear and pulled into traffic. "That scared the hell out of me, knowing you were in there in the middle of all that. I don't know what the hell is going on with me, but I know it has everything to do with you. This friend thing... not going to work. I'm already way too far gone for you."

He chuckled mirthlessly. "I'm usually a quick fuck and done sort of guy. I did promise to not have sex with you, but... it's been rough." He managed to keep his gaze directed steady out the front windshield but couldn't suppress the hungry growl in his voice.

Pensively, Sophie studied his features, looking downright irritated. Shit, he'd explained that badly, as usual. "What's going to happen when we do have that sex, then? You sure you're not going to be done with me?"

"What? Fuck no. I'm trying to say that you're so much more to me than an easily accessible lay. Or a friend. I can't get you out of my head. Once is most definitely not going to be enough."

She smiled, reassured, and turned back to the window, watching the quiet afternoon of the small town. "Good. I'm not looking for a one and done. I've been there, done that. Let's wait until after the wedding, so we don't both break our promises just yet. Let her mull things over after she's all honeymoon-happy and the stress of the wedding is done."

Grinning, she turned back and this time, rotated her whole body to look him straight-on. "And, you clearly haven't been with the right woman. I promise, you'll be begging for more. Again, and again." Raising an eyebrow and smirking with a fucking sexy come-hither look, Asher's mind went straight to the gutter, as she'd clearly intended.

"Oh, before it's done, you'll be on your knees begging." He smirked back, knowing she was right. He was a breath away from begging right now.

As they left town proper, Asher added one more addendum, "You know, it's not because I, uh, because I slept with a few of her friends, way back when I was a spoiled shithead... It was more that I didn't ever call them back." Reaching across, he grabbed her hand and pulled it to his lips. "That's not going to be a problem this time."

Chapter Twelve

T-Minus 8 Days

Floating on the drive to the clothing shop, Asher tried to lose the smitten grin that just wasn't going anywhere. He'd slept with Sophie pasted to him all night again. No sex, just some good old fashioned making out.

And cuddling. Fuck, when had he ever cuddled? Even the word was scary. A little too teddy-bear. With Sophie, it was critical; made the air fresher and the blankets warmer.

This time, they'd ensured his bedroom door was locked and the bathroom door unlocked. They'd wedged shoes under both doors to ensure one stayed closed and the other open.

He'd managed to hide her birthday presents in his closet and couldn't wait to surprise her tonight. His mother hadn't been at all surprised by the fact that it was Sophie's birthday.

"I know," she'd said. "Sophie's been dreading this birthday for years, knowing her aunt will come, manipulating as she does."

"Shouldn't we celebrate anyway? Something lowkey? She's been a trooper with all the crazy wedding business."

Denise flashed him a sly grin. "Of course we're celebrating. I was going to say something sooner, in case you wanted to pick up a gift or something, but I actually haven't seen you without her around in a while. Just us, plus I invited Freya and Grady to join us. Lincoln too, of course."

Why was he surprised? Denise didn't miss a trick. "I was at Larissa's yesterday and ordered a few pies for today; thought I'd pick them up after the fittings are done. Sophie mentioned she likes a seasonal fruit pie."

With no more than a whisper of a questioning eyebrow raise, Denise quickly covered her reaction. "That was very thoughtful. I was just going to pick up a cake from the grocery store later."

He sighed, not quite sure what to make of her response. Was she surprised that he was being considerate or that he had done something special specifically for Sophie? "I'm a thoughtful guy."

Was he a thoughtful guy? It could rarely be said that Asher Sutherland performed acts of selflessness. Making for the door, he started to leave for the damn fittings, but paused at the doorknob. Turning, he added, "Mom, I'm sorry about all the shit I put you through."

Her expression unreadable, she managed a half-smile that only puzzled him more. "I won't say you were an easy kid. Too smart for your own good, but too foolish to do anything useful with that brain. The more your dad tried to reign you in with structure, the more you pushed away. So, I compensated by babying you, which didn't help you build up much resilience, I suppose. Somehow, despite us, you turned out pretty darn great." By the time she finished, her eyes were glossy, and she bit her upper lip until it turned white.

Closing the distance between them, he pulled his mom in for a bear hug, and rested his chin on her head. "It took me a while to figure it all out. Thanks for always letting me just be me." He kissed the top of her head and pulled away again. "My ducks are finally starting to line up, so hang in there with me a little longer."

She winked at him. "I know it, honey. As soon as you figure out how to make your own dinner, I think you'll be just fine."

Opening the front door, he winked back. "What fun would that be?" Heart a little fuller than it had been an hour ago, he sauntered out to his truck.

Until he saw his watch. Shit. He hoped he made it in time. He had to reschedule therapy for the stupid fitting today but hoped to report good news to his therapist next time.

Last week had been intense. He'd been *encouraged* set a goal to tell his dad his career plans by the end of the week. That prospect was stressful enough. He could broach the Sophie topic with Pippa later. Despite her fury, she scared him a little less than Paul.

Pulling into the last parking spot on the block, Asher dove out of the truck and headed for Tracey's. The shop was pretty typical, he supposed, for the sole clothing shop in town. Foothills had been pretty stubborn in resisting big box stores, so they were lucky to still have locally owned shops like Tracey's and Sutherland's and the diner.

A limited, but diverse selection of dresses, bridal, and other event wear was tastefully displayed on the back wall, and the right half of the store was dedicated to men's ware, including the dreaded tuxedo and suit options. Not his style, but it was perfect for what they needed.

As soon as he entered, Tracey made straight for him before he could head to the fitting rooms. Setting down the dress she'd straightened on the hanger, she smiled as she stopped his beeline for the back. "Asher Sutherland. I heard what you did at the bank. Lorna Stephens tells me you saved her life; all of their lives. The whole town is talking about it. I already wrote off the price of your tuxedo. It's the least I can do to thank you."

Tracey perhaps should have retired a decade ago, the tremor in her hands was a terrifying prospect for anyone needing alterations. He tried not to stare as he imagined the potential injury in his near future. "That's generous of you. You didn't have to do that."

"I wanted to. It's good to have good men like you in town." She shrugged with a slight blush in her cheeks. "That maid of honor is running a tight ship. Kicked out the bride when she panicked that the bridesmaid dresses were slightly more peach than pink. Apparently, Pippa is now relaxing and getting a massage. Much calmer back there now, but Sophie sure is keeping Lucy busy."

She paused, realizing Asher hadn't been back in town long enough to catch up on all the gossip. "Lucy's my granddaughter. Just moved here from Anchorage, and I'm hoping she'll let me retire soon. She'll be seeing if we need any adjustments and should have everything ready to be picked up the day before the wedding."

Suddenly all business, she led him by the arm and sent him to the back like she was launching a paper airplane. "And remind that maid of honor she needs to try her dress on still."

He masked his sigh of relief that tremoring Tracey wasn't going to use him as an oversized pincushion. Sophie caught him at the door to the fitting rooms and wordlessly directed him straight toward the rack, with more determination and accuracy than her inept dart throwing.

The back was actually pretty cool. Sort of a private gathering space. An oversized trifold mirror with a pedestal in the middle for standing took up one section, with two couches and a chair forming a U around it. Greenery warmed up the room, and along the wall there were glamourous black and white photographs from past events. There were four fitting rooms along the wall, each with full length plantation-style doors.

"Three down, three to go." Sophie had an official wedding tablet with a running list of notes from today's fittings. She looked quite official, albeit not the prim looking wedding planner, in her distressed skinny jeans, flip flops and strappy tank.

All work and no play, she directed him to fitting room four. "Alright Sutherland, you're up next."

Grabbing her by the waistband, he dragged her into the fitting room, stole a quick kiss, and patted her on the ass as she escaped back to her duties. Laughing, she went to check on Lincoln. Asher quickly changed into the tux, having no idea how to tie the... was it a tie? A cravat? What the hell was this excessive piece of fabric?

Coming out in the pants, shoes, and unbuttoned dress shirt, he held up the rest and begged for help. Lincoln came out of number two at the same time, back in his street clothes with the tux neatly hung on the hanger.

Lincoln laughed out loud, slapping his leg when he saw Asher. "Need a little help there?"

"Shut it," Asher growled affably.

Putting his hands up in defense, Lincoln backed out of the room. "I didn't pick it out. Speaking of, I'd better go check on Pippa. Poor thing was hyperventilating until Sophie made her an emergency appointment for a massage."

Lucy flitted into the room with refreshed supplies. "Oh my. Let's get you started." Although fifty years her grandmother's junior, she was remarkably alike in mannerisms... and the tremor. Cringing, he recalled all the acts of bravery in the last eight years of his life to muster his courage.

Humbly, Asher let Lucy poke and prod until she was satisfied. Standing isolated, feeling oddly vulnerable on the pedestal, his reflection all around, he felt like a fucking Ken doll on display. All with a tremulous hand holding a needle frighteningly close to a rather sensitive area.

The humiliation was complete as Lucy then awkwardly tied his stupid neck-thing. Humming while she worked, likely to distract herself, she finally nodded in satisfaction and set him free. Thankfully, he hadn't needed many pins.

Finally able to turn around, Asher's breath caught in his throat as he saw Sophie waiting patiently in her bridesmaid gown. Fucking knockout. The slip-style silk dress clung in all the right places, accenting the subtle curves of her long, lean frame. It flowed like water as she walked, the slit revealing her spectacular legs.

Shyly, she bit her lower lip as his eyes explored every inch of her appreciatively when she was on full display standing on the pedestal. As quickly as he could muster, he changed out of the ridiculous penguin suit and back into his jeans so he could watch the action.

Tsk'ing, Lucy shook her head at Sophie in disappointment. "Do you have another bra?" She whispered so Asher wouldn't hear such naughty talk.

In an ordinary speaking voice, Sophie shrugged. "No. What's wrong with this one?"

Scowling, Lucy walked around her a few times. "It's just not quite right. Why don't you go slip that one off and hang on a minute? I have another one that might work better."

Sophie slipped out of the bra while remaining on the pedestal. Sighing with pure satisfaction, Asher tried to not let Lucy see his response as the silk draped low, the details the bra had been hiding now nicely visible through the silk. She'd clearly been cautious of his lecherous ways as she hadn't wanted him to even hear the word *bra*.

Blushing, Lucy skittered to the front of the store.

Joining Sophie on the pedestal, Asher approached and stood almost close enough to feel the smooth silk of her dress. "You embarrassed her," he admonished with a teasing lilt in his voice, his eyebrow raised in challenge.

Rolling her eyes with a goofy grin, Sophie teased him back. "You embarrassed her more. Besides, I think she has a crush on you. Your tailoring was quite meticulous."

Shuffling in her homely steps, Lucy hurried back as fast as she could muster. Out of breath, she shot Asher a glare until he moved off the pedestal. Holding up a strapless, well-padded pushup bra, she handed it to Sophie. "Try this."

She unzipped the back of her dress and looped the bra through her top, just managing to keep covered. Lucy tried to hide her blush this time but failed miserably.

"That looks awfully difficult to secure. I'm good with my hands; I can help," Asher offered quite magnanimously. Poor Lucy's cheeks turned a fiery red.

Working a few contortions, Sophie finally managed to secure the bra herself. Pulling and tucking, she figured it out better than he had his tie. Zipping up the dress, she turned to show off her new look. Breasts fully on display now, like a busty barmaid from the good old days, she flashed Asher a come-hither wink.

Voice downright shrill now, Lucy backed away. "That bra works much better with the dress. You're all set then. I'm going to take a lunch break. I'll have my grandmother notify me when that other groomsman arrives."

Watching the mousy little thing run out of the fitting area, Sophie stifled her laugh. "I'm told she's an excellent seamstress. Don't scare her away."

"Hey, you're the one that winked at me with those spectacular breasts on display." Lucy actually was pretty under all the shyness with her big, expressive chocolate eyes; she just didn't quite seem to have a comfort with people.

With a final show-off turn on the pedestal, Sophie stepped down to go change. Without waiting for permission, Asher followed her into the dressing room, closing the door behind them.

Facing away from him, Sophie pulled her hair up and out of the way. "Mind getting my zipper for me?"

Leaning against the door, he folded his arms across his chest. "I liked watching you do it better."

"If you're not going to be helpful, then get out." She sounded like she wanted to be serious, but her heart just wasn't in it.

"Fine. If you insist." Stepping up close, Asher gently pressed his body against her backside. Painstakingly slowly, he lowered the zipper, grazing his hand along her skin as he went. Lowering each thin strap separately, he kissed her shoulders in turn. "Happy birthday," he whispered against her skin.

The silky dress slid down and draped delicately at her feet. Reaching around, he ran his hand along the tops of her breasts, still extraordinarily ample in the pushup bra. Slipping his hand into the bra, he teased her tight bud. Sophie let out a soft whimper before she caught herself and quieted.

With a quick flick of his wrist, Asher had the bra off and flipped it across the room in a flash. Breasts free, standing in nothing but strappy heels and a whisper of a pink satin thong, Asher watched her reflection in the mirror. Caressing, grazing his hand along the side of her breasts, then grasping her perfectly shaped breasts with both hands from behind, he watched as her head tilted back in erotic response.

"Open your eyes," he whispered in her ear. "You are so beautiful." Sliding his hand into her thin panties, he rubbed her center.

Her skin heated against him. Listening to her breaths coming quicker, he increased his pace and firmly circled, driving her wild until she panted faster and faster as her climax approached.

Loving how he could make her feel, he broke contact for the briefest of moments, turned and backed her against the wall. "Keep watching," he insisted.

"Hurry."

Not a sound from outside the dressing room, he continued his exploration. Dammit, he should have waited until they were at home, where he could draw this out. When he could truly let her know how beautiful she was.

Slipping the scrap of satin she wore out of his way, he dropped to his knees in front of her. As she stood there wearing nothing but stiletto heels, he about came at the sight. Warm velvet against her slick petals, he ran his tongue across her core. She moaned before remembering where they were and bit her tongue.

Spreading her legs apart at his silent urging, she held his head for support, and pulled his mouth against her in desperate need. Flicking, vibrating, sucking, he drove her rapidly into overwhelming, triumphant orgasm.

The sensation coming so quickly, she shuddered and clung to him before she collapsed. Pleased with himself, Asher kissed her inner thigh before pulling away.

Catching her breath, Sophie suddenly remembered where they were, blinked away the moment and abruptly searched for her underwear. Asher grabbed it off the floor and returned it reluctantly. Fuck, she'd tasted so good.

It had taken every last scrap of willpower to not beg for more. "I don't think that counts as sex, right?"

Sophie laughed as she pulled on her jeans. "I'm really not sure that's true, but let's not argue semantics and just go with it."

"Thank god. Me too."

Sophie fastened her pants and slipped on her shoes, but looked frantically for her own bra.

She didn't need to say anything, he offered, "You left it out there."

"I'm a little naked here still; mind grabbing it for me?" She gave him a winning smile he couldn't refuse. Glancing down at his raging erection, she added, "Although, you may want to deal with that, or poor Lucy will have a heart attack."

He managed to pull his gaze away from her topless with jeans look. Damn. Wasn't easy. Her expression hazy, she was as lost as he was.

After a stern talking to, looking away from her gorgeous body, his erection was mostly calmed down. Asher dashed out to grab her bra from the pedestal. Tossing it in the air, he juggled it a bit on his way to return it to Sophie.

"Something I should know?" Grady stood in the doorway where he'd clearly just come in.

Or hopefully just come in. Shit, if he'd heard anything... Asher may know he was in it for the long haul with Sophie already, but others wouldn't know that yet. Or would believe it of him.

"What?" Asher blinked and played dumb while he figured out exactly how much Grady had observed. Out of the corner of his eye, he saw Sophie pull closed the dressing room door. "Oh, this. Lucy, the seamstress, she helped Sophie change her bra out to one that fit the dress better. I'm just grabbing it for her so she can get changed."

Daggers coming out of his eyes, it was clear Grady wasn't born yesterday. Glancing down, he saw the lingering tenting action going on. Gritting his teeth, Grady went to the rack to grab his tux. He opened his mouth to say something but managed to hold it back.

For now.

A disembodied arm shot into the dressing room, her bra dangling from the hand.

"Thanks," she said in a shaky breath. Shit. Grady totally knew.

Dressing as quickly as possible, Sophie hung up her dress with the new bra and added it to the rack. Asher was gone by the time she got out. Guilt left a nasty taste in her mouth, but not because of what they'd just done. That she wouldn't, couldn't regret.

Despite some of her rebellion on escaping from her aunt, she'd never been excessively promiscuous. Never would have had the gall to do something like that in a dressing room. Not that she planned to make a habit of it, but around Asher, she was overwhelmed with exciting sensations of lust and thrill and... a deep-seated happiness.

Lucy shuffled back in a few minutes later. Wordlessly, she grabbed her tailoring gear and waited at the pedestal for the final groomsman.

Looking dashing in a perfectly completed tuxedo, Grady came out of dressing room number one a moment later. He barely spared Sophie a glance. Good thing, as Sophie had no idea what to say. Knew the word *GUILTY* was pasted across her forehead in big, bold red ink.

Lucy was well into her inspection when Grady couldn't stay silent any longer. "How long?" He glanced at Sophie through the mirror. His expression dark, lips drawn tight.

She wanted to act like she didn't know what he was asking but was never one to lie. Omitting the truth was bad enough. "It's not what you think."

"So, you weren't just fucking Asher?" Acid spit from his mouth, somehow his tone even more callous than the harsh words he spoke. Lucy's hand shook as she pinned the cuffs. Too bad she wasn't working on the crotch area and pricked the prick.

"I said, it's not what you think. I... Asher... Yes, we've been sort of seeing each other. Yes, we had a... moment in the dressing room." Why was she answering to him? She didn't owe him anything. Pippa and Lincoln had certainly been trying to push them together, but she didn't think she'd ever led him to think they were an item.

"Hey, if you're looking to be another bedpost notch, I'll accommodate you. Likely with a little more finesse." His words were still acid, but his expression was rapidly revealing more hurt than anger.

Hoping she hadn't hurt him, hadn't led him on, she didn't know whether to smack him upside the head for being an asshole or let him down easy. She settled for somewhere in between. "So far your finesse is seriously lacking. I like you Grady. I did, anyway. It's none of your damn business what goes on between Asher and me. But... I'm happy."

Expression pained, his brow scrunched, he glanced again at her through the mirror. Lucy continued her pinning, feigning disinterest and thankfully not acknowledging the conversation. In this business, she might as well get used to dressing room talk.

Sophie fought the threatening tears, terrified she'd lose her best friend, Asher, or both. "With the wedding coming up and Pippa already stressed out, we don't want anyone to know just yet. Please. Whatever your feelings, for Pippa's sake, and by extension Lincoln's, please don't say anything."

Inhaling deeply, exhaling slowly, Grady nodded. "I won't say anything. But, when he does exactly what everyone expects him to do, I'm not taking sloppy seconds." Poor Lucy's hands were quivering uncontrollably.

"I think you can finish up here by yourself." Shoving Pippa's wedding tablet into her purse, she stormed out of the building.

Sophie slammed the CR-V door, furious with Grady. Furious with Pippa. She didn't regret one minute with Asher. If she'd just brought her stupid bra to the fitting room. None of Grady's business, that was for damn sure.

Trying her best to not exceed the speed limit or run any stop signs in her fury, Sophie drove home overly cautiously. She did let herself kick up a bit too much dust on the driveway in her anger. Asher's truck was in the garage, his legs sticking out from under it again.

Calming herself as best she could, she walked over and hunched down to get his attention. "Hey," she said.

Wheeling out from under the truck, he smiled sadly when he saw her. "Hey." Rising to stand in front of her, Asher brushed a stray lock of hair out of her eyes but didn't linger.

"Grady's pissed, but he won't say anything." She stood inches away, afraid to touch him or she'd fall apart.

"What did he say?" Asher raised his hand to touch her again, but pulled away before he made the contact they both craved.

"Nothing that would surprise you. Comments about bedpost notches, sloppy seconds." Before she knew it, her fingernails were right in her mouth. Dammit, not again. After getting that one last bit that she just couldn't resist, she shoved her hands in her pockets.

Clenching his jaw so tight she was afraid he may break a tooth, he seethed. "I've said it before, but maybe we really should hold off for a bit. Everyone's tense, ready to pounce on anyone for just about anything."

A stray tear rolled down her cheek. Stupid emotions. Sniffling before any other emotion tried to trickle down her face, Sophie nodded.

She liked angry better. Unleashing a taste of the resentment she'd been holding back, she stomped her foot. "No. I like you. Even if *this* fizzles..." She gestured between the two of them, "I'm not going anywhere. This is my life, and I get to decide who I date. I've given up enough on behalf of others. No matter how much I love your sister, this is my life and my decision."

She paused, briefly, but clearly was on a roll. "I'm a grownup. I'm not going to stop being Pippa's friend if I get mad at you. Decent people don't judge others based on the behavior of others."

Still standing back, hands shoved deeply in his pockets, Asher looked torn. "I haven't given up enough for others. Certainly not my family. For that, I should give you up–"

Heart already breaking, she turned to leave. Not wanting to hear the rest.

Running to catch her, Asher didn't touch her but stopped in front to slow her progress. "Wait, I wasn't finished, dammit. You're so certain of rejection... I'm not giving up on *this*..." Like she had, he gestured between the two of them. "As much as I've always come off as a selfish bastard, I've also spent my entire life floundering, not finding anything that mattered enough to stand up for."

Shaking his head, he searched the cluttered garage for the right words. Satisfied with his next words, his gazed bored into her. "I want you. I'm going to fight for you. Whatever it takes."

Asher, someone she was attracted to beyond reason, a man she enjoyed even just coexisting with, was pledging to fight for her. There wasn't anyone she trusted to truly fight for her in a really, really long time, and he had a hell of a reputation working against him. Despite all that, she believed him.

Brushing away her tear with his thumb, his tone became less strained, his tense muscles easing. "You're gorgeous, thoughtful, intelligent. Stubborn, fierce. Sexy as fuck." He grinned at her, gulping down the final lump of uncertainty. "It was clear Pippa and Lincoln had wanted you and Grady to hit it off. He wanted it, too. Looked at you longer than I like. Checked out your tits enough I wanted to sock him."

With a small, teary chuckle, she teased, "My tits?"

"Hey, when an opponent is staring at your girl's magnificent breasts, it's easy to get a little crass. He was making some pretty obvious moves in your direction. You just weren't paying attention." Asher pulled her against him and wrapped his arms around her. His cheek rested on the top of her head.

"I was too busy noticing someone else's moves." She chuckled as she burrowed in.

"I do have some good moves." His chest expanded as he inhaled deeply. "As usual, I fucked up everyone's plans. I'm having trouble regretting it this time."

Her face nuzzled against him, she nodded. "We'll figure it out." Feeling so remarkably at home in his arms, she knew it was true.

Chapter Thirteen

I nvigorated after a refreshing swim on a hot day, Sophie walked up the stairs and grabbed her towel. Warmed from the sun, the heat from the towel radiated into her bones. Her stomach was starting to growl, reminding her again that she had missed lunch.

Well past four in the afternoon, it was nearly dinnertime. Maybe she could spend a quiet birthday dinner in her room with some reheated lasagna and a massive glass of wine. If all went well, she could have her way tonight without any arguing about how birthdays should be spent.

After enough lonely birthdays, she certainly didn't mind another quiet evening alone. Preferred it, actually. Especially with this being one of the biggest birthdays of her life, financially anyway. Lingering to let the sun dry off some of the drips, she didn't rush back to change.

She should have. A thick cloud of dust came barreling down the driveway. Everyone she knew was either already here or at work for at least another hour, maybe two for Paul. Emerging from the dust cloud, she could see a white convertible Camaro coming down the drive.

Sliding on her flipflops, she wrapped the towel around herself and tried to sneak in the back door of the house to avoid talking to a stranger in her swimsuit. Pippa and Denise were both inside and could answer the doorbell. Looking across the way, she could see Asher poking his head out of the garage to see who would be driving up so recklessly.

Before Sophie could reach the house, the car came to a screeching halt, kicking up another puff of dust. Stepping out was a busty, platinum bleached blond in a leopard print dress and heels. Shit. No sense putting it off, Sophie stepped into view.

"Happy birthday." Suddenly calm and gracious, Yvette walked across the entrance to the pool area. She held out a small, wrapped package.

"What are you doing here?" Niceties were long gone. They had disappeared years ago.

Right around the time Yvette sold off the few heirlooms she had from her parents. Her mother's wedding ring, her father's military medals, the quilt her grandmother had made for her shortly before she passed away. Sophie had stuck out the last two weeks of high school and was gone.

At eighteen and three months, she lived out of a motel for the duration of the summer before starting at UCLA. During those months, and her first year or two at college, she'd gone a little nuts after six years of feeling miserable. Tried a few bad habits she quickly learned were not her style.

Yvette looked all innocence. "I wouldn't miss your birthday for anything." Looking Sophie up and down in her bikini, towel, and flipflops, she cringed. Gesturing awkwardly, she poorly attempted to compliment her. "And I wanted to see that you're looking well. That these Sutherland folks are taking good care of you."

It ached to know her aunt may have remembered her birthday every year, as she clearly knew the day, but hadn't bothered until it meant a few hundred-thousand-dollar payoff. Too little, too late.

"Didn't I just give you enough money to last until you nailed the Netflix job?" Sophie made to leave, but Yvette grabbed her arm. Her long, fake nails dug into Sophie's skin before Yvette remembered Sophie didn't respond to violence. She'd only tried it once, but Sophie already had a decent right hook by then. Bruises didn't get Hollywood wannabes jobs.

"Yes, and thank you. My landlord has backed off a bit. Really, I have apologized more than enough for missing your birthdays." Yvette's expression was all regret. *Ha.*

"And selling my family's belongings. And tarnishing my reputation, more than a few times. Oh, and for never being the grownup."

There was always another job she was counting on soon. But, if it was her own money that she'd actually earned, Yvette *needed* to invest it in the next job, not frivolities such as food and electricity. Investment usually meant more plastic surgery, makeup, hair stylist appointments, mani-pedis. "You are so much better of a person than I could ever be. Your sweet mother passed that on to you. I appreciate everything you've ever done for me."

Moving onto excessive sweetness was never a good sign. Sophie tore free of her grip and continued toward the house. She knew exactly what Yvette was here for. Wasn't sure she could handle it.

"Please. I took you in–" Yvette's tears were in full force, her body limp with hopelessness.

"Because I was a nice source of steady income. Someone to tell you how nice you looked, what a great actress you were, how generous you were." Letting loose the final resentment she'd been harboring, Sophie kept her voice calm but was vibrating inside. "I didn't have anywhere else to go. My mother would never have chosen you if she'd had any other choice. Perhaps you should have skipped the last Botox, nails, the airfare to come here, the fancy car rental... and not bothered to show up here."

That was enough for Yvette. Like flipping a switch, she was in full-bitch mode. "You'll have had full access to your funds since this morning. If you cared about me and my future at all—"

Sophie scoffed, astonished somehow. "How do you think you're entitled to a share of *my* inheritance? You blew through yours before I was even born." Sophie knew this day would come but couldn't help being astonished at her aunt's narcissism. Couldn't help her disgust.

"For putting up with your antics, yes." Yvette walked as close as she dared, standing tall in her stilettoes to drive the point home. Her voice low, she sneered, "I'll make you a deal. You give me half, and I'll stay out of your life. Forever."

Sophie backed away, turning toward the house again. Yvette wasn't done yet. Anticipating the threats, Sophie couldn't decide whether to hear them out or to run away, plugging her ears and yelling *la la la la la*.

"What do you think will happen if you don't? This is sure a sweet little town you've decided to settle in. It would be too bad if all of your clients found out about the embezzlement scandal I helped get you out of a few years back. Or perhaps that little prostitution ring you were running before you left LA? I could keep going, it just depends on how quickly you come through for me." Yvette was almost giddy now from her deviousness.

Seething, Sophie stood tall, eye to eye with Yvette in her bare feet to Yvette's heels. With all of Yvette's creativity, it was astonishing she was so unsuccessful in life. "I actually should thank you for teaching me how to be practical, frugal, and love myself for who I am. You're not getting one more cent from me. Go home. Don't ever contact me again."

Her hand finally on the front door, she ignored Yvette's finally plea as she started sobbing melodramatically in the driveway. "Please," she cried.

A rumbling voice from behind them spoke up. "If you don't leave this property immediately, I'm calling the police." Sophie's hand stilled on the doorknob mid-turn. Asher had been clearly listening in. He'd let Sophie handle it, then he was there to back her up when she needed it.

Instantly switching to the charming vixen, Yvette strutted like a hungry cat towards Asher. "What's this? Little Sophie find herself a handsome boyfriend? If she won't share her money, maybe she'll share you."

Holding his ground, he didn't flinch when she ran her long red nails along his shoulder. His arms folded across his chest, he remained expressionless, unmoving until she got the point. Wow, she certainly was dense. Her hand ran down his back and slapped him on the ass as she circled her prey. Still ignoring, he didn't move.

Sophie would have socked her by now. Was tempted to intervene, but it was interesting to watch Asher not reacting in the least. She could use a few lessons on ignoring.

Putting on a pouty, dejected expression, Yvette finally stepped back. "Well, you're no fun." Glancing back to her niece, she used her innocently sweet expression that could have won her an Oscar. "My dear, dear Sophie. You have four days. Au revoir."

Turning on her heel, Yvette sauntered back to her shiny rental convertible. Suffocating dust billowed behind the wheels as she flew down the driveway. Yvette meant what she said. And could pull it off, as she had many times before. Conniving bitch.

Biting her lower lip to keep from crying, Sophie breathed slowly in and out. Refusing to shed a single damn tear on behalf of that witch again. How could that woman be related to Sophie's mother? They were from different stock.

Sophie doubted her mother had a clue what she had turned into, or she might have written for foster care, rather than letting her go into the care of her only living relative.

Frozen in place, her hand still clutched around the door-knob, she blinked away the threatening tears. Once the car was out of sight, Asher turned towards her. Seeing her about to lose it, he closed the few steps between them in a heartbeat.

His arms wrapping around her, he held her close against him. Melting into Asher, she let him hold her up so she didn't crumble.

Still in her swimsuit, towel slipping down, Sophie soaked two perfect breast prints into his shirt. He didn't care. What a damn witch. Her aunt was a real piece of work.

"Why can't she just leave me alone? I tried not sending money for a while, but that just made it worse. I had to take time off of school to clean up her mess." Sophie buried her face into his shoulder, her hair tangling in his short beard as he kissed the top of her head.

"I'm no psychologist, but there is something seriously wrong with that woman." His voice was gruff, struggling to restrain the emotions that were boiling to the surface.

Fury at Yvette. Fear that Sophie was going to have to live with this for the rest of her life. Regretful that Sophie had suffered this woman for so long.

He could feel Sophie's damp nod of agreement against his chest. "Should I just wire half my damn trust fund to her and tell her that's it? I know it won't stop her, but it should buy me a few years of her pestering, anyway."

Pulling away only slightly to see her face, but hesitant to let her go, Asher looked down at her. He wiped away the stray tear she hadn't been able to withhold despite her efforts. "Why don't you change your phone number tomorrow, before you start work and start establishing yourself in Foothills.

Change your email. You'll be moving soon. Make her at least work to find you."

"She'll find me."

Expression stern, Asher was on a mission to make this harassment stop. Not exactly within his repertoire of skills, unless she wanted Yvette watched, abducted, or assassinated. If he officially got the police job, he'd be well-equipped to help. He'd submitted everything the moment he'd gotten home, now it just depended on how fast Jonah worked. If she spread the lies she was threatening, Sophie should have a damn good case. Maybe Lincoln could help? "If she does, you call me."

"Thanks for coming to my rescue."

"Anytime. Always." A crushing ache in his chest, Asher wished he could do more for her.

They stood there for minutes, hours, who knew. He couldn't seem to let go, and neither could she. Since age twelve she'd lived with that monster of a woman. How did she turn out so normal? His dad was downright patient and supportive by comparison.

"I'm okay now." Sophie pulled back and managed a soft smile. "I'm going to get changed."

Asher didn't want to let go, but knew he had to. She knew he was here if she needed him. Needed anything. He managed a nod and watched her walk into the house.

Giving her a few minutes, he tried to calm whatever the hell was going on inside his head. Sophie was nothing he'd ever expected. Like no one he'd met before. She was a fascinating mix of enduring character and determination to make her way in the world. An open book he still didn't know enough about.

He trotted over to the garage and shut the door, giving up on his truck for the night. It had made a few decent drives now, but it wasn't long for this world. Despite the knowledge that it was time to invest in a replacement, he didn't want to give it up. His grandfather had driven that truck since he bought it off the showroom floor, and it had always been a safe haven for Asher.

Feeling more than a little at loose ends, but damn tired and ready to crash, Asher headed into the house. After the day he'd had, he should have expected the tirade as soon as he walked in the door. Couldn't catch a break.

Pippa stood staring, her accusing scowl boring a searing hole into his soul. "Why is Sophie crying, and why are you wet with a lovely boob-height bikini imprint?"

Done with her attitude, done apologizing for ancient mistakes, he blew up. "Because lovely Aunt Yvette just stopped by demanding money from Sophie. Threatened her while she was at it. I'm sorry for being there for your friend. And mine, by the way."

His angry bridezilla sister immediately softened. "Oh no. I wish I'd been out there. I assumed it was UPS or something. Did you give her a piece of your mind for me?"

Eyebrows raised, jaw clenched, he nodded. "Hell yeah. What a witch."

Simultaneously looking up the stairs, his heart broke for Sophie, and he saw Pippa hurting for her friend as well.

He stared up the stairs, wishing he knew what to do. Wondering if she was doing okay, if there was anything he could do to help. Unsure if she would prefer a moment alone or a distraction.

"I'm glad you're friends with Sophie. I feel bad. She's in a new town and hasn't started work yet. Pretty much just living at my beck and call these days, and I've been terrible company. I almost forgot her birthday. Mom said you brought home pie for tonight and we're having a quasi-surprise party for her?" Pippa lowered herself into the living room couch, looking downright forlorn.

Hoping this was the moment, he sat in the couch opposite. "She's pretty awesome. I can see why you and she are such good friends."

Smiling reflectively, Pippa nodded. "She is. Got me through grad school, I swear."

Here goes nothing. "Pippa, about Sophie—"

After a quick knock, the front door opened as the intruder let himself in. Grady. Dammit, not now. Worst timing ever. For the second time today. "Hey there. Sophie around?"

Asher held firmly in his spot on the couch, not trusting himself to say anything decent. Pippa answered for them. "She's in her room. I'd give her some space, though. Her aunt was here, and it was a pretty unpleasant interaction."

Grady nodded, looking quite sympathetic. "I'd like to talk to her anyway. I owe her a huge apology, so maybe she could use some kind words."

Selfish prick. Just let her be. Asher mentally berated himself. Maybe Grady was right; maybe he could at least right wrongs from earlier today and bring some relief to Sophie. Or he could make her day much worse.

Puzzled, Pippa raised an eyebrow at Grady but apparently didn't think she should pry. "You know which room is hers? I'll bet she could use a good friend right now."

As Grady neared the top of the stairs, Asher hopped off the couch. "I'm going to go get changed into a dry shirt." He headed straight for the bathroom that separated his and Sophie's bedrooms. Not that he was intending to listen in, but, hey, what if Sophie needed backup?

He could hear Grady's voice easily through the door. "I'm so sorry about earlier. I'm sure it's obvious, but I was rather hoping to ask you out myself. Guess I moved too slow, which I'm notorious for."

Sophie mumbled something he couldn't hear.

Grady continued, "I guess when I realized you and Asher had something going on, realizing I'd missed my window, I blew up. He's got a reputation, and I know you haven't dated much, so I worried that you were being taken advantage of."

Speaking louder this time, he could hear Sophie. "Apparently I give off that vibe. Thank you for worrying about me, but whatever it is about me that gives off this vibe, it's not innocence. I just know myself well enough to know that I won't pursue anyone that I can't see myself with fifty years from now. Not anymore, anyway."

Silence reigned for a moment. A hopeful twinge fluttered in his gut. Fifty years from now, huh?

He tried to picture what was happening. Grady was sitting down now? "And that's not me, huh?"

"Sorry, no. I really wanted to feel that way about you. You're everything I'm looking for, but as Freya would put it, the pheromones just aren't there."

"What is it about Asher? I was worried it was because Pippa warned you off about him and you had a forbidden fruit complex." A long pause. Hopefully Sophie was giving him a good death glare. Or laughing in his face. "I heard about his history with Pippa's friends."

Sophie's voice was surprisingly calm. He wanted to punch him in the Adam's apple. "First, that was a long time ago, and I don't think Pippa sees her brother for who he is today. Nor was Pippa as good of friends with those particular few as she cares to recall.

"Not that it's any of your business, but we haven't had sex. Second, if you got to know Asher at all, I think you'd like him too. He's clever and thoughtful. He's only been out of the navy for a short while and went through a lot. Give him time."

Somehow, Grady redeemed himself. "Okay. Lincoln likes him, and thinks you're pretty capable, so I won't tear the guy apart just yet."

As if. Navy SEAL. Expert in the kicking ass business. Not that he would; he was also trained when to use restraint. Tempting, however.

"You going to tell Pippa or just send her a wedding invitation when the time comes?"

He could hear Sophie calming, a genuine smile in her voice. "We're holding off on saying anything to her until after the wedding. Pippa has enough on her plate right now. I just need to find a way to let her know she and I will always be friends, no matter what happens with Asher."

"Your secret is safe with me. For now. But, if he tries to pull anything, I'm raising the alarm, got it?"

"Thanks, Grady."

Asher could hear Grady closing the bedroom door as he left. Moments later, he was about to sneak away when the bathroom door opened, the doorknob nearly smacking him on the ass as he tried to sneak away, undetected.

"Get all that?" Sophie's eyebrow was raised in challenge. The grin on her face destroyed any chance she may have had at appearing menacing.

"I won't kick his ass just yet." He leaned down and pulled her against him. Wrapping her arms around his neck, her body molded against his. Pressing his lips to hers, he savored the sweet, easiness of the kiss.

Pulling back, Sophie sniffed the air, and a satisfied smile passed her lips. "Did I smell Italian for dinner? I'm starving."

Ignoring the mouthwatering scent of dinner wafting about the house, he stared at her mouth and growled, "Me too." Lifting her up onto the bathroom counter, he devoured, feasting on her warm lips, soft neck, hands running along the smooth skin of her back.

Ending the building tension before things got out of hand, he ended the kiss and shook his head to clear his one-track mind. Sophie did the same, hopping off the counter. He was falling so deep and so fast for Sophie, it was becoming painful to be unable to shout it from the damn rooftops. Not to mention, sexual frustration was a bitch and a half. A little release would go a long way to improving his mood.

Turning, he headed out through his bedroom to change into a dry shirt. Just to piss off his dad, he pulled on a ripped up old

Disturbed concert tee to match his dark mood. He was itching for a fight but wouldn't start one. Unless provoked.

Chapter Fourteen

The shirt had the desired reaction. Paul didn't say anything, but his pinched expression said it all for him. Leaned up against the kitchen counter as Denise pulled a piping hot pan of something delicious and Italian out of the oven, Paul took a swig of his beer to avoid commenting.

Wordlessly, Paul pushed off from the counter and grabbed a beer for Asher from the fridge. He poured it into a glass and handed it to his son. His mother was oddly silent. Not good.

"Join me out on the deck for a few." Yep, the beer was not a peace offering but a blow-softener.

Asher grabbed the offered beer and followed his dad out to the deck to the Adirondack chairs where he and Sophie enjoyed their coffee together each morning. A cool breeze was kicking up for the night. Shadows grew long across the deck as the sun dipped behind the house.

Something more than the t-shirt was up. Paul kept starting to speak, then silencing himself. Denise and Pippa pretended to be deep in conversation... right next to the open window off the living room.

Not realizing anyone was in earshot, or not caring, Paul finally let loose. "If you weren't planning on working at Sutherland's, why didn't you say anything?"

"I'm really sorry, Dad. I really was planning on working there. Couldn't say I'd planned to stay forever, but I was planning to give it a chance." No longer thirsty, Asher set his beer on the wide arm of the chair.

"Then why did Old Chief Larson just tell me congratu-fucking-lations on my son getting hired on at the police department? I sure looked like a moron telling him he was mistaken." Prickly heat rose up Paul's neck to behind his ears.

Asher couldn't hide his surprise, and his delight. "I got the job?"

"According to Old Larson. He hates your guts, so I'm betting he wouldn't lie about something like that. Why didn't you tell me you were looking for other jobs? I would have hired somebody else weeks ago." Paul set his beer on the armrest so brusquely, half of it splashed out the side. He shook off the spilled liquid from his hand as if personally attacked by the frothy beverage.

Asher knew he should have said something, but he'd wanted to wait until he knew for sure. "I'm really sorry you found out that way, Dad. I honestly wasn't looking for other jobs. Jonah, Young Larson, I guess, is chief now. He offered me the job, pending formal application, background checks and references, of course. I was waiting to hear back from him before I said anything."

"When did you see Jonah–" Paul thought before he finished speaking, for once. It was clear when it dawned on him. "The bank incident. I got so caught up with this whole wedding drama, I completely forgot to say anything. Now I'm the asshole around here. Asher, you did an incredible thing, rescuing those people. I'm guessing Young Larson was more than a little impressed with your skills?"

Rare praise from a hard man. Trying not to make too much of it, hiding the warmth that nestled inside at hearing his father's compliments, he nodded. "Yeah. He pretty much offered me the job right then and there. Guess they've had a hard time hiring folks with any sort of relevant work history or education these days."

Smile wide across his leathery cheeks, Paul marveled. "Or the balls to put himself in front of a bullet to save somebody else."

And that was the end of the moment. Paul went on a rant about folks lacking in common decency anymore, which led to a diatribe about his daughter's future in-laws shirking any share of the cost burden, citing their own daughter's wedding someday. Thank goodness she wasn't marrying some slouch despite his questionable family. Complaining about money or the degradation of society was always a neutral topic, according to Paul, anyway.

They weren't questionable, they were actually really nice people, but Paul wasn't in the mood to hear that right now. Asher bit his tongue and listened politely. Best not to endanger the truce that was still so fresh.

Saved by the bell; Asher's phone rang with a local number he didn't recognize. He walked to the far end of the deck and stopped at the short stairs leading to the lawn to answer with a reasonable amount of privacy.

"Asher," he answered in his acquired crisp military accent. Couldn't seem to shake it.

The voice on the other end was kind, casual. "Hey, Asher. Jonah Larson here. Your application and background checks cleared our screens, and those were some pretty great references from your old Navy colleagues. If you're sure want the job, we'd love to have you on the force. Being the new guy, you'll get stuck with a lot of nightshifts to start."

Overcome with an optimism he hadn't felt in a long time, Asher almost couldn't find his voice to accept. "Absolutely. When do I start?"

"Glad you're eager to join us. Next training starts in about four weeks, that work out okay for you? You'll join the rest of the recruits from across the state in Burien, undergo physical and psychological evaluations, polygraph, PAT test. Then the formal academy training; takes about three months to graduate. It's a long haul."

"I made it through SEAL training; I'm sure I can handle it." Asher's chest was tight with nerves and excitement.

"Great. Greg will be in touch with more details and have you come in for some paperwork to start the process."

"I'll look forward to it."

Larson ended the call, thanking him for taking the position. Right place at the right time, that was for sure. As Sophie had pointed out, maybe his impulsivity wasn't such a bad thing. He turned to see the rest of the crew had joined Paul outside.

Lincoln and Freya must have appeared sometime in the last few minutes. Pippa and his mother ran over and gave him bouncing, bubbling hugs, topped off with high pitched squeals.

Looking over their heads, Asher caught a wink from his dad. Having something his family supported him in wholeheartedly was a brand-new, overwhelming sensation.

Sophie stood in the doorway wearing a huge smile that lit up her face... the brilliancy of her look struck him like an arrow to the heart. Denise and Pippa pulled away and continued their fussing as they returned to their party setup. More than anything, he wanted to pull Sophie against him and spin her in his arms. Maybe drag her upstairs to celebrate.

Warmth filling her like hot chocolate with marshmallows on a blustery, January day, Sophie stood back and watched as Asher smiled so enthusiastically. Maybe it wasn't so bad of a birthday after all. She'd come downstairs a few minutes ago in old jeans and a ratty t-shirt to find Pippa and Denise glued to the open window overlooking the deck. Asher and Paul were having one of those testosterone-overload, stiff-postured arguments.

Freya and Lincoln had clearly just entered and were setting gifts on the entry table. Pippa shut everyone up with a glower and a wave of her arm. Rolling her eyes, Freya headed straight for Sophie and shook her head.

"Birthday girl, get your butt straight back upstairs and make yourself presentable." Smiling deviously, Freya turned Sophie by the shoulders and pointed her up to her bedroom, following right behind until they entered the bedroom.

Pulling open the closet doors, the hinges squeaking in protest at her gusto, Freya flipped through the hanging items. "You have some cute clothes. I'm going to do some shopping in here later."

Sophie rolled her eyes playfully, enjoying having another girlfriend. "I don't think any of it will fit you. You're taller by at least two or three inches and have triple the boobs."

Grabbing out a pretty pink sundress that was girl-next-door sexy, Freya shoved it at her. "This."

"I love that one but it's a little short, so I never wear it." She held it in front of herself, demonstrating the mid-thigh length.

"Today's a perfect occasion. Asher will love it." Freya winked knowingly.

Sophie couldn't hide her confusion. She tried speaking but her tongue was frozen in surprise; she didn't even know where to start.

"It's obvious to anyone with eyes that you're into each other. Pippa will come around." Freya headed into the bathroom and pulled out Sophie's makeup bag. Seeing the open door connecting to Asher's bedroom, she turned and looked meaningfully at Sophie. "Naughty girl, are you sneaking through here at night?"

Sophie snagged the makeup bag and dress out of Freya's hands. "I like you, Freya. For now." She shot her a teasing death-glare. "Now get out so I can change."

Feeling boosted in her confidence, thanks to Freya's sparkling demeanor, Sophie was deliriously happy, despite Yvette's little visit earlier. By the time she got back downstairs, Pippa had moved on from the window and stood at the foot of the stairs, waiting for Sophie with a beer.

"Happy birthday! Surprise!" Pippa beamed easily, much more her normal, thoughtful self now that her wedding wasn't the focus of the evening. "I figured you'd argue if we told you we were throwing you a party, or that you'd be uneasy by us all sneaking around then shouting surprise at you. So, you get what I'm calling a *subtle* surprise party."

Accepting the beer and adding a hug, Sophie smiled gratefully at her friend. "Thanks. I was hoping no one noticed it was my birthday. But I'm glad now."

Heading out to the deck, aglow in the dusky light with twinkling Christmas lights and candles, they joined the others. Sitting around the outdoor table with her friends... and family, Sophie felt fantastically at home. Thing was, she didn't give a shit about the inheritance she gained control of today. But, out of pure respect for her kind, good-hearted mother, she wouldn't let a penny of it go to the one person who was the polar opposite of *this*.

She wasn't allowed to help with dishes. Instead, she relaxed, visiting with Pippa, Freya, and Denise, who had shoved the boys in to handle the dishes tonight. "Thanks for a great dinner, Denise. You'll have to give me the recipe. Pippa can attest that my cooking has come a long way since our first apartment in LA."

Snorting so hard she bumped her own elbows off the table, Pippa chuckled. "That's a fact. Boxed macaroni and cheese shouldn't be that crunchy."

"Yeah, you're one to talk. Who screws up frozen pizza?" Sophie mischievously knocked her bare toes into her friend's shin under the table.

Denise rolled her eyes. "You're both excellent cooks. At least, you are now. Perhaps you could teach Asher a thing or two, but I've never even seen him try."

Testing the waters, Freya took the final sip of her beer that had warmed over the course of dinner before commenting. "Or maybe he'll find himself a pretty little wife that enjoys cooking for him."

Pippa and Denise sighed wistfully. Sophie tried to play along. She felt an unfamiliar pulling sensation deep in her chest. A yearning she couldn't suppress. Certainly, not to become a pretty little wife that cooked for her husband, but something along the lines of maybe being his pretty little wife. With more equitable sharing of tasks.

Leaning forward, Denise conspired, "I think he's ready to settle down. Now we just need to give him a little push in the right direction. Have anyone in mind?"

Freya mused over the thought, responding dryly, "I'll keep an eye out."

Considering, Pippa didn't seem to be coming up with anything. "What makes you think he's ready to settle down?"

Denise's eyebrows pulled together, her lips pursed in deep consideration. "Things he's said. Just the other day we were talking, and he mentioned that when he gets married, he'd rather just have a small ceremony here at the house."

Nodding enthusiastically, Pippa ran with the topic. "He did turn down Irene's come-on at Ahab's. Maybe he's already seeing someone. Lincoln seems to think so."

Denise shook her head. "I don't think he had anyone in mind, I mean, he hasn't left the house except for errands and appointments. If he is seeing anyone, he sure isn't showing her much of a good time."

Gulping the last of her own tepid beer, Sophie hid behind the glass to mask her blushing reaction. He certainly was showing his girlfriend a very, very good time. Who needed restaurants and flowers when one had late-night make-outs, dressing rooms, and morning coffee?

Just to irritate Sophie, or so it seemed, Freya leaned into the whispering hens and added, "No, I think he's found one. When he's sitting alone, sometimes he gets this dopey grin on his face like he's thinking about something sweet."

"Dessert," a deep, rumbling voice behind her announced. Chills ran up her spine as Asher approached behind her. Setting a pair of scrumptious pies on the table with a mass of candles, a rapidly melting twenty-seven of them, glowing bright. Mostly slanted, but all still lit.

Sliding in the seat next to her, Asher reached under the table to subtly take her hand under the cover of the tablecloth. From across the table, Pippa led an enthusiastically offkey round of *Happy Birthday*. Sophie couldn't remember the last time she'd had such a normal birthday.

Feeling like the little kid she'd been last time she was presented with so many gifts, Sophie tore into the stack of presents. Lincoln and Grady went in on a collection of nice wines set in a stylish repurposed wooden wine rack. Denise and Paul gave her some fragrant nature-scented candles and vases with a gift card to the Sutherland's Hardware for when she moved into her own place—with a note ensuring there was no rush, she was welcome to stay in their home as long as she liked.

Pippa had gone solo on her gift and found her a set of quirky Pottery Barn dishes that Sophie had been drooling over for months, with a simple note on the card, *If I get the dishes, at least you get a cute new set.*

The package from Freya was huge. Sophie tore back the paper, revealing a gorgeous a hand-painted mountain sunrise. "Is this yours?" She knew Freya was a talented artist, but had no idea her work was so vivid, stimulating yet tranquil.

Freya rolled her eyes. "It's yours. And you'd better like it. I haven't slept in days trying to get that done for you. I was going to give you an old one I had laying around, but when I discovered how much I actually liked you, I had to make you something unique. Something that was purely you."

Sophie stared at the painting, feeling she could walk right into the glowing sun rising over the Cascades, a well-traveled trail weaving through the foreground. She hadn't known Freya long, but her new friend had certainly captured exactly what would call to her.

Allowing her to first get lost exploring the painting, Asher waited before handing her an adorable package wrapped in a paper map, tied with a blue utility rope. A pink flashlight, a handy multipurpose tool, and a gift card to Sporty's, the outdoor shop she'd seen in town. "I thought you'd need some hiking boots, but you ought to pick those out yourself. Have you ever been camping?"

She shook her head, in awe at the thoughtful gift. She'd never been camping but had always wanted to. Despite her mother's doting, the woman hated camping. Probably something about being a single mom with a young child living in the city.

Snorting, Pippa commented, "I can't believe you want to sleep out in the middle of that mud. I'm not sleeping outside; you're on your own with that one."

Laughter bubbling through her, Sophie teased her friend, "Message received. I believe that's what you told me the last thirty times I asked." On several occasions, she had requested a hiking or camping trip while visiting Foothills, but for a born and raised country girl, Pippa sure didn't like getting dirty.

Cleaning up garbage, dessert plates, nearly empty pie-pans, the crew started clearing out. In the commotion, Asher whispered in her ear, "Next week. I have a perfect spot picked out." Happy butterflies paraded through Sophie's gut, her ears ringing in anticipation.

The party cleared out painfully slowly. Freya tried to help her cause, shuttling out Grady and attempting to expedite

Lincoln's sloth-like departure. Apparently, Lincoln and Pippa couldn't quite decide where to spend the night. Pippa was too tired to go anywhere, and Lincoln had a meeting early the next morning, but both wanted to stick together.

Sophie bit her tongue to hide her impatience. "How about I pick you up tomorrow for a late breakfast or early lunch and we'll have more of that scrumptious pie at Larissa's?"

Pouting, Pippa nodded. "Okay. At least then I don't have to drive my own car tonight." Lincoln finally, mercifully dragged his sleepy fiancée out the door.

Denise and Paul had already disappeared to their bedroom in the chaos.

Freya grabbed her purse on the way out. "Have fun." With a wink, she popped her head back in the doorway. "Don't let that girl go to bed too early on her birthday."

Living room quiet for the first time all night, Asher dashed to the front door and locked it before anyone could change their mind and come back in. Nodding, he motioned Sophie upstairs. "I've got one more present for you."

Eyebrow raised, full flirty smile engaged, Sophie felt those butterflies wrestling again in her gut. "Is this code?"

Mouth quirking up at the side, Asher shrugged mischievously. "It can be. But I actually have one more present."

Anticipation building, Sophie followed Asher upstairs. Where he trotted up the stairs in an eager rush, she was too nervous to move so quickly. "Thanks for remembering that I like pie. Did your mom or Pippa think it was odd when you brought home pie for my birthday?"

Each stopping outside their bedroom doors, Asher shrugged. "Not that they said. I'm not hiding the fact that you're my friend. Give me ten minutes."

What was Sophie supposed to do for ten minutes? The wait was killing her. They'd built quite the routine of going to their separate bedrooms each night, then once it seemed the household was asleep, she'd climb into his bed. Maybe make out a little first, maybe curl right up and sleep.

Tonight was new. There was something different about him.

She brushed her teeth. Shifted and re-parted her hair. Checked her legs for stray hairs the razor had missed. Washed her face for the evening, then added a touch of makeup. Changed into a nightgown. Changed back out of the nightgown into her normal cami and panties. Then back into the nightgown. Washed the makeup back off again.

Finally, a knock at the bathroom door. Asher poked his head in. "Okay, come on in."

A scattering of candles left a soft glow in the darkened bedroom. Flickering serenely, the candles cast a romantic glow around a large, zipped-together sleeping bag set spread out over the middle of the bedroom. "I love it."

"I didn't want to give you a sleeping bag in front of everyone. Seemed oddly intimate given the circumstances. See how they zip together? Genius that came up with that. Sex in a mummy bag is not easy." Suddenly shy, Asher stood back and watched as she stood in front of him and pulled off her skimpy nightgown with a wiggle of her hips.

"Can't say that I've ever tried," she remarked, feeling so unreserved around him. His shyness and the uniqueness of his gift triggered something in her, she wasn't sure exactly what, but she was overcome with the need to find out more of who he was, who they were together. Some of that would come with time, some with intimacy.

Empowered, she slid her panties down her hips and stepped past him, grazing her hand along his abs in a playful gesture. She otherwise passed right by him, naked and tormenting, knowing it would drive him wild. His eyes grew wide as she was now fully undressed and stood over the sleeping bags.

A knowing look crossing her face, her lower lip pulled between her lip and breasts rising and falling with eager breaths. "There is one dessert I like better than pie." Fuck, he was so done for.

She was so hot. Lickable, strawberry red nipples, those pert breasts, waist narrow with slim hips and legs a fucking mile long. He was dreadfully, overwhelmingly out of his league.

At her mercy, he stepped forward and stopped in front of her. She teased her fingertips lightly under the edge of his shirt before pulling it over his head. Not quite tall enough, she stopped with their arms both raised over their heads. Rather than laughing it off, silly like they had been before, she took complete advantage of his trapped hands, and pinned his arms above his head. Kissing him deeply, aggressively, sucking his tongue hard before releasing him and allowing him to finish peeling off his shirt.

Sliding his jeans down over his hips, she pressed her body tightly against his. She fit so perfectly against him, tormenting him. His cock, already iron-hard, twitched against her, desperate to bury into her.

Not tonight.

His body tensing in anticipation, she didn't tease him with her light touch this time, instead she took his rigid length in her hand and gripped firmly, driving him out of his mind at the sudden sensation. Stroking, grasping, she massaged until a rumbling, gravelly groan escaped his lips.

Gliding her tongue across his chest, she nipped his nipple before lowering down to her knees in front of him. Fuck, he was about to come at the sight.

Cupping his balls, she teased, taunted. With a long, savoring lick, like he was a fucking popsicle on a hundred-degree day, she trailed her tongue along his cock and flicked the tip before taking him deep in her mouth.

Lush, pink lips wrapped around his girth, soft and giving to his hard. Her slow, methodical rhythm pulled at him, his hips instinctually thrusting with the pace she set. "Oh fuck, Sophie—"

Accelerating, she sucked him hard, taking him deeper into her mouth as she stroked him. He lost his voice. Lost all coherent thought as she swallowed him. Shuddering, he felt his climax and barely managed to warn her. "I'm coming—"

Gripping him tighter, she wouldn't let him pull away, but took him deeper. With a deep groan, his vision went black as he released into her mouth. She bit her lip as she rose to her feet and smiled smugly.

Hell no, she was not the innocent people seemed to think. Something about her gentle demeanor, who knows, but she knew exactly how to drive him completely, totally out of his mind. Pulling her against him, he wrapped his hands around her narrow waist. Looking up at him, he could see the twinkle of satisfaction in her eye.

"We've got lots to keep us entertained without sex in the traditional sense." She ran her hands along his ass and pulled him against her.

S ophie had never been so turned on giving head before. It was taking every shred of willpower to not drag him down on the sleeping bag bed he'd made and ride him to both their undoing.

As if reading her mind, he said, "You absolutely undo me. Make me feel things I didn't know were possible. And I don't just mean the incredible things you do to my body," he whispered as he kissed along her collarbone. She tipped her head back as he ran his tongue along her throat.

Lowering them down to the plush, slick fabric of the sleeping bags, Asher was... different. Fiercer, more intense. She'd seen so many sides of him, but tonight was so much more vivid.

Taking her mouth with his, Asher kissed her deeply, exploring, tangling. A soft sigh escaped her lips; heat spread from low in her belly to the tips of her extremities.

Was it just this morning he had taken her in the dressing room? Remembering the ecstasy, the rapid pulse of need that had driven through her, she was ready for him.

"This time, I'm savoring." And he did. Taking his time, he ensured every inch of her body received his undivided attention. Never having felt so exquisitely aroused, Sophie was overwhelmed with sensation. Again and again, she came at his touch, cried out in delicious, victorious orgasms.

Limbs heavy from the molten lead that filled her veins, Sophie could hardly move. Letting her down gradually from the most intense orgasm—correction, orgasms—she'd ever experienced, Asher rested his head low on her belly.

His deep voice rumbled against her, "I felt a bit rushed this morning and needed to take my time this go around. Hope you don't mind."

She managed to speak, barely, not yet able to find her full voice. "I like my new sleeping bag."

"You'll like it even more when we're out in the middle of the woods, far from the ears of the house." His voice croaked with something she couldn't identify. Emotion? Exhaustion?

Realizing what he was implying, she vibrated with a rich belly laugh, bouncing his head against her abdomen. "Sorry about that. I've never been a noisy orgasmer before."

"You are welcome." She could feel him smiling against her skin and place a soft kiss on her tattoo. They laid there for a long while, breathing together in silence. Peacefully, she started to fall asleep.

Asher sat up briefly to move up next to her and pulled the cozy satin lined with flannel sleeping bag around them. She'd never slept in a sleeping bag before. By the time she would have gotten to have sleepovers as a kid, she was stuck with Yvette and wasn't allowed.

There were a lot of firsts the last few weeks. A lot of surprises. Like that she was a freaking voracious bundle of lust, apparently.

More, the feeling that she could lean on someone, entirely, and help carry his burden as well. A fluid give and take with someone else, their joy and their pain. She never wanted to need anyone, so the idea was a little frightening, yet oddly reassuring at the same time.

Chapter Fifteen

T-Minus 7 Days

Rising before the sun, as usual, Asher placed a lingering kiss on Sophie's forehead before sliding his arm out from under her. As she had the last few mornings, her sleepy figure wasn't releasing him. This time, however, her cheeks were rosy from a long night of not-quite-sex.

They were curled up in their makeshift bedroom campsite that he was loathsome to clean up. Wrapping her other arm around him, she clung to him like a koala on a eucalyptus tree.

Chuckling quietly, he whispered her name, "Sophie... Sophie, I'm getting up now."

Stirring, but not releasing him, she groaned. "No."

Grazing his long fingers along her side, he traced a circle around her belly. She bit her lip to suppress a laugh. Pleased with his progress, using a feather light touch, he grazed his hand further until he reached her breast.

A soft sigh escaped her lips, her eyes still sleepily closed. Mischievously, he gave the tight nub a quick pinch. That earned him an elbow in the ribs.

Lowering himself, he circled her breast with his velvet tongue before pulling her in with a deep caress with his mouth. Her gasp not so soft now, her eyes flashed open in sensual shock, her arms releasing him. Nipping the side of her breast, he pulled away now that she'd unlocked him from her unbreakable grip.

"See you on the trail." He hopped out of bed and dashed to the bathroom before things got carried away. Slipping on his running shorts and shoes, he was out of there before she could retaliate.

Sophie made good time; they crossed at about their usual spot at his favorite lookout. He should stop there more often. Maybe they could have one of her favored picnics there one of these days. Or even set up camp.

They didn't stop to talk, as was their routine. Instead, they flashed each other a satisfied grin and kept on their way. Today, he made it back first.

After a quick shower, he threw on some cargo shorts and a NAVY t-shirt per his usual. Bringing their coffees out to the deck, he only had to wait a few minutes before she came out the sliding glass door.

"Morning," she greeted with a contented smile. They sat in silence for several minutes, enjoying the peace of the morning.

Neither said anything about last night. Not yet. They'd hashed and rehashed the nuances of their situation more than either cared to. Both hated keeping secrets, but both knew Pippa would be thrilled once she understood they were in it for good.

He sort of assumed Sophie was in it for the long haul. She was, wasn't she? It would be a painful, sweet revenge against him if Pippa's friend dumped him and left him broken hearted this time. Rubbing a gnawing ache under his sternum, he tried to shake off his self-doubt.

Finally, he remembered the awful run-in with her aunt to give him something else to focus on. "I know you want to deal with it yourself, but do you mind if I speak with Larson about your aunt?"

Poor timing, as usual. If he'd thought before speaking, he might have realized the topic was a bad choice. Foot in mouth, as usual.

She adjusted in her seat, her spine ramrod straight. "I don't want to involve anyone else in this just yet."

Crap. He didn't want Yvette to get ahead of them and ruin Sophie's chances of success in her new venture. Mostly for her, knowing how much she was hanging her dreams on this opportunity. But he didn't deny the not-so-small amount of selfishness he felt in her settling in locally.

If she left Foothills, he didn't know what he'd do. If she'd let him follow. He didn't tend to plan ahead well, but damn, when he found what he wanted, he didn't hesitate. He knew. And he knew Sophie was his future.

"I get that, I really do. I don't trust that woman."

Sophie drained the last of her coffee with swift finality and stood from the chair. "Neither do I, but I'm not giving her the satisfaction. I'm sick of defending myself, of suffering her lies. If she tries anything, I'm facing it head-on."

Knowing when to pick his moments, he bit his cheek before he said anything to upset her any more than he already had. "Okay." She headed for the door while he remained glued to his chair, feeling absurdly helpless. "Sophie... if you need anything, I'm here. Don't hesitate to ask for help."

She offered him with a glum smile. "I know."

"Really. I know you hate asking, but I'm in this with you." If only he could tell her just how much he had her back. Not yet; not when she was turning inward. He was terrified that she'd disconnect further.

Hesitating, but otherwise not acknowledging, she left him alone on the blindingly sundrenched deck.

Angry at himself and his poor timing, he stalked into the kitchen and made a quick piece of toast. Impatient, he snatched the barely warm piece of floppy whole wheat from the toaster and stuffed the dry bread in his mouth on his way to the garage. If he just had the right words, the right approach, maybe he could make this a little easier on Sophie. Her aunt would inevitably make her life a living hell for years to come, as she'd done since Sophie was just a kid.

Waiting for the painfully slow rise of the garage door, listening to the familiar clanking of the metal gears, he stared at his truck as it came into view. The engine had been running oddly yesterday, occasionally missing. Worse than usual. Something wasn't right, but he couldn't figure it out. Since he'd been back from that awful last deployment and the engine quit the first time, he'd poured weeks of repairs into the damn thing, but every time he managed to get something fixed, something else went wrong.

Sliding beneath the engine, then looking from up top, fiddling with every bolt and cap, then inspecting even the damn axels and tires, he couldn't find anything wrong. Couldn't come up with anything that might be nonfunctional. Connections were secure, nothing rusted through, nothing leaking.

He hopped in the driver's seat and cranked the engine. It fired up no problem. Okay. It's okay.

Just when he was about to shut it down, he heard the sound again. Not exactly missing, more like a systemic weakness. The rumbling started to slow.

Gently pushing on the gas, he managed to bring a little life to the engine. Removing his foot again, it slowed again. Again, it revved a little with a little gas, but not as strong this time. Fucking death rattle.

Revving the engine with the pedal pushed to the floor, he poured all of his hopes and frustration into the dying engine. Not now, dammit. Not one more loss.

Screaming, the engine tried to cooperate with the influx of fuel. With a final, pathetic puff of black smoke from the exhaust, the engine slowed and came to a quiet stop. He turned the key again. Nothing. No activity.

A fierce growl rose from deep under his diaphragm, filling his chest, his arms, with fury. Desperate, helpless, that energy funneled into his fists and he slammed into the dash, the steering wheel, again and again, until his knuckles bled.

Leaning forward, his forehead met the steering wheel and stayed. An aching, burning sob rose from his chest.

The passenger door opened. Glancing to the side, his forehead glued to the wheel, he saw Sophie sliding in through his glassy vision.

Not wanting her to see his loss of control, his voice barely above a whisper, he pleaded, "Let me be, okay?"

Hand on the door handle to leave, she nodded. "Okay. I'm here if you need anything."

He knew she got it; he just couldn't even say it to himself yet.

"Let me know if you want me to call anyone, you know, a mechanic or a tow or anything, okay?" Her voice was so gentle, so caring, with an understanding of loss and pain better than anyone.

"I don't need a fucking tow truck. It's going to be fine. I just need to see what's wrong." The snap came out of nowhere. What sort of monster yelled at someone like that? Someone he cared about? That was just trying to help?

Her face darkened with something he couldn't read. Now he felt like an asshole. Voice soft, kinder than he deserved, she said, "Okay. I'll be inside if you need anything."

S unset came later than usual. Not actually, but it sure seemed to. Dinner had been long and painful, awkward. Most wouldn't have noticed the black pall that clogged the air, but the silence between Sophie and Asher was palpably thick.

After a tasteless dinner filled with Pippa's frantic worries about centerpieces and playlists, Sophie's brain was numb. She'd gone out to the garage to apologize for her closing off before. Yvette tended to have that effect on her; worrying about her sent her into the shell she'd adopted early on. Instead of finding him pleasantly tinkering as usual, he'd been so broken.

Stupid; she can't believe she'd mentioned a tow or a mechanic when he was so freshly grieving. She'd expected him to be angry with her when she finally saw him at dinner, but he'd looked as miserable as she felt. His eyes were bloodshot, but the sweet smiles he'd snuck her way had melted her.

Finally, the house was settling in for the night. Sneaking through the bathroom, as she had grown accustomed to, she didn't even reach the door when he was on his way to her. Those whisky eyes overflowing with regret, his smile still was struggling, but adorable.

Neither spoke, neither hesitated. He pulled her into his arms so quickly, so completely, filling her with everything she'd ever needed or wanted. "I'm sorry," he whispered against the top of her head, his voice hoarse, his stubbled beard brushing against her hair.

Leaning into his neck, she inhaled his musky scent. "I'm sorry, too."

Standing together until her blinks lasted longer and longer, her eyelids heavy, they moved into bed. Snuggled close, lulled to sleep by the steady rise and fall of his chest, Sophie drifted off into deep, soothing sleep.

Chapter Sixteen

T-Minus 2 Days

S ophie would have said she could handle just about anything, but she would have been wrong. Had suffered
more than her fair share of bad parties that her aunt had
dragged her to when her agent had decided Sophie could be a
star. Her stardom would have elevated Yvette right along with
her, or so Yvette had thought.

What a nightmare that was. Yvette had talked up their wonderful relationship in the hopes that Sophie could land her a
part in the midst of a long dry spell. When Sophie didn't play
ball, Yvette proceeded to rake her over the coals to everyone
she met. Including Sophie's teachers, friends, coaches, whoever would listen.

A rehearsal dinner should be a relaxing evening. One in
which everyone is so excited for the upcoming wedding. All
about the bride and groom and the fun day planned, with
their closest friends and family together to make the big day
happen.

"Did you hear about Pippa's friend from Los Angeles? I hear her aunt is a sweet, delicate thing that Sophie turned her back on when her aunt got a part in a movie that Sophie had her eyes on." The chipper voice sounded a little too thrilled to be raking the maid of honor over the coals. Yvette must still be in town somewhere. As promised, the campaign had begun, and would get much worse before she was done.

And what sort of minister spoke such nasty gossip to the mother of the groom anyway? Sophie was heading out of the bathroom when she stumbled upon the nasty bit of conversation. Groaning, she ducked out of the way to avoid having to face it head-on. Her ears burned, her breath forced in and out as she tried to ignore the tripe.

Thankfully, Lincoln's mother sounded to be as considerate as he was. "Lincoln has known Sophie for a number of years now and is quite fond of her."

Having heard the sort of bullshit Yvette enjoyed spreading more times than she cared to recall, she closed her eyes to steady her rapid pulse and let the nonsense roll off her like the graywater it was. Shoulders back, chin up. Sadly, just like her aunt had taught her when she thought she might be molded into her image. Regardless of the source, it was a good strategy.

The wedding venue was amazing. A garden sprawling out from a renovated barn overlooking the mountains, aptly known as The Barn, it was an incredibly serene locale for a joining of two people in love. Looking across the valley, Sophie took the fragrant, afternoon mountain air into her lungs.

She knew it was him before he even reached her. Didn't have to look back; echoing in her chest was a pair of timpani drums with Animal from The Muppets hammering away with unrestrained enthusiasm. "Incredible view." His deep voice rumbled, stirring a yearning deep in her chest.

"Isn't it?" she agreed with the newcomer, wishing he'd wrap his arms around her, savoring the moment together. The last few days had been like a dream. Hours of not-sex lovemaking every night with Asher. Waking before dawn for a satisfying run and enjoying their ritualistic morning routine. Sneaking out for quiet picnics when the rest of the house was too busy to notice.

Only a few more days of the secrecy that was tearing her apart inside. Turning, she saw Asher standing a few feet away, his eyes on her rather than the evening sun glowing on the rugged Cascades in the distance.

"How's Pippa holding up? I needed some air and didn't see her arrive." Needing air was an understatement. Yvette was devious and cunning when it came to getting what she wanted. Unfortunately for all, Sophie in particular, she didn't choose to use her powers for good.

Standing a few feet away still, Asher maintained his distance. It felt like miles. "She's hanging on by a thread. Lincoln's calming her down now. Mom already tried. I don't think I've ever seen her this wired before."

Sophie knew Pippa tended to take stress to epic levels of anxiety and overzealous control freakishness, but Pippa's behavior the last few weeks had set records. She'd heard of weddings turning perfectly normal people into monsters, but she'd never imagined it of her friend. Today's behavior especially, and she'd spent the last four years living with Pippa. No one would ever describe Pippa as laid back, but neither was she quite so intense or emotional. "I'd better go check on her."

Loathsome to leave the serenity of the moment, watching the warm evening sun set an orange glow over the Cascades, standing next to the man she was growing increasingly attached to, she turned and headed for the converted barn. She could feel Asher's eyes on her as she walked away and wished he could follow. Teasing, hoping to drive him mad, she added an extra swing to her hips. His chuckle melted her insides into silky chocolatey fondue.

Back in The Barn, things weren't looking so hot. The seating wasn't going to be right. Where was the wedding party going to walk in from, with the ready rooms behind the small stage? Pippa was in full exasperated panic.

Steadying herself for her friend, Sophie confidently strolled into the room like nothing was wrong. Like there wasn't a frantic, hyperventilating bride standing in the middle of the room. Ignoring the bride and her soothing–although more likely enabling–entourage, she scoped out the room. Grabbing a few folding chairs, she carted as many as she could carry outside.

Carting them out to the field, she set one not far from the idyllic spot where Asher still stood. Chair by chair, she set a few more as markers. As expected, a very confused Pippa walked to the wide barn doorway that opened to the field. Silence was a highly underrated method to getting someone's undivided attention. Pippa had shared that helpful tip from her teacher's training.

From her spot in the field, she hollered, "Paul, what's the weather report tomorrow?"

Grinning, he caught on immediately. "Wedding ceremony at five pm. Predicted to be seventy-eight degrees with scattered clouds, ten percent chance of light showers."

Shielding her eyes from the cloud-filtered sunlight, she hollered again, "What time is it now?"

Checking his watch with dramatic motions, he ensured he was heard by all, "About four-thirty."

Walking back to the barn, she grabbed the bitch of a minister and linked arms with her. Whispering on the way to the makeshift markers she'd set out, she ended this little string of gossip before it spread further. "You may wish to get to know someone before you start spreading such nasty lies about them." Taken aback, the minister stood where she was told and scowled. Maybe a little guilt in the scowl, maybe not, but Sophie liked to think the subtle upbraiding would have an effect.

Next, she pulled Lincoln along. Not that he needed any dragging, he winked in acknowledgement and did as he was told. Next, she directed the parents, except for Paul just yet, to the few folding chairs she'd set up to model the audience. Asher followed her back to the barn, smiling the whole way. Turning on her phone, she played the song Pippa had painstakingly selected for the bridal party's entrance.

Pippa watched the entire proceedings, looking humorously stunned. Asher and Freya linked arms and walked the length of the field to the waiting ceremony practice scene. Winking at her, Grady took Sophie's arm and escorted her down the aisle.

"Nice save," he whispered as they walked.

Grady was becoming a fast friend now that the air was clear, and she enjoyed the moment with him. Leaning into him amicably on the walk, she wordlessly let him know they were okay. "She has a severe case of decision fatigue. Just trying to make her life a little easier."

Flipping the music to the wedding march Pippa had selected, Sophie turned the volume as high as it would go so Pippa would hear. Paul extended his arm and walked Pippa down the makeshift aisle. Her lost sheep look started to look a little more like joy.

Reaching Lincoln, she found her full smile. Taking a deep breath, the bride found a little peace. "This is where I want to get married."

The whole group sighed together, immensely relieved they were out of the woods. Close one. Poor Pippa had put too much energy into one day. An important day, but still just a party.

The rest of the rehearsal part of the evening went smoothly. They walked through the ceremony, reception, discussed when and where photos would be, working out wedding day details. With the ceremony outside and weather predicted to be cooperative, for Washington anyway, they really could sprawl on the property, so The Barn could be designated for food and dancing.

After a painful hour of hashing and rehashing, they finally headed to dinner. Lincoln's parents had rented out the big room at the finest—and only—steakhouse in town. They'd called the restaurant when things were looking bleak to have dinner pushed back a bit.

Arriving at the restaurant, Sophie went straight for the bar. Asher wasn't far behind. Grabbing a glass of white, she waited while he grabbed a pint.

Primed for catered gatherings, the multipurpose entertaining space was perfectly designed for a relaxing evening. There were scattered high and low tables for visiting, a massive dining room table in the center to seat the entire party, and a few collected couches and chairs arranged into cozy sitting areas next to the gas fireplaces.

She'd worn her favorite olive-green linen sundress for the occasion. It was a new and rather pleasant feeling to be shorter than her date, or not-date, when wearing her tallest heels. Not just tall, his shoulders were broader, stronger than the guys she'd dated in the past. Just existing, he exuded testosterone and made her identify with the Asher groupies she had heard about.

Making her way to one of the cushy sitting areas, Sophie sat and leaned back, crossing her heeled feet on the ottoman. Settling in next to her, Asher did the same. For a moment, they sat in silence, finding a small corner of peace in a chaotically enthused party, watching as the guests filtered in.

As the wedding party and associated families settled and found their own chill-spaces, Asher broke the silence, his deep voice soothing her more than the crisp wine ever could. "Tell me about your mom. Colette, right?" Asher rested his beer in his hand at his side and watched for Sophie's reaction, clearly hoping he'd chosen a safe topic, because he was genuinely interested.

No one had asked her that in a really, really long time. "She was incredible. Dad was in the military and died in combat when I was in kindergarten. Tough as nails, she made sure I could handle anything that came my way. That I was never the helpless damsel."

"After meeting Yvette, I figured your mom must have been something special. You turned out pretty fantastic despite that witch." He flashed her a heart-wrenching smile, one side of his mouth turned up adorably, his eyes warm as honey.

"She really was. I never wanted for anything. We had plenty of money, as she had grown up well off. Didn't blow through her inheritance like Yvette had. But that's not what I mean. I never wanted for love or attention. We had a sweet little house right down to the white picket fence. I was on whatever team I wanted to join. We travelled a lot."

Sophie was glad he'd asked. Few did, fearing she wouldn't want to reminisce over painful memories. It was hard for a long time, but she still missed her mom as much today as the day she died. Speaking of her now made her feel connected.

"What was your favorite place you and she travelled to?"

"Here, actually. We did a little tour of the Pacific Northwest. Stayed at little inns around the Puget Sound, the Olympics along the coast, the Cascades." They'd about worn through their hiking boots on that trip.

"What did she die of?" His expression mournful, brow heavy with regret, she felt him sharing her pain, a deep empathy she wasn't sure others knew he was capable of.

"Cancer. An aggressive lymphoma." Sophie's heart still ached recalling the day her mom had given her the news. She'd been tired for a few weeks, already losing weight before she realized something was wrong. Being a single mom, she was used to running on fatigue.

"I'm so sorry. I hate to ask, but I'm liking having you around; was it something that could be hereditary?"

She smiled, understanding his concern. Her mother had asked that almost immediately; it had worried her until the oncologist had reassured her. "No. Just one of those things."

Without regard for the rest of the room, he took her hand in his. Sophie needed the contact. She hated keeping this secret from her best friend. From Paul and Denise. Her friends.

Eyes locked on to each other, they stilled for longer than they should. Visiting quietly in their private corner, they nearly forgot the rest of the party existed.

Grady came to the rescue. "You know, it'll make it harder to keep this quiet if you two blow it before you break the news to Pippa." He raised an eyebrow at the indiscreet couple.

Remembering where they were, Sophie pulled her hand out of Asher's and sat up a bit in the cushy sofa. "Thanks, Grady. I hate lying to Pippa. Love her to death, but she's a little scary right now."

Raising his eyebrows, he nodded. "Lincoln's going nuts trying to keep her sane. I find I'm inspired to consider eloping when my time comes. Even if I found a partner that could handle it, I don't think I could handle my mother."

Sophie had to agree, although something about getting married in such a beautiful spot was pretty tempting. Her parents had been married in a courthouse and apparently had lived quite happily together, never having loved each other any less for lack of a big wedding. Colette's parents hadn't exactly been thrilled about their nineteen-year-old daughter marrying an enlisted guy in the army. Despite their initial misgivings about the marriage, they came around and had been doting grandparents, for the few years that she had them.

"Your mother can't be half as bad as my aunt," she goaded, suddenly wanting to know more.

He took a big gulp of beer, rolling his eyes deep in his skull. "Maybe, maybe not. She's just rich and entitled. Me, being me, she enjoys criticizing like it's a hobby."

Chuckling, Sophie couldn't imagine anyone thinking Grady were anything less than perfect. Before she could call him on it, Asher sat up in his seat and raised an eyebrow. "Seriously? You're a mother's dream. Hell, my parents know I'm a screw up."

"Not my mother. Anyway, I'm sure you'll get to meet her eventually. Not that she would stoop to using a local accounting service or call the police when she could call in her own team of Seattle bodyguards if needed." He shrugged and toasted the air. "Enough about dear old Patricia. What's the deal with your aunt?"

Immediately defensive, Sophie tried to hide her reaction. No good ever came from questions about Yvette. "What have you heard?"

"Nothing good. Sophie, I've heard you and Pippa talking about her, as well as a few rumors here and there. I know she's a pretty terrible person."

Rolling her eyes, Sophie nodded. "That about sums it up."

Turning into full lawyer-mode, Grady wore his serious face. "There are some pretty vile stories floating around the party. Maybe even around town. Mostly about how you abandoned your feeble, benevolent aunt and left her destitute."

Sophie smiled through threatening tears of boiling hot rage and resentment. Her fists balled up tight, nearly crushing the wineglass she'd forgotten she held. "Oh, is that all? She threatened worse."

Asher covered her fist with his hand in attempt to comfort her, but it would take a whole lot more than empathy right now.

Voice harsh, Grady was pissed on her behalf. "How much worse?"

Asher went to speak up, but Sophie wouldn't let him. She didn't want to let this get out of control, as things so quickly could with Yvette. Better to let it go, reduce the blast zone when things got too hot.

"I can handle it." Realizing her tone was a bit harsh and not helping her case, she added a cursory, "Thanks though."

Making meaningful eye contact across her, she knew Grady and Asher weren't going to take her objections seriously. Plotting how to defend her without her consent. She sort of appreciated that they cared so much, but more, she feared their help might make things worse. She'd been on her own when it came to Yvette for too long... for a very good reason, and she couldn't help but fear the repercussions if she actively resisted Yvette.

"Look, if she's threatening you, you may have legal rights. Please, let me help if this gets out of hand." Grady tensed his jaw, his eyes full of hatred on her behalf.

"I will. Really. Thanks, Grady." She mustered up an appreciative smile and a nod.

Lincoln's father hollered from the massive dining table set to host the entire party, "Alright, folks. Come and get it." Smiling, happy guests descended hungrily on the table.

For now, Sophie relaxed a bit. The rest of dinner went by relatively uneventfully. Fortunately, most everyone knew not to mention her dear old Auntie Yvette around her.

Chapter Seventeen

By ten that night, the household was finally quieting down. T minus forty-two hours until I-Do's. Sophie got ready for bed then went straight to Asher's room. Despite their exhaustion from a trying day, they found comfort in each other's arms.

They'd had to be careful in case his mom decided to clean his bedroom again. A habit she was slowly starting to step away from as she silently, lovingly gave her son a little shove out the door. Never leaving a trace, Sophie even adjusted her pillow and made her side of the bed before leaving it each morning.

Sated from an intense, passionate bit of not-sex, Asher laid awake, holding Sophie in his arms. Exhausted as they both were, she was already falling deeply into dreamland. Wrapping his arms around her, he pulled her up tight against him.

He wasn't falling asleep so easily. How had this happened? From the moment he'd laid eyes on her, all snarky and playful in his garage, he'd been hooked. Correcting himself, he realized it had started a lot sooner. A sucker for her untamed, indecisive hair, that lush pink smile, and those stormy gray eyes that revealed the secrets her sweet expressions masked, he'd tanked when he first saw that graduation picture on the mantle.

He'd been with more than his share of bed partners, but none had even tempted him to settle down. Somehow, before they'd even met, he'd known.

Just as his thoughts were drifting into nonsensical imaginings as sleep finally enveloped him, a shrill series of chirps from his phone jolted him awake. Sophie stirred beside him but didn't open her eyes.

Sliding the answer button, he answered the unknown number. "Yeah?" He must have been more deeply in sleep than he realized, his voice was full of gravel.

"Jack's in the ICU." The voice was terse, gruff.

"Zane? Where are you?" Zane was due to get out of the navy any day now, last he'd heard. Not that he'd heard much since he'd been home. Zane and Jack had been his best friends in the navy, his only friends, really, for years.

"San Diego. I was listed as Jack's emergency contact."

Heart thundering in his chest, Asher slipped out of bed and pulled on the closest pair of sweatpants. Found them crumpled on the ground now that he was generally stuck doing his own laundry lately. "Is he okay?" Juggling the phone, he snuck into the bathroom, so he didn't risk waking Sophie.

"Fuck no, man. He's in the ICU. On a ventilator and god knows what other shit they have him hooked up to. Sepsis; bacteria in his blood or some shit like that." Zane's voice was as croaky as his own.

Asher froze, knowing this wasn't a good sign. Jack had been seriously injured in the op that had taken a good chunk of their team. Asher and Zane had left the battle with hardly a scuffed knee between them and a bitter aftertaste of survivor's guilt.

Not Jack; he'd never walked again.

"What hospital?"

Zane gave him the information. "Come quick man, I don't think he has much time left."

"I'll be on the first flight out." Fuck. Not Jack.

Until the injury, he'd been the heart and soul of the team. Both the obnoxious, impish little brother and the got-your-back buddy. It had been devastating for Asher, but Zane was a damn mess afterwards.

Asher had at least known he was getting out soon and had a family to go home to, so he'd stayed afloat on the hope of distance from the mess. Zane didn't have much else in his life.

They should be as dead or amputated or concussed as the others, but Asher had seen someone moving down the street and had taken Zane to investigate. The impulsive decision had spared the two of them, but those left behind weren't so lucky. Would he ever be able to stop reliving it?

Hanging up the phone, Asher moved back into the dark bedroom and sat on the side of the bed. Searching his phone, it took only minutes to book a flight. Next Seattle to San Diego left at 0400, best he could do. *Going to be a long fucking night*.

Restless, no way he was getting back to sleep just yet, he slipped out of the room. Tiptoeing down the stairs, he headed for the kitchen to grab a drink.

Sniffling from the moonlit living room caught him off-guard. "Pippa?"

A wet voice answered, "Nothing. I'm fine." She stood from the couch and wiped her eyes, looking ridiculous, pretending all was well as she cried alone in a darkened room, when the rest of the house was asleep.

"I think you may need a drink as badly as I do." He continued on his mission for liquor. Opening the pantry, he pulled out a dusty bottle of Jameson.

Pouring each of them a finger, or two, of whiskey, he brought both glasses to the living room. Pippa didn't argue when he handed her the glass, but she made a face as she hesitantly nursed the strong drink.

"What's up, Pip?" Worrying about Jack... And Zane, for that matter, wasn't going to help anyone right now. He was actually grateful for the distraction, but admittedly felt a little guilty that his relief was at his sister's expense.

"Am I a total nutcase?" She sniffled again but washed the threatening return of weeping down with another sip of whiskey. Grimacing, she swallowed the liquid fire.

He managed a sympathetic smile. "Not usually." He stared at his own glass, debating whether it would actually help or just make things worse.

"I'm sorry I've been so crazy around this whole wedding business. It doesn't even matter, that's what I can't figure out. I love Lincoln, he loves me, so why do I care so much about the stupid party to make it official?" She stared out the window at the bright moon.

"For one, it's a big damn party that's going to be amazing. For another thing, this is a lot to take on and you've shouldered most of it. You have always been single-minded." He quickly added, "In a good way. That's why you always seemed to be able to do the right thing."

"I don't always do the right thing." She rolled her eyes and snorted indelicately.

"Sure about that? You went to college, graduated on time, took a break to get some experience in the field, to ensure you knew for sure you wanted to be a teacher, then arranged your life to attend grad school near each your high school sweetheart. Right on schedule you're getting married, probably starting a family soon. You have a job lined up already, doing what you always wanted."

All their lives, she'd seen what she wanted and meticulously planned so things panned out exactly as she envisioned. Dove in with everything she had. Didn't dick around with indecision and discontent like he did, acting on impulse and relying too heavily on luck.

She nodded with a watery smile. "I do like to plan." Raising her glass, she saluted him mockingly.

Biting his lip, he hid his agreement. "And you like things to go your way. Hence, wedding crazies. That's a lot of variables to ensure go your way."

"I'm sorry I try to control your actions and behaviors." That was out of nowhere.

Had she always realized she did it to him? Bossy and over-bearing sister from day one? Hell, she'd hardly been able to talk, and she'd grab his hand and drag him to the kitchen so he could climb up and steal a cookie from the jar for her.

Nudging her shoulder with his companionably, he didn't ask when or how she'd realized it. "You and Dad have a lot in common. You know what's best for others and strive to make them realize it too." He paused, but knew it was time, so he added, "Even when you're wrong."

She smiled at that. "Sadly, that is true." Downing the last of her whiskey, she reached for his untouched glass to steal the rest.

Pulling his glass away, he took a long pull and then set it out of reach of them both. "Sometimes I know what's best for you, too."

Finally realizing it was the middle of the night and her brother had come seeking a rare hit of liquor, she puzzled at him. "Why are you up at this hour?"

Now would have been a perfect time to bring up Sophie, but he couldn't handle the possibility of an argument. Not when he had other priorities tonight. "I'm sorry, Pip, but I have to fly to San Diego in the morning."

Sitting bolt upright, she stared at him as if he'd just told her he was wanted for stealing a herd of cows. "Why?" she managed to ask as calmly as possible, her breaths quickly becoming shallow and rapid. Well, maybe it wasn't the best time to bring up Sophie after all. Good thing he hadn't.

"Did I ever mention how I got out shortly after a fucking awful mission? You know Jack, my buddy that was hurt just before I got out?" His chest clenched as he realized he may not have even mentioned his friend.

No wonder Pippa didn't trust him, he never showed her who he was. Never opened up to her. Let her think he was an uncaring asshole, living for his own hedonism.

She stared at him, knowing his news wasn't going to help her out at all. Still, he could see the empathy starting to seep through.

He continued, "He's in the ICU. Sepsis. I just hope he makes it until I get there."

At last, here was his sweet sister. Thankfully. Her face went long with grief on his behalf. "Oh, Ash, I'm so sorry. What time does your flight leave?"

"0400. I already booked a return flight so I can be back before the wedding. I'm sorry I won't be there to help with setup. Going to be a bit of a photo finish as it is." He flashed her a regretful smile.

Committed now, she searched around the room as if looking for supplies for his journey. She shook her head. "Don't worry about it. We'll make it work, whatever you need. Why don't you borrow my car?"

He didn't want to think about why he couldn't take his truck right now. "Thanks. I really appreciate it. Now, Lincoln is probably upstairs wondering if you're ever coming to bed. You go to sleep. I'm going to catch a few hours rack time before heading to the airport."

The drive was miserable. Dark, sleepy, painfully long. Fortunately, not many folks on the road at this hour. He drove Pippa's Corolla a smidge over the speed limit, wanting to grab another cup of coffee at the airport before his flight left. If anything was even open yet.

Sophie woke when his alarm had gone off at 0130 in the damn morning. She'd slept through the call from Zane, but somehow, she knew something was wrong. She didn't question the alarm or try to drag him back to bed like she usually did. He filled her in as he rubbed the fog of fitful, inadequate sleep from his eyes.

She'd been amazing. While he took a quick shower, she'd taken care of him. Made him a massive cup of coffee. Packed him a backpack with a change of clothes, phone charger, basic toiletries, and some protein bars, knowing he wouldn't stop to eat on his own.

Looking adorably rumpled in his t-shirt that ended just above her mid-thigh, she finished packaging a breakfast sandwich she'd thrown together for him. "Don't worry about at thing. I'll bring your tux along to The Barn so you can come straight there. I-5 traffic should be okay since it will be a weekend, but who knows."

Pulling her in for a long, sleepy kiss in the dim light of the kitchen, he almost asked her to come. Wanted her support, her nearness.

Didn't want to watch another buddy die.

Cradling his face in her hands, she softly pressed her lips to his one last time before releasing him. "Do you want me to come with you? Things will be just fine here. I'll do whatever you need, sit in the waiting room or come in with you. I don't want you going through this alone."

He knew she was needed here, knew he could handle this, even if he didn't want to. Knowing she wouldn't hesitate to come along was enough.

"I really appreciate that. Any other time, I'd jump on that offer. Not right now. Too much going on here. I need to know someone is keeping things calm here so I can take care of things and not worry that I'll be missed. Besides, I think Zane's worse off than I am."

"Keep in touch. I'm here if you need anything." Walking him out, she quietly closed the door behind him.

Chapter Eighteen

T-Minus 1 Day

S leeping restlessly for the next few hours, Sophie managed to make it until five before tossing back the covers. Asher had been gone for a few short hours, and already the bed was cold and lonely. Groaning from achy muscles after tossing and turning, trying to fall back to sleep after Asher left, she managed to drag herself out of bed.

Despite the aches, she ran her normal route in record time, then hopped in the pool for a few laps. Trying to enjoy her morning coffee alone on the deck, she snapped a picture of the sun just as it was rising and sent it to Asher. Long after her coffee had gone cold, she sat curled up in the Adirondack in her coziest distressed jeans and an old Bob Dylan t-shirt.

Shortly after, right as his plane must be touching down, her phone chirped with a photo he'd taken of the sunrise out the airplane window during the flight. Smiling, she felt like they'd spent their morning together after all. This was a perfect example of how she knew he didn't see her as a convenient lay. Maybe she could show Pippa and explain why she didn't need to worry. Not that the simple gesture would be so obviously a sign of love to anyone else.

Slowly opening the sliding glass door, it made its usual grinding sounds as it moved across the weathered track. Armed with an oversized coffee cup and a warm blanket around her shoulders, Pippa wordlessly joined Sophie in the other Adirondack. "Morning," she greeted with a sleepy smile.

Both stared at the ever-brightening mountains in silence for a few minutes. Finally, Pippa sighed before saying what she'd been bottling up all night. "I'm sorry I've been so crazy. I've not been a very good friend since we left Seattle."

Sophie patted her friend on the knee before wrapping her arms around her own knees. "You're only a little crazier than when you were studying for your GRE's, finals, moving–"

Chuckling, Pippa interrupted the list. "Okay, I get it. I don't do stress well."

"It's not that you don't do stress well. You just feel everything so fully, that when it exceeds your usual impressively vast comfort zone, you sort of... lose your filters." Glancing at her friend, she saw her sheepish smile forming.

"How do you always manage to stay so calm?"

"Look at my poor stubby fingernails. I thought I had quit the habit years ago, yet they're already about chewed to nothing. Besides, once Yvette's threats come to fruition, I doubt calm will be a word anyone uses to describe me. Is it considered premeditated if I'm plotting my own self-defense?"

Pippa pondered on that one for a minute. "You'll have to ask Lincoln or Grady that one." Voice quieting, she appeared afraid to even say the rest out loud. "I heard some of the rumors last night. I fired our minister."

Aghast, Sophie's head whipped around so fast she nearly gave herself a neck cramp. "You can't do that. Who's going to officiate?"

Appreciating Sophie's less-than-calm reaction, Pippa shook her head in amusement. "I don't want that gossip-happy bitch marrying us. Lincoln agreed. Aunt Jane coincidentally has one of those licenses you can get online. She did a wedding for a friend a few years ago. Actually, I wish I'd known sooner, as I like her better anyway."

"That's a huge relief. She's pretty great. I can't wait to start working with her. I've got education and internships to keep me afloat, but I'm so nervous. She showed me my desk and my schedule. For the first few weeks, she's making me take a light load until I get a feel for things." Stealing Pippa's massive coffee mug, Sophie poured a few more sips into her own cup so she could have a little extra caffeine jolt. Pippa didn't need it anyway; she was running on adrenaline.

Denise came flying out the glass door. "Did either of you talk to Asher? Is he okay?" She pulled a chair up in front of Pippa and Sophie, disturbing their pleasant moment.

Crap. No good way to say she'd seen Asher off at oh-dark-thirty this morning. Fortunately, Pippa had seen him too. "I talked to him last night. He should be back before the ceremony tomorrow. Poor Asher."

Tearful, Denise nodded, already knowing some of the basics from the note Asher had left. "Jack. He has been such a good friend to Asher. One of the guys hurt right before he got out. My poor boy, this must be so hard on him."

Hating being so far away and still not convinced that her not going with him was the right decision, Sophie rose from the deep-seated Adirondack. "Why don't I fix some breakfast."

Denise was such a nurturer, never admitting when she was hurting. It was clear she was hurting for her son now. Sophie could help, feeling a similar pain. "Asher has been through worse. He'll be okay," Sophie added as she stepped inside.

In the kitchen, Sophie pulled out a large bowl and whipped up a double recipe of Dutch babies to go in the oven. She tossed some pork sausage on the stovetop griddle. Pulling out the fresh strawberries she'd picked up to share from the local farm stand the day before, she sliced and tossed them in a small saucepan for a yummy summer topping.

Yep, her cooking had come a long way since their first apartment. It had been top ramen and PB&J with Yvette. Now, Sophie enjoyed creating delicious foods. Usually nutritious, but today was an exception. Comfort food was very necessary today.

It's not like she and Asher were an established couple or anything. They'd been dating what, a few weeks? Not even dating, exactly, as they were trying to keep things on the downlow.

She'd never fussed like this over a boyfriend before. Stupid. You didn't just fall in love with someone this quickly. This easily.

A lively chirp from her phone interrupted her distress. She juggled it out of her pocket with strawberry covered hands before she could check the text. *Doesn't look like he'll make it thru the night. Will call you later.*

Her chest ached thinking of what he must be going through. He'd implied a lot of his counseling was to help with his survivor's guilt, and Jack was a big part of that. Hopefully he and Zane would be able to help each other through the next few hours, both coming away unscathed when others were hurt then and still dying now.

A minute later, her phone chirped again. *Miss you.*

Well that just wasn't fair. Whatever her issue was, feeling maybe more deeply involved than she should be this far in, she realized he was right there with her. Part of her still expected him to be the love-'em-and-leave-'em sort.

Delaying sex hadn't just been about keeping a promise, it had been about protecting herself. Damn it, even without the sex, she was falling head over heels for him.

H opping out of the cab he'd tipped well to take the quickest route to the hospital, Asher ran into the lobby. There was a glowing, colorful map in front of him, but his mind was too unfocused to try to figure out how to find the damn ICU. Scanning the lobby, there were dozens of arrows and hallways. And a freaking Starbucks.

A friendly, arthritic eighty-something year-old saw his clouded vision as he tried to figure out where to go. "Are you here to visit someone?"

Ears buzzing with worry, he managed to nod.

"Do you know what unit? I'd be happy to show you the way." The poor volunteer, designated by a clearly marked blue vest, hesitated, unsure whether to splash cold water over Asher's face or wait him out.

Shaking off the fog that had muddled his brain, remembering he was here because he needed to be here, he managed to respond. "ICU. Jack Holden."

With a gentle nod, the volunteer pointed towards the far hallway. "This way." Following behind the painfully slow pace of his new best friend, he tried to not sprint ahead. Wouldn't help to lose one's guide, only to get lost around the next bend.

After an interminable trudge to the ICU, Asher tried not to panic when he saw the staff running in all directions, a cacophony of life-saving machines beeping in alarm. He was about to ask the man at the front desk to point him towards Jack's room when Zane approached him from the side and whacked him on the back.

"About fucking time. This way." Zane didn't wait for his response.

The nurse, however, wasn't having it. "One at a time."

Desperately, Zane took a step forward. Towering over the nurse, his scowl could have caused the poor guy to combust, but his tone was all plea. "Call security if you need to, but our friend is dying. One more body in there won't change a fucking thing."

Taking the nurse's hesitance as approval, whether it was intended to be or not, the pair stalked back to Jack's room.

Sliding open the glass door, Asher pulled the privacy curtain to the side to enter the room. His friend lay pale on the bed, hooked up to more wires and tubing than he could make sense of.

Fucking shit, Jack.

"How the hell did he get sepsis? I thought his injuries were all healing?" Taking the only seat next to the bed, Asher sat at the bedside and stared at Jack's pasty complexion.

Zane stood back with his arms crossed over his chest. "Heroin."

"What? You're fucking kidding. He couldn't have been that stupid." Running his hands through his hair, Asher saw the scattered scabs that marred his friend's skin where he'd been injecting.

Seething, Zane held his post in the corner of the room, his jaw clenched tightly. "Apparently, he was that stupid. I don't know if he just got hooked after all the damn pain pills he'd been taking after... After. Or, if he was abusing because he was too lost and depressed."

"I haven't seen him in what, two months, and he lost it that quickly? Wasn't he planning another surgery soon?" Maybe if he hadn't been so caught up in himself, he would have noticed Jack wasn't okay. Could have said or done something.

Zane shook his head briefly. "Guess he stopped going to his appointments a week or two ago. I think he gave up. Took the most painless way out he could come up with. Not that it worked out quite how he wanted."

"Why didn't he... Why didn't we... was it suicide?"

Zane shook his head, his eyes red with fury. "No way to know. Don't think so, as there was no note and he had stuff out like he'd been in the middle of something. Whatever, though, we should have realized something was wrong. I should have been paying more attention."

"He'd have dragged our loser asses out of the ditch." It was hard to imagine the gaunt, lifeless figure in front of him as his colossus of a friend that had pulled him out of a number of scrapes. "I was too fucking busy putting a band-aid on my scuffed knee to pay anyone else any attention."

Not caring about the plethora of cords attached to Jack, Asher rested his hand on his friend's and gave a gentle squeeze. Whispering his apologies for not realizing how much he was hurting.

"Too late now. I've been out of the navy a grand total of forty-eight hours and have spent most of my free time at this damn hospital. Fucking depressing."

Looking up, Asher saw Zane hadn't moved. His jaw was clenching a mile a minute, tense as the rest of him. "I didn't even know you were out. You going home?"

Eyes still glued to Jack, Zane managed to shake his head. "Nah. Not much home to go to." Zane's parents owned a snooty architecture firm in New York and had never shown much interest in their children. His brother was last rumored to be somewhere in Nepal, and his sister lived and breathed Air Force life.

Knowing Zane was heading to an early grave right alongside Jack, not from drugs, but certainly something self-destructive, Asher couldn't let another friend go. "Come on up to Washington. Foothills is a good place. I just got on with the police department."

"Fuck no. I'm not going to be a damn cop." Zane's brow furrowed in pure disgust.

Laughing under his breath, Asher almost found humor in the dark moment. "I'm not saying come be a cop. Doubt they'd hire your lazy ass anyway."

That got the desired response. Zane unfolded his arms and rubbed his temples with flat palms, blinking rapidly to wake himself, reminding Asher of all the long nights they'd had on missions. "Just egotistical, fly by the seat of their pants pieces of shit like you, huh?"

"Damn straight. If it helps, I know a lot of hot, willing women in Foothills."

"Any you haven't slept with?" Lightening up, Zane grabbed the wheeled doctor's stool from under the computer and rolled it up to the bedside across from Asher.

"I can let you know who's worth the effort. Just not my woman. Or my sister. Maybe my cousin, but that might be pushing it. Not sure you could handle her anyway."

Sitting opposite over their dying friend, they almost enjoyed feeling normal with their typical banter. Messing around got them through some tough, emotional shit when there was little to do but wait. Along with Jack, the three had been inseparable for years. Would never be the same, but it felt good to be together again, all three, one last time.

"You got yourself a woman already? You move fast." Raising an eyebrow, Zane smiled mischievously.

Pulling out his phone, Asher scrolled through to find the picture he'd snapped of Sophie at the rehearsal dinner. The smile she'd given him when he'd found her looking out over the valley, escaping the crowd.

Whistling, Zane ripped the phone out of his hands. "Not bad, Sutherland. Not bad at all. She have a sister?"

"Sorry, she's one of a kind. An accountant. All responsibility but gives as good as she gets."

"And fucking hot. You keeping her?"

"Hell, yeah." Taking his phone back, he stared at her photo a minute. Her mouth was quirked in a flirty smile, her multi-toned blond hair wild in the breeze. He'd updated her throughout the day by text but needed to hear her voice.

"She know that yet?" Damn, Zane knew him too well. In all the years they'd known each other, both had initially enjoyed the company of SEAL groupies.

After their first major op, the appeal had seriously worn off. Neither had dated much after that, Asher least of all. The guys enjoyed ragging him for being a commitment-phobe or some shit like that.

"Working on it."

One of the machines, which had been beeping an almost soothing rhythm before, suddenly started to alarm incessantly. Crashing into the room came the nurse from before along with three others close behind. Not arguing, Zane and Asher stepped outside the room and watched through the window.

Asher tried to pull his eyes away but couldn't shield himself from the awful image as they tried everything to save Jack. CPR, pushing meds, adjusting the oxygen. Everyone cool and composed in their voices but frantically fast in each call and intervention. Minutes passed before the doc in the room called it. "Time of death 1026."

He was gone.

The nurse pulled the sheets back up to cover most of Jack and let Asher and Zane back in the room to sit with his body. Words of sincere apologies came from the code team, devastated to have been unable to save their friend. With grim nods, they thanked the team for trying.

Sitting in silence across the bed again, neither felt any shame at the flood of tears that poured down their faces.

"I'll let the rest of the guys know. He didn't want a funeral or anything; he'd told me that when we weren't sure he was going to make it after the injury. But I feel like we should at least spread his ashes somewhere decent." Zane wiped away the last tear from his cheek and sat up with a clearing snuffle.

"Let's not call it a funeral then, but bring up his ashes and we can toast a drink in his name when you get to Foothills."

Zane shook his head with a small smile. "You're not giving up on me coming, are you?"

Reaching across, Asher extended his hand. "You have two weeks. Get your ass up there."

With a teary half-smile, Zane shook the offered hand.

Exhausted from a sleepless night and an emotionally draining day, Asher finally staggered into his hotel room. Looking out the window, he watched the planes coming and going from the airport. Wished he could have found an early flight home, but maybe the extra time away from the chaos wasn't such a bad idea.

Dialing Sophie, he was worried she wouldn't answer. It was after nine, and she'd likely be distracting Pippa from her wedding night jitters. Or already turned in for a good night's sleep.

She answered on the first ring. "How are you?"

God, it felt so good to hear her voice. Worried, but he liked that she was worried about him. It meant she was as deep in this as he was. "He's gone. I'm at a hotel for the night."

"I'm so sorry. I hoped you'd call tonight. Zane holding up okay?" Her voice cracked in sympathy. She didn't miss a beat. He'd mentioned Zane with some of the stories he'd told her about his time in the navy, but she'd paid attention. Knew it would be just the two of them with Jack.

"Think he'll be okay. I convinced him to come up to Foothills; he just got out two fucking days ago. Nice way to reenter society. Anyway, I gave him two weeks to get his ass up there." He chuckled picturing Zane grudgingly, efficiently packing his things. Maybe even tonight. He wouldn't linger.

"Good. You both could use a friend close by." He could hear shuffling in the background, the sound of her pulling up the blankets and settling in for the night. Hopefully in his bed like usual, even if he wasn't there.

"He doesn't have someone like you. Sophie, I don't know how I'd be getting through this without you. Thanks for understanding I needed to be here. For letting me just be."

"Of course. I'm so sorry you have to go through this."

"Me too. I'll help Zane with some of the arrangements in the morning. He'll have to shoulder most of the burden, which I hate putting on him. But he's a survivor. He'll roll." Hopefully. "I'll do as much of the legwork as I can by phone and fly back down in a few days."

Asher would be able to coordinate with the funeral home for his cremation. Leave Zane with the sole task of picking up the ashes. Shit, and dealing with Jack's belongings. It felt like too much to leave for Zane, but the timing just sucked, and Zane had insisted.

Kicking off his shoes, Asher quickly brushed his teeth while they talked. Dead on his feet, he stripped down before sliding into the stiff hotel sheets. "Distract me. I'm not going to be able to sleep with my head on fire like this. Did Pippa calm down at all today?" He flipped off the light and sprawled across the bed.

"A bit. It felt like one long, drawn-out girl's day like we had in our first apartment way too often. Seemed to be the old Pippa shining through; glad to see she's still in there. I love that girl, but holy crap she's been a stranger lately. We went for a walk and baked cookies and painted our nails. Well, our toenails..."

The image of her glaring at her bitten down fingernails struck him. She bitched at herself every time she discovered she'd started gnawing unwittingly. He found it an endearing habit; she didn't see it that way.

"...Then, I sent her off to bed early to rest up for tomorrow. For a bossy thing, she didn't seem to mind me ordering her around."

They chatted about somethings and nothings for over an hour. Asher struggled to keep his eyes open, but he couldn't seem to disconnect from her. "If I fall asleep, I'm sorry. I'm enjoying listening to you. Keep talking."

Her sexy, wholehearted laugh echoed through the phone. "I'll try not to be offended. I know you must be exhausted. Hate to say it, but I'm out of conversation topics. I'm tired too."

"Why don't you talk dirty to me, then? Tell me what you're wearing and all the naughty things you're doing to yourself in my bed. I'm not sure I'll be able to get any sleep otherwise."

Her amused laughter tickled into his bones. "Yikes. Not my forte. Let's just call it a night."

"Please? I'm perfectly willing to beg."

"It would take a hell of a lot more alcohol than my small glass of wine after dinner."

"Not even if I tell you I'm already hard just thinking about how you're wearing nothing but that little black lace thong? You don't want to tell me about how you're rubbing your sweet, wet pussy and dreaming of me?"

With very little begging, she accommodated him and left him with much better dreams than he could possibly have imagined. Despite her initial hemming and hawing, she was a natural. Impressively creative with very little prompting.

Could run a fucking call service. Not that he'd ever tried one, but if they sounded anything like Sophie, with her soft, soprano moans as she came over the phone...

Chapter Nineteen

The Big Day

C heers of, "It's my wedding day," echoed through the house. Sophie glanced at the clock. She'd never seen Pippa up at six in the morning without a very good reason. And she was certainly never happy about it.

In the distance, Sophie heard a knock on a door. Shit, her door.

Leaping out of Asher's bed, she ran through the bathroom and into her bedroom. Realizing she was still wearing nothing but the thong he'd begged for last night, she tossed on an old shirt and shorts. She wasn't overly creative and had to immerse herself in character last night.

It had taken forever to fall asleep last night after their dirty conversation, she was so wound up. With his enthusiasm on the other end, getting off on her words and her voice, describing her body, how she touched herself and how it felt, she grew increasingly confident.

Hell, she'd about come just at the sound of his deep, rolling voice telling her all about what he wanted to do with his tongue. Add that and a little manual stimulation and she'd come three times over the phone. It would be a miracle if she didn't jump him on sight.

Quickly catching her breath, she opened the door.

"You look awfully out of breath for so early in the morning." Pippa was still in her bathrobe with her hair standing on end, in adorable disarray, but was all smiles.

"Sorry, I was in the bathroom and didn't hear you right away. Happy wedding day." Pippa's good mood was actually rather contagious. Although, she'd woken with a perma-smile herself this morning.

"Be down in ten. Okay twenty. Maybe thirty. I'm making breakfast." Without waiting for an answer, Pippa danced down the hall and down the stairs.

At least she wasn't frantic and self-pitying anymore. Maybe a little manic, however. In twenty-four hours, she might have her friend back again. Hopefully.

Complying with the very reasonable request, Sophie had run, showered, dressed, and was downstairs within thirty minutes. Paul and Denise, equally sleepy after the abrupt awakening, were sitting in the living room sipping coffee, looking very much like sleep-deprived parents on Christmas morning.

Sophie poured her own coffee and, at Pippa's urging, joined them on the couch. Her phone chirped an incoming text, *Morning gorgeous. I'm going to try to catch an early flight, but not looking good so far.*

Bleary-eyed, Denise turned to Sophie. "You're getting updates from Asher? Why am I not getting any?"

Oh boy. Sophie had figured at least his mother would have started to notice, but she was as blind to her son, apparently, as everyone else. Denise must not have read the full text over her shoulder, or she would have answered her own question.

Paul bit his cheek to hide his smile. Apparently, he wasn't so oblivious. Entertained by her ignorance, he patted his wife on the knee but didn't say anything. He flashed a conspiratorial wink at Sophie.

She'd already had her defense planned. "One of my maid of honor duties. I'm the communication hub."

Her phone beeped again, this time from Freya. *On my way*. "Case in point. Freya is on her way." Phew. Good timing. Shouting to the kitchen, she made sure Pippa was cooking enough for Freya as well.

The morning actually went pretty smoothly. Pippa's chipper, and seemingly relaxed mood, lasted throughout the day, even after they arrived at The Barn and started set up. Having the planning done so thoroughly, the big day ran impressively smoothly.

Sophie felt like she was directing traffic. Pippa's aunts were displaying flowers and centerpieces around the venue. Various capable looking folks were setting out tables and chairs from the rental trailer, mostly extended family that Sophie hadn't met yet. The small outdoor tent had already been set out. Paul was setting up the less expensive arbor, rather than the massive portable gazebo Pippa had given up.

All was going well. So far, so good. Bride getting ready. Groom present and accounted for, still hasn't seen the bride.

Grady wandered over to Sophie as she stood in the center of the field and ensured everything was going smoothly. "This looks amazing. I'm grabbing Lincoln a shot of something strong; I've never seen him so nervous."

Chuckling, Sophie linked arms with him and walked toward the portable bar. The bartender was setting out the evening's available drinks for display. "Can we bother you for a bottle of whiskey for the groom and some white wine for the bride?"

"Sure thing," offered the brunette with an affable demeanor, a metallic jingling sound as she nodded, shaking the long string of earrings lining her ears. "I'm still setting up, so go ahead and grab what you need for glasses and such."

Accepting the bottle, she turned to Grady. "Pippa's doing surprisingly well. I think she got most of her wedding crazies out of the way already, thank goodness." Sophie grabbed a handful of glasses for the ladies as Grady grabbed some for the guys.

"I guess now Lincoln's making up for his prior calmness."

Freezing, Sophie had to confirm, "He's not having second thoughts?"

Rolling his eyes lightheartedly, Grady shook his head and refuted her brief panic. "Hell, no. He's well and truly hooked. I think it's just the whole drama of the day. He's stayed calm this whole time; he's allowed a brief freak out."

Looking her up and down, Grady noticed Sophie was still in her jeans. "Shouldn't you start getting ready?"

Sophie's phone chirped in her back pocket. Setting the wine and glasses on the nearest table, she checked her text. *Thirty minutes out.*

"Yes, I really need to go get ready. Fyi, Asher should be here in half an hour." She shoved her phone back in her pocket and juggled the glasses until she held them all securely.

"Sophie?" Grady was suddenly serious, his expression genuine. Smiling hesitantly, Sophie didn't know what to expect, what he was getting at. "I'm really, really happy for you and Asher. Really."

"Are you sure? Because you just said *really*, like three times," she teased.

He grinned back. "Yeah, that sounded bad. I mean it though. I haven't known you as long, but I sort of knew Asher growing up. What I'm getting at is, I sort of watched Asher grow up from the periphery. Always a little jealous at how confident he was, especially with women. How he followed the beat of his own drummer. Honestly, I thought he'd end up a lifelong military playboy. Lately, with you, he's seems so much more settled than he's ever been."

Sophie nearly dropped the load of glasses in shock. She hadn't realized Grady had even known Asher, they were so distant now. It wasn't a big town, and they were pretty close in age; of course they'd known each other. "Thanks. Really. I'm happy."

Starting to relax, Sophie was feeling a sense of peace that everything was going to be okay. Wedding set to go. Bride relaxing; bridezilla exorcised. Groom appropriately nervous. Groomsmen happy and almost all present.

Knocking with her foot on the bridal ready room door, Sophie didn't dare risk the glasses she'd commandeered, juggling the breakable load as she was. Freya appeared at the door a second later, almost completely ready. "I thought you were the photographer. She should be here any second."

Setting her load on the table, she pulled out the cork the bartender had loosely recorked for her. "So sorry to disappoint you." She rolled her eyes and started to pour the wine. "The photographer is here and is taking some scenic shots first."

Standing in her stunning, sleeveless lace wedding dress, Pippa beamed. "My hair's almost ready so she'd better get here soon before I mess it up." Denise gratefully grabbed her offered glass of wine and continued her now one-handed smoothing and straightening of Pippa's gown.

Speak of the devil. Freya let in a stunning redhead wearing practical but feminine slacks, heels, and a sleek top. "Hey there. I'm Bree for those of you who don't know me yet." She pulled around an expensive looking camera and winked at Pippa. "Don't move, Pippa, you look amazing. Can I snap a few candids in here?"

Dazzled, smile wide and genuine, Pippa agreed. "Sophie, when's my brother getting here? We can start with couples photos, but I have him planned for a bunch of family and wedding party shots."

Handing Pippa a glass of wine, Sophie glanced at the time and reassured her. "ETA twenty minutes."

The ladies finished getting ready. After Pippa left for photos with Lincoln, Sophie quickly slipped on her dress, including the excessively helpful pushup bra that Lucy had insisted on. She tugged a little to hide the hint of cleavage the bra had created. Carefully, so as not to wrinkle the delicate silk dress.

Freya tsked. "You're not used to having cleavage, are you? Just own it. You look amazing."

With one last fuss, Sophie managed to stop tugging at her dress. She could use a touch of Freya's free-spirited confidence right now. Touching up her makeup and hair, she strapped on her tall heels and checked her reflection. Not bad. Maybe she'd try the fun bra with a few other outfits when she was feeling daring.

From behind, Freya handed Sophie her untouched glass of wine. "Quick, gulp for courage."

With a chuckle, Sophie took a big sip and set the glass down on the table. Burning down her esophagus, she immediately regretted the bite-you-back swig; wine was generally not recreationally guzzled for a good reason. After a painful cough and watery eyes, she turned to Freya. "Ready."

"I hate getting my picture taken; let's get this over with." Freya pushed Sophie out the door of the dressing room ahead of her.

Freya dragged her feet as she followed Sophie across the grounds. Toned down from Pippa's original plans, the site was charming. Dramatic lighting still established the ambience, but with glowing fairy lights rather than trendy paper lanterns. Scattered tables and chairs surrounded the dance floor, topped with simple bouquets of seasonal flowers in country jars. Against the far wall, the buffet table was dressed with plain blue rather than layered translucent tablecloths. Sophie actually preferred the modified design.

Venturing outside through the massive, open barn door, Sophie let the sunshine wash over her bare arms like a warm shower. Most of the wedding party and family members that had come early to help with set up were now visiting in small clusters while they waited for the official guests to arrive. Freya abandoned her to mingle with cousins she hadn't seen in years. Keeping to herself in the background, Sophie observed as the photographer took the bride and groom to the overlook point to snap some scenic shots.

They looked so much in love. Relaxed, finally. This was what it was all about. Sophie couldn't deny the pang of envy that fluttered in her belly as the couple could publicly pronounce their love and intentions.

Pippa had better come around quickly. The secrecy was pecking away at Sophie's soul, more with each passing day. She wouldn't deny the stolen moments with Asher were thrilling, but acceptance would be better.

Out of nowhere, Sophie remembered the daisy bouquet Pippa had picked herself that morning. Sophie dashed back to the dressing rooms to grab it for Pippa. She'd want it in the photos.

Rounding the corner, she ran smack dab into Asher. Catching her before she toppled to the ground, he laughed out loud. "You ought to take corners a bit more cautiously. This time, I was ready for you."

Melting in his arms, Sophie snuggled into him, appreciating his reference to their first collision. As he had then, he embraced her securely so she wouldn't get hurt. She absorbed the heat emanating from his body, feeling his heart thundering synchronously with her own.

He was frazzled. His hair was a bit wild but had been neatly trimmed a few days prior, so it couldn't become disheveled beyond repair. Sleep deprived with dark circles under his eyes, t-shirt and jeans wrinkled from the flight, he looked like he needed a long nap.

Arms still wrapped around her, he leaned his forehead against hers. "I missed you. Thanks for talking me through the night."

Craving his touch, his kiss, Sophie slid her hands up his chest before pulling his body even more tightly against her, as much so as the laws of physics would allow. Pressing their lips together, the familiarity, the comfort, the thrill it stirred was a perfect triad of everything she needed. Gliding her tongue along his lower lip, she silently begged for more. Unrestrained for a brief, stolen moment in the empty hallway, they lost themselves in the kiss.

A throat clearing behind her quickly brought them back to reality. Paul and Denise stood in the doorway; Paul was blushing but not surprised, Denise looked completely aghast, her face more of a furious beet red. Admonishing her grown child, Denise put her hands on her hips and glowered, "Asher Harold Sutherland. What on Earth are you—"

Paul cut her off with a good-natured smirk. "Dear, I think you know what they were doing. And I'm quite certain they know what they're doing."

"But—"

Asher held one arm around Sophie's waist and shifted her to his side possessively. "Mom, it's not like that. Just please, please don't say anything to Pippa just yet. We'll tell her when she gets back from her honeymoon."

Her exasperation faded to mild vexation, but the confused groove between her eyebrows wasn't going anywhere. She didn't bother to hide the suspicion in her eyes. "Tell her what, exactly?"

Paul gave Asher a wink. "I'll explain when you're older, dear." Guiding his wife away, he whispered in her ear.

Denise's response was priceless, her sudden about-face was adorable. "You mean it? Another wedding?" She ignored Paul shushing her and laughed aloud with joy.

Blushing, Sophie tried to avoid Asher's gaze. He turned her toward him with a gentle nudge of her chin. "He may be getting a bit ahead of things, but I'm looking in the same direction. I know it's quick, but, Sophie, I love you."

Legs turning to overdone noodles, she tried to breathe. "It is soon." Terrified of the new emotion, the change it would bring, yet thrilled at the truth of it, the future it mapped out, she locked eyes with his. "I figured it out pretty quick though. I love you too."

"Yeah? How quick?" Twinkle in his eye, he looked eager to hear her response, his hands still splayed around her waist.

Looking up at him, not as far as usual in her freakishly tall heels, the corner of her mouth quirked up in enjoyment before she responded. "About the time you took your shirt off to wipe the grease off your face and hands. Call me shallow, but I couldn't wait to get my hands on those abs."

Her teasing elicited the chuckle she'd hoped for. "I believe they call that falling in lust. Not love."

"Well, that's when it started. I was sold that day sitting over the creek. You weren't quite the womanizing lecher I'd been led to believe. Easy to visit with, fun to joke around with when I needed a distraction. As always, you made me feel respected. Normal. Sexy but not objectified."

He continued to hold her close. "It started a bit sooner for me."

"You hadn't even met me yet. Now who's confusing lust for love?" She knew they would be missed soon, but had trouble caring.

"I've been dreaming of those lips of yours for years. Was a little hesitant that you'd be as uptight as my sis, maybe more so as an accountant, but I knew there was more to you with all the secrets you try to hide behind those stormy eyes."

From across the grounds, they heard Lincoln bellow their names.

"Shit, we are absurdly late for pictures." Sophie dragged Asher at full speed to the men's suite. "Be quick. Your tux is hanging right inside. I brought a bag of your toiletries; should be on the bathroom counter."

Pulling her back for a quick, but profound kiss, he gave her a quick pat on the ass. As she walked out of sight, he whispered just loud enough for her to hear, "Don't work too hard. I've got plans for you later."

Chapter Twenty

A Long Day

L eaning back in her chair under the stars, Sophie held her very full stomach. "I think I ate too much."

A very satisfied and mellow Pippa nudged her in the side. "You're not getting out of dancing at my wedding that easily."

Lincoln leaned across Pippa. "Hey, we paid good money for that cake. You'd better have saved room."

Sophie chuckled and sipped her wine. "Not as much as you think. It's actually three birthday cakes from the grocery store bakery that Denise stacked and scattered candied flower petals over."

Overall, they'd done pretty well shaving off some of those big expenses. She tried to not toot her own horn often, but it was well deserved in this case. Lincoln and Pippa got up from the table and made some rounds, chatting with their guests as others finished their dinners. Sophie couldn't imagine knowing so many people to invite to her own wedding; half the dang town was here.

As many of the guests finished eating, others wandered the grounds and socialized before toasts, cake, and dancing. Timed to the minute thanks to Pippa's meticulous planning, they had about twenty minutes until the next set of wedding obligations. Who knew weddings were such hard work? No wonder Pippa had lost her mind planning it.

Heading to the back to freshen up a bit and escape the crowd for a few, Sophie caught an earful from someone she'd never even met. Stopping abruptly in front of her, a short, wiry old man shook his finger at her. "You must be Sophie Jones. I heard about what you did to your poor aunt. Framing her for an embezzling scam and sending her to prison in your stead? For shame."

Wanting to argue, but knowing it was an uphill battle, Sophie brushed past the strange man. She made it a few paces before she heard a weeping sound she knew only too well.

"She really is a sweet girl, just misdirected. I don't blame her for the conflict that has occurred between us, really. I manage just fine now that Sophie's involvement in that prostitution scandal has calmed down."

Turning slowly, dreading what she would see, Sophie approached her dear old Auntie Yvette. Hair a homely shade of brown, attire toned down to a lavender pantsuit and flats, she hardly even recognized her. A small crowd had gathered to hear Yvette's woes and the incriminating gossip about the town's newest accountant. The stranger from the big city.

Sophie was done with it. Placing her hand sweetly on Yvette's arm to capture her attention, Sophie interrupted the hurtful conversation. Yvette feigned a chin quiver when she saw Sophie.

"Lovely to see you Yvette, but I can't say I'm surprised. I guess you didn't get the Netflix role. Need a few thousand more for another boob job? Or is it more Botox this time? I'm really not sure your landlord would appreciate another blowjob in lieu of rent this month." She'd thought of all kinds of accusations. Maybe something about the jail or to ask after her pimp. It was tough to choose just one, so she went with the truth as it was equally damning.

She felt Asher's fingers link with her own as he came up from behind her to stand at her side.

Those damn butterflies in her stomach were flipping out. Holding her ground, she was terrified yet exhilarated to stand up to her vile aunt so boldly. So publicly.

Asher didn't hesitate to reprimand Yvette. Unflinching, calm and collected, as Sophie had discovered him to be in a fight, he called her out, "I don't recall my sister inviting you. It's time for you to go."

Grady stepped up her other side. After a disgusted glance at Yvette, he turned to Sophie. "I believe I offered legal assistance regarding your aunt's threats, should you need it. I would be happy to write up some documents to protect you from any further slander or defamation of character."

Before Sophie could fully process the wall of support forming around her, Jane appeared next to Grady. Voice steady and even, Jane didn't bother to hide a superior smirk. "You must be Yvette. I am Sophie's new employer that you called yesterday. As I mentioned on the phone, Sophie has my full support, and I will not lend credence to your lies."

Jane's tone abruptly turned harsh despite Yvette's wide, moist eyes and meek façade. "What kind of aunt tries to get her niece fired? Very creative tales you spun, but Sophie's record is quite clean. I would know, as I recently ran the appropriate background checks I would for any prospective employee." She reached across Grady to pat Sophie on the shoulder. "I hope you don't mind, but I already filed a complaint with the police department."

The crowd no longer looked so sympathetic towards Yvette. Looks of disgust were swiftly redirected. Sophie no longer felt the dread, the exposed sensation that rotted and festered in her stomach that she'd grown to expect when in public with Yvette. Warmth from the show of support from her friends filled her veins.

Another voice boomed from behind her as he approached. Chief Larson pulled his badge from his suit pocket and flashed it at Yvette. "Ma'am. I'm the Chief of Police here in Foothills. I understand you were not invited. I'll ask you to leave the premises immediately."

By then, a small crowd had gathered behind Sophie in a show of support. All these years, she'd been too afraid, too proud to ask for help, despising the weakness that was her only relation. She felt an emerging sense of optimism, bolstered by the support of her new community.

As one could have predicted, Yvette didn't take well to the tide turning against her. "Chief, please. I'm so glad you're here. Sophie has been harassing me. She's the reason I haven't landed a decent role in years. Her illegal deeds always come back to haunt me." Abundant tears flowed down her cheeks.

Oh boy. Here we go.

Larson wasn't easily manipulated. "If you continue making accusations without legal support to back them up, I will recommend a restraining order and that she accept the offer of legal counsel from Mr. Mallory, here."

And that was about all Yvette could handle. With the emotional intelligence of a preadolescent child, her tantrum wasn't pretty. Yvette brushed her hair over her shoulder dramatically, whacking the guest next to her in the face.

She screamed. She hollered. She stomped her feet.

Plodding right up to Sophie, she stopped inches away. It was oddly gratifying for outsiders to see the nightmare of a woman she'd had to suffer all these years, yet humiliating at the same time. "Please, leave. Now," Sophie demanded through gritted teeth.

From out of nowhere, Yvette's hand flew into the air to strike Sophie across the cheek. With quick reflexes, Asher caught her hand before she could succeed. Ripping her hand away brusquely, Yvette smacked Asher across the face, the loud crack echoing across the grounds.

Self-righteously, he smiled as he rubbed the glowing hand-print on his cheek.

As usual, Yvette was so self-centered she begged for help. "Officer, you saw that. I'm pressing charges against this man. He grabbed my wrist."

Larson seemed to be enjoying himself. Tongue in his cheek, he tried not to smile. "Actually, you just assaulted the newest recruit to the Foothills Police department; he's already proving himself to be an impressive asset. I'll have to double check on the nuances at this point, but as he's officially been hired, you may have just assaulted an officer of the law." He glanced at Asher briefly. "Sutherland, you looking to press charges?"

He considered a moment. Looking to Sophie, he left the decision to her. Sophie felt the connection between them growing deeper, more elaborate. How could she not fall more in love with him, feeling such support, such respect for her opinion?

Yvette was digging her own grave, and a little legal protection might just help solve this once and for all. "Absolutely."

Stepping forward, Larson took Yvette by the arm and led her away. "Nice work, Sutherland. I'll escort her out; I was about to head home soon anyway. Sophie, Asher, mind stopping by the station tomorrow? I believe you have eager legal counsel here if you'd like to invite Grady along."

"I'll do that. Thanks, Chief Larson." She smiled, again, appreciating that Asher's new boss was a pretty decent guy. After all the shit he'd been through, the self-doubt lately, he could use a supportive boss.

"I believe I told you it's Jonah. Enjoy the rest of your night." Yvette wasn't so feisty now. Head hung low, she played the cooperative prisoner, no doubt to downplay her punishment.

After accepting a few quick words of support from her friends, and several new acquaintances that inquired about her start date with Foothills Accounting, Sophie continued on her path back to the dressing rooms for a moment of peace and quiet. Maybe a good crying jag.

She paced the room, restless. Was it really over with Yvette? Or was the nightmare just beginning? The whirlwind of uncertainty was suffocating. Thank goodness no more than twenty people had witnessed the scene. Particularly Pippa; she'd hate for Yvette to ruin her friend's special day.

Sophie sat on the awkwardly squishy velvet couch and buried her head in her hands, waiting for tears that just wouldn't flow. Over the years, she'd cried so much over Yvette she didn't have anything left. As much as she hated crying, the pressure behind her eyes was almost painful, begging for the soggy release.

Giving up, knowing she needed to get back out there, she headed into the bathroom for a quick refresh of hair and makeup before rejoining the party. With any luck, the pent-up sob-fest wouldn't strike her during the reception. Or during her toast; that would be humiliating.

Cautiously, the door opened. Asher popped his head in and searched the room for her, finally finding her peeking her head out from the bathroom to see who the intruder was.

"You okay?" He closed the door behind him and locked it.

Her gut torn to pieces, filled with confused butterflies, she nearly knocked him over she ran so anxiously into his arms. "I hate that woman so much." Anger was a decent emotion, better than the hollow nothingness.

Remembering the slap, she studied Asher's cheek. "I think she left a mark." Sophie gently ran her fingers over his smooth cheek, missing the stubbled beard he normally wore, wishing her vile aunt's handprint hadn't taken its place.

Scoffing, he covered the mark defensively. "Not exactly the worst assault I've sustained." His voice softening, he grazed a knuckle across Sophie's cheekbone. "I'm just glad she hit me and not you."

"Thanks for that. Nice catch." On her tiptoes, Sophie kissed away the hurt. Asher pulled her tightly against him, burying his face in her hair.

A wiggle of the doorknob, followed by a demanding knock, startled her out of the peace she'd enveloped around herself. *Shit.* Probably Pippa coming to check on her. Word would likely be spreading fast to those that hadn't witnessed the humiliating scene.

Might as well rip another fricking band-aid off while she was at it, shatter all of her protective coatings in a twenty-minute period. Stepping in front of Asher to face the music head on, she bravely opened the door.

Not Pippa. *Phew*. She didn't actually want to rip that band-aid off just yet, but found she was proud of her courageous attempt. Instead of a flabbergasted bride, Denise rushed in the doorway as soon as it was open.

Throwing her arms around Sophie, Denise started talking a mile a minute, her voice shaking with fury. "I am so sorry that woman got in. Are you okay? What a nightmare for you. Oh, I just hate that bitch."

Now the waterworks started with an annoying combination of relief and irritation. She hated crying, but the release was welcome. Wishing she hadn't already retouched her makeup, Sophie gave up her last shred of control and let it all out. Between sobs, she managed, "I'm fine. Really." Denise held her, letting her cry out the last fifteen years of humiliation and fear.

Finally, the tears started to slow, and Denise stepped back. Smoothing Sophie's hair maternally, the side of her mouth rose in a kindhearted smile when she saw the dark mascara smudges. Linking arms with Sophie, she guided her back into the bathroom. "I'm so proud of how you stood up to her. Now, you'd better get cleaned up and back out there before you're missed."

Asher stood back and watched, face pinched in indecision and concern. Tugging at his tie, he finally ditched the excessive swath of fabric and tossed it across the room. Leaving Sophie to clean up her now irretrievably destroyed makeup, Denise grabbed her son and pulled him in for a squeezing bear hug.

"You did good out there," Sophie heard Denise complimenting her son. "I'm glad Sophie has you to stand up for her." She added, "And vice versa."

A long pause. Sophie almost had the inky black scrubbed away from under her eyes but wasn't sure the I've-been-crying red and puffy appearance was going anywhere.

Denise continued as she embraced her son, "I'm really happy for you both. Don't worry about your sister. I don't blame you for waiting until after the wedding to tell her. She's a bit high strung as it is. It may take a while for her to come around, but she will."

After another moment, Sophie heard the door shut, and Asher popped into the bathroom and leaned back against the counter. "Don't you have to give a toast pretty soon?"

Nodding bravely, Sophie checked her reflection one more time. Not quite as put together as she'd been a few hours ago, but she looked halfway decent.

Shoring up her courage, Sophie led the way, Asher following right behind. At the door, she dropped his hand. Tomorrow would be much better, when they didn't have to hide. This was stupidly stressful.

As they entered the crowded barn, dusk was imminent, and the twinkling lights cast an enchanting glow on the room. Clinking his glass, Grady cleared his throat and began his toast. The room immediately stopped their reveries to listen. No wonder he was already a popular attorney in town despite being in practice little more than a year; his words, spoken in the rich tambour of his voice, were mesmerizing.

Sophie wasn't sure she could come close to matching that toast. A few fun lawyerly jokes, childhood stories, and hopes for the future. Damn, he was good. She'd had several toasts written and rewritten, stuffed in her coat pocket in the bridal suite. In the chaos, she'd forgotten her notes. She didn't like any of them now anyway.

Cheers rang out and glasses clanked together.

Okay, here goes nothing.

Walking up to the dessert table where the bride and groom waited, Grady flashed her an encouraging wink and handed her the glass he'd reserved for her. For all their issues a few days ago, he'd sure turned out to be a good friend now that the air was clear.

The room went silent, waiting to hear her speak. Sophie had never had the ability to speak easily in front of a crowd, but she'd never feared public speaking either.

"As Grady just described, we are all incredibly lucky to be in the presence of such a beautiful union. I don't have quite the oratory skills he has, so don't mind me while I gulp down my champagne for courage," she joked and took a big swig. She didn't need it, but it bought her a second to collect her thoughts.

Worked every time. The crowd chuckled right along with her, boosting her confidence the shred it needed so she could continue. "Alright. Ready now."

Sophie would like to think that she wowed them with her oratory prowess. Maybe, maybe not. She got a few laughs talking about the oddity of Washingtonians and their distaste for umbrellas. A few tears when she talked about how Lincoln and Pippa reunited and had fallen even more in love after the years spent apart.

She'd seen Pippa and Lincoln take things so painfully slowly in their meticulous planning, she wouldn't have been able to stand it. She'd been the result of a rushed, but devoted relationship, her parents marrying and having her when they were still children themselves. Although she hadn't been old enough to notice, she'd heard stories of how the first year or two of settling in were rough on the young couple.

Things between her and Asher had become so powerful, so quickly. But she was certain their love for each other was so very real. Perhaps the truth to a successful marriage was somewhere in between?

Her gaze wandered to Asher standing a few feet away as she wrapped up her toast. "Falling in love is easy. Fostering a relationship that survives time and hardship... that's a sign of a special bond." Raising her glass, she saluted her friends, "To an enduring, loving marriage."

Pippa was watery eyed by the time she finished. Politely, they cut the cake, not smearing too much frosting on each other. Just enough to tenderly kiss away the stray frosting bits. Sophie had little doubt the adorable and non-messiness had been premeditated.

Joining her as she backed away from the dessert table, Asher pulled her to stand with him for cake cutting and dancing. He whispered in her ear, distancing himself just far enough to avoid looking intimate. "Nicely done. But you forgot to give a special announcement to Pippa, 'and please don't kill me when I tell you I've completely fallen in love with your brother and plan to ride him like the stallion he is. All night long.'"

Taking another sip of champagne to hide the lusty blush heating her cheeks, she laughed. "Actually, I considered threatening all the women here to stop giving you their numbers. Announce that you're off the market."

He grabbed her glass and set it on the table next to her. Pulling her over for a dance as the music started, he whispered again, "None of them hold a candle to you. It's a small town; word travels fast. I'll tell five people here that I'm madly in love with you and the whole town will know within a week."

Grinning, she twirled into his arms and glided with him across the dance floor.

Chapter Twenty-One

All Night Long

L aughing, Sophie grabbed Asher and pulled him directly into her bedroom. Smiling against his mouth as he kissed her again in the doorway, she demanded, "I'm not hiding this anymore."

Dragging her through to his bedroom, despite her protests, he added, "Agreed. However, your bedroom is directly over my parent's, and I want to hear just how loud I can make you call out my name."

It had been unbearably difficult to wait until the bride and groom left the wedding. After throwing birdseed, cheering, and doing a cursory initial clean-up, Paul had waved them off when Asher had attempted to stay and help. "We got this. You two get home. You've had a rough couple of days. I'm real sorry to hear about Jack."

"Me too. Thanks, Dad." At the mention of it, Asher's features looked drawn as he thought about his trip to San Diego. Rubbing the exhaustion from his eyes, he hadn't argued when Sophie dragged him out to his borrowed car. Knowing he'd be wiped out after the last few days, she'd caught a ride to the wedding with his parents, so she could drive him home early, if needed.

Lifting her into his arms, he'd clearly caught his second wind as soon as they got upstairs. So much had led up to this moment. Glad they waited; Sophie was ready to take the next step. Call her old fashioned, but knowing he loved her made this moment that much more miraculous.

Setting her down in front of the bed, he was tearing off his suit jacket and kicking off his shoes before she could even catch her balance, then moved on to getting her clothes off as quickly as possible. Struggling with her zipper to slide the dress off, he laughed out loud. "What the hell? I had this off of you so easily, what, a week ago? I feel like a green, virgin groom."

Normally remarkably adept with his hands, his clumsiness was endearing. Any other time, Sophie would have found it humorous. Maybe she did, but more, she was thrilled he was as nervous as she was.

Reaching behind her, Sophie slid the zipper down and let the gown pool at her feet. Down to her panties and heels again, he groaned in response. Eager, she reached for the waistband of his pants.

He stilled her hands. "Slow down. I'm not going to make it very long as it is." Looking her up and down, the hunger in his eyes was enough to drive her over the edge. It's not like they hadn't explored every inch of each other's bodies already, but tonight was different.

Reaching behind her, he unhooked her overly helpful strapless bra and tossed it across the room. "I hate that bra. You have magnificent breasts." In stark punctuation, he wrapped his hands around each perfect breast and pulled one deeply into his mouth.

Gasping, the sensation rocketed like an electric current through her entire body. Writhing in his arms, sensation scorched from deep in her core. Urging him on, she buried her hand in his hair, gripping him tight to let him know she was close.

Gliding down across her sensitized skin, his hand reached her center and cupped her soft curls. Tantalizing, stroking her core, he brought her to the edge. Already, he knew her so well, knew exactly how to drive her wild.

"Yes," she chanted breathlessly, crying out for more as her climax neared, letting him know how he affected her.

Shifting his body downward, he trailed his tongue along her abdomen, circling her navel before reaching her core. As he had that day in the dressing room, he grasped her hips and pulled her against his waiting mouth. Licking, sucking, velvety heat stroking her slick nub, an eruption of sensation tore through her.

Already there, her veins rapidly filled with molten lava. She called out his name, unable to contain the crushing orgasm. Hand still gripped in his hair to steady herself, she rode wave upon wave of pleasure that built inside of her until her vision blurred and her legs couldn't hold her up any longer.

Supporting her, grinning with pure, primal masculine ego, he scooped her in his arms and tossed her onto the bed. Before her sighs even began to diminish, he'd ditched the last of his clothes and was sheathed in protection. Propelling the orgasm that still tremored through her, he drove into her with a dynamic thrust.

Exhilaration, desire, and love consumed her as he buried into her. They fit so perfectly; she knew he was it for her.

Carefully building, he tried to steady his movements.

Climbing higher and higher in the delirious pleasure that resonated through her, she wouldn't let him slow. Tightening around his thick, pistoning cock, she cried out as orgasm overtook her.

As she rode the crest of bliss, she dug her fingertips into his shoulders, urging him faster. Wild, he drilled on. Coming fast and hard, powerful and vital, he climaxed with her, letting out a rough groan as both collapsed, lost in a haze of euphoria.

Drained, exhilarated, Asher collapsed atop her. His muscles had turned to heavy lead, yet he soared like Icarus. Pounding in his chest, his heart clenched with unfamiliar emotion. He'd known they were more than compatible, but this was something record-breakingly miraculous.

Taking her with him, he rolled onto his back, so her head rested on his shoulder. His hand lightly trailed along her arm as they caught their breath together. From the moment she'd cocked her hip out and taunted him with that damn bolt that he'd lost in his engine, he'd been a fucking goner and had known it would be different with Sophie.

Couldn't even count the number of women he'd been with before, but none could hold a candle to Sophie in or out of the sack. Nor would there ever be anyone else for him. Ever. His heart was well and truly hers.

"Confirmed. You have made me a noisy orgasmer," she breathlessly proclaimed. "I see why you moved us to your room."

A satisfied chuckle rumbled through his chest, jostling her head on his shoulder. He wanted to counter with a quippy response but was too busy feeling quite pleased with his discoveries. As much as he hated to admit it, he'd never been so anxious about a partner's response before. Historically, he'd been more focused on getting a quick, yet satisfying, bang and getting the hell out of there.

"You might be right. We'd better test this out, maybe run a few trials. You could build a spreadsheet for us." He traced his hand along her side and splayed his hand around her waist.

"If we're running a complete data analysis, I'm game as long as there's a spreadsheet involved. No control groups, though." She lifted her head off his chest and raised an eyebrow at him.

He knew that she knew that he was all-in when it came to their relationship. But did she know exactly what that meant? "Sophie, I love you so much. You're the only one for me. I've been waiting for you a long fucking time."

He craved her again, cock already thickening. "Just so you know, I've never not used a condom. Protecting you; I just didn't know it until recently. Sappy as that sounds, I'm feeling rather poetic at the moment."

Her lips turned up in a provocative grin. "Me neither. I'm on birth control... I wonder what it feels like, the smooth skin of your cock gliding into me..." Damn; just like on the phone, her words shattered him.

Shifting atop him, she straddled him like riding a stallion and rocked against him. Moving rhythmically atop him, not yet letting him in, she explained *exactly* what she had in mind. Drove him out of his fucking mind at her words, her motions.

At her command, he leaned up and sucked on her breasts with the pressure she demanded. Pulling and suckling until she cried his name, he felt her need building as she rocked against his rigid erection.

Fuck, he already could feel her slick heat ready for him, and he wasn't even in yet. Reaching between them, rising up to the challenge of bringing her to unrestrained, unmatched orgasm, he circled her clit with his thumb to bring her just over the edge, more intensely than before. Instinctively, she pressed against him and climaxed again at his touch.

Breathless, she looked down at him. Gazes locked together, he was lost in her gray eyes that had shifted into full thunder storm.

Slowly, with all the control he could muster, he slid into her tight, wet heat. "Fuck, you feel so good."

Deliberately at first, each savoring the exquisite sensation of the intimate contact, they moved stronger, fiercely together. Crying out in ecstasy as he gripped her hips and drove deeper inside her, she rode him to his undoing, stars flashing in his vision. More than he could ever have imagined, he was completely, forever hers.

Chapter Twenty-Two

The Day After

Trapped in a Sophie-cage of arms, legs, and her wild blondish hair, Asher tried to roll out of bed the next morning. Limb by limb, he attempted to free himself, but she just gripped more tightly. Those long limbs were incredibly nimble.

"Wake up. Let's go for a run," he pleaded, his voice raspy from too many sleepless nights. Although, as long nights went, he would happily repeat last night as often as possible.

Sophie had been worth the wait. Not that most would consider three weeks waiting, but for him, it had felt like an eternity. Hell, his longest wait before Sophie had been about three hours. All that pent-up sexual frustration for both had led to a fucking amazing night.

Brushing her hair out of her face, she squinted at the sun shining in the window. She pouted, "Didn't you get enough exercise last night?"

Grinning, he dragged her out of bed with him. "Yeah, but if we move along, we can do it in the shower before anyone else wakes up."

By eight o'clock, they'd run, enjoyed a spectacularly erotic shower, and were downstairs to enjoy the quiet of the morning. As usual, his parents either slept in late or had taken their coffee to bed to watch the morning news.

Asher carried his coffee out to the front patio and held the door open for Sophie. "I think I'll go shopping for a new truck today. Wanna come?"

Bundled in his sweatshirt to combat the cool breeze that had blown in overnight, Sophie curled up in her usual chair. "Fun as that sounds, we have to go to the station today."

Shaking his head, he scowled as he settled into his chair. "Shit. I forgot. After?"

Sophie nudged him playfully with her foot. "How about I drop you off at the dealership while I go look at some rental houses? As much as I appreciate your parents letting me crash here, it's time."

"Fine. I'll shop alone. I hate dickering. If they give me the runaround, mind coming down to make sure I'm not getting fleeced?" He waggled his eyebrows at her.

"I can do that. I'll play dumb, then tear apart the crappy deal they've proposed."

Nodding, he was already turned on by her brain. When had he found math skills so damn sexy? "It's a date."

She rolled her eyes playfully. "I'm starving." Pleasantly sore from head to toe, she stretched like a sleepy cat as she rose from the chair. Asher liked seeing her wear his sweatshirt; although she swam in it, she looked adorable.

If he played his cards right, maybe she'd take pity on him and cook a real breakfast rather than the toast he'd likely stuff down out of laziness and culinary ineptitude. "Eggs? Bacon?"

"Only if you're cooking. I was thinking yogurt." Her accusatory glare was comical.

Moping, Asher followed her into the kitchen and stared desperately into the fridge. "You don't want to suffer my cooking." He could cook some basics, but nothing anyone wanted to actually eat. Alone, he could survive off of rubbery eggs for breakfast, bagged salads and PB&J for lunch, then an overcooked steak for dinner. Didn't enjoy it, but it was something.

"I know. Your mom implied you may be looking for a sweet little wife to cook all of your meals for you." Reaching around him to grab herself a yogurt, she leaned against the opposite counter and opened the container.

"Looking to help me with that?" He shut the fridge, no longer interested in breakfast, and stepped up to her. Pressing his body against hers, he nibbled along her neck, her jaw.

"Fifty-fifty, pal," she teased as he traced his hands up her sides, gently pulling up her shirt. Laughing, she set the yogurt down so she could tug her shirt back down.

He nipped her ear. "How about we work out a mutually satisfying system. You cook and I find other ways to balance our relationship." Skimming his hand along her skin until he reached her pert breast, he left the shirt in place this time as a compromise. See? He could be fair.

A soft, breathless sigh escaped her lips. Continuing his exploration of her body under her clothes with his hands, his mouth explored hers, plundering in hasty urgency. Increasingly desperate for her, he scooped her up and set her on the counter. He pulled her against him, and she wrapped her legs around him, holding him securely.

Realizing the kitchen was a stupid place to start this, he tried to pull away. Sophie gripped the waistband of his jeans and pulled him close again. "Let's go upstairs," she whispered breathlessly.

Before they could release each other, he suddenly became very aware they were not alone. Pippa stood in the doorway,

her eyes wide with horror. Biting her lip to keep from screaming out, she fled, slamming the door shut behind her.

"Shit." Asher raced full speed for the door. Sophie tried to
follow. Holding up his hand, he pleaded, "Give me a minute."
Shit. Shit. Shit. She'd never forgive them, finding out like this.

Tearing out the front door, Asher ran and caught Pippa
before she could climb back in the car. He leaned against the
passenger door to block her from running away. Lincoln was
just getting out of the driver's door and knew immediately
what was up.

"Please, Pip. Let me explain." Asher's chest throbbed with a
deep, gnawing ache, hating that he'd hurt his sister. Knowing
she'd understand and maybe even be happy if she could just
hear him out. Folding his arms across his chest protectively,
he braced himself for her disapproval.

"Explain what? That you needed a little something last night
and slept with my best friend? Again?" She was furious, pacing
and kicking dirt. He'd never seen her quite this angry before.

From across the car, Lincoln tried to speak, but she shot
shut-up arrows out her eyes at him.

Asher clenched his jaw in rapid fire, panic rising. "Yes."

As anticipated, she had not expected an admission of guilt.
Simple wording. She'd expected defensiveness and long explanations. Spinning on her heel, she stepped a few paces
closer and stood stiffly with her hands gripped at her sides.
At least she was listening for a moment.

"Yes, I slept with her last night. And I plan to again. Every
night for the rest of my life, if she'll have me." He paused,
allowing for the inevitable retort. Out of the corner of his
eye, he saw Sophie coming out and waiting at the front door
looking worried. He didn't dare break eye contact with Pippa.

"How could you do that to me? You're not driving away
another one of my friends because you're so damn impulsive
you can't think about how it affects me."

She stomped her foot and stalked a few feet closer to Sophie, but didn't get too close. "And you? You knew how I felt. You. Knew."

Tears flooding her eyes, she stalked back to the car before Sophie could respond and shoved Asher out of her way. Broken hearted for his sister, he didn't try to block her this time.

"Lincoln, let's go. I'll buy a new hair dryer on the way. Mine was old anyway." Sliding into the car, she refused to hear anymore.

Before getting back in the car, Lincoln looked to Asher. "Sorry, man. She'll come around. Give her time."

Asher stood in place, watching as they pulled away. Dammit. Absolutely not how he wanted this to go. When Pippa got into a rage, she couldn't see or hear anything. Missed the whole *rest of my life* comment.

Walking to his side, Sophie was teary-eyed. "Let's go to the station." She clearly didn't want to dwell any more than he did. Subject change approved.

Nodding, Asher ran back in and grabbed his wallet and phone. Behind him, Sophie grabbed her purse, and shot a quick text to Grady that they would meet him at the police station. Neither said a word the whole way into town.

It didn't take long. Jonah took their statements and reassured her he'd do what he could to help sort things out with Yvette. Grady had met them there and helped with all the necessary paperwork, promised to follow up on everything.

At this point, Sophie didn't give a flying fuck what happened to Yvette. She could threaten all she wanted, spread all the rumors she could come up with and even try framing Sophie for something. Sophie was done with her. And, she had good legal support.

"Do you still need a ride to the dealership?" She wasn't in the mood to look for a rental but needed something to focus on.

Nodding grimly, Asher responded, "If you don't mind."

Sophie dropped him at the dealership and started driving. She'd compiled a list of places to check out. Maybe it was her mood, but none of the houses appealed in the least so far.

Until the last on her list. She pulled up to a stunning three bedroom outside of town. Overlooking the valley, the spot was perfect. Sadly, the place was way outside of her price range, so she'd only been looking to torture herself.

The place could use a little love, but nothing major. Although it was a one-story craftsman-style, it looked surprisingly light and airy. Lots of windows. Could use a new paint job, the trim in particular. In front, the curb appeal was lacking, but nothing some decent landscaping couldn't fix. She wouldn't mind learning a little home repair if she could have this house, especially with its expansive view of the valley.

A bit sooner than she'd planned, but maybe worth making an offer to buy it? Flashing to Asher, she considered asking what he thought. If he was ready.

Moving in together... sounded fantastic. She was outrageously, head over heels in love with him. That wasn't changing. But this was officially his longest relationship.

Freya was moving back into town soon and needed a roommate. She was an artist, maybe she'd agree to cheap rent in exchange for help fixing up the place.

Her phone chirped with an incoming text. *Mind bringing your brain? Found a good truck, but the math isn't adding up*.

Smiling weakly, she responded, *ETA ten minutes*. Taking one last, longing look at the house, she headed back for the dealership.

Everything about Asher was amazing, everything she'd ever wanted. More than she'd dared to hope for. Supportive, generous, fun to visit with. Damn sexy.

But so very new.

A sher ran his hand across the pristine dash of his new truck, admiring the fancy touch screen and buttons with all kinds of alien symbols. Like Sophie, it had been worth the wait. The thing was all shiny and new with all the bells and whistles.

Done with any more bullshit in her life, Sophie hadn't given the dealer an inch and had gotten him a killer deal. Calculating the interest rate and payments in her head, she hadn't given them a chance to catch up to her. Fucking knockout. He'd never grow tired of looking at her. But something about that sexy brain of hers. Her quiet calculations, how she formed that cute little crease between her eyebrows when something didn't add up.

The morning had really messed with her. With both of them. They'd worked so hard to protect her, only to ruin it in one brief second. He had to get Pippa to accept this. How could they build a life together with such strain on the foundation?

Following Sophie back home again, he didn't know what he was going to say when they got home. If she'd talk to him. She'd hardly said a word all day.

Sophie was already in the house by the time he pulled into the driveway. With his new job starting soon, he hadn't wanted to risk the embarrassment of a speeding ticket from a future coworker, but she'd had hauled ass to get home.

If Pippa would answer her damn phone, maybe he could talk her down a bit. She'd been ignoring his calls and texts all day. Phone turned off in a big fuck-you gesture.

Paul came out of the house as soon as he arrived. "Nice ride."

He'd already alienated his sister today, and his unspoken truce with his dad was fragile enough. As much as he wanted to go after Sophie, it was probably better to give her some space and spend a little quality time with his dad. "Thanks. Fancier than I was going for, but Sophie talked them down. Took one look at the deal they'd come up with and tore the poor sales guy a new one."

Climbing in the driver's seat as Asher got out, Paul started playing with the buttons, fiddling with the touch screen. Hell, Asher couldn't figure the dang thing out either. "She's a smart one. Good choice. I was afraid you'd end up with someone like Pippa's old friends back in the day, at the rate you were going."

Utterly confused, Asher raised his eyebrows in question.

Laughing, Paul shook his head at his clueless son. "I figured of anyone, you'd remember some of the halfwits she brought home. Hardly a complete brain between the lot. Flighty, giggly bunch they were. Drove me nuts. Although, you didn't seem to mind." He gave him a knowing look.

"I guess I hadn't thought about it." He had often wondered about Pippa's taste in friends. With all of her attentions devoted to Lincoln in high school, then the book nerd she turned out to be in college, she really hadn't had much in the line of decent girlfriends over the years.

"Sophie came in the house a few minutes ago. Tried to hide the red eyes, but Denise figured things out pretty quick. Once I made sure you hadn't been the one to make her cry, I was out of there." Hopping back out of the truck, Paul had the hood popped and was performing his perfunctory paternal inspection.

"I don't know what I'm going to do if Pippa doesn't come around." Running his hands through his hair, still longer than he was used to, even with the recent trim for the wedding, Asher tried to focus on the engine rather than the crappy turn his love life had just taken.

"She'll be fine. Despite her bitching and moaning, your sister is a romantic at heart. Give her a few days." Paul fiddled with a few of the nobs and wires before dropping the hood. Asher couldn't wait to get his hands in there and figure out the mechanics of it. Technology had changed quite a bit. He'd definitely need an updated manual.

"Hey, you tend to know these things. Sophie's looking for a rental house outside of town. Any of your customers updating their rentals for new tenants?" Asher shoved his hands in his pockets, not sure how to phrase it. He knew it was too soon, but he was sort of hoping Sophie would agree to finding a place together.

Paul considered for a moment, then nodded as his face lit up with a bright idea. "Actually, Grandpa's place just opened up."

"You still renting that out? I thought you'd sold it by now." Grandpa's place was perfect. The view was to die for. Without a doubt, the house would probably need updates, but Paul would have kept it in adequate repair.

"Sure am. I wanted to keep it in the family, if one of you were interested when the day came. Grandpa built that from the ground up. Needs a lot of work, but that's all superficial. For Sophie, I could give her a good deal."

"How much you want for the house?" Both stood a few feet apart, legs spread wide and arms crossed. Scary when one looked so remarkably like one's father. It was promising that they wouldn't always be at odds.

Shifting his feet, Paul looked beyond pleased but tried to hide it behind his considering scowl. As he hadn't mentioned anything in all these years, Asher suspected he didn't want to pressure anyone. Again, not like him, but the house was a bit of a sensitive topic. "You thinking of buying it?"

"Hell yeah. I need a few paychecks first though. About drained my short-term savings for the down payment on the truck." The place was gorgeous. Asher had wanted it for years but was never sure if he would be moving back or staying in the navy or who knows what.

"How about this. We'll lease it to Sophie for a few months while you're getting settled in the police department. Then, we'll see about you making an offer." Paul gave him a wink that almost looked pleased. Maybe even proud.

"Probably a good idea. I..." Asher tried to explain his thoughts; his brain twisted in confusion as he struggled to say something emotional to his inflexible father.

Suddenly, he felt full sympathy for when Paul had attempted to give him the sex talk. *When a man and a woman fall in love... babies... and... diseases... just use a damn condom*. Little did Paul know—or maybe he had but realized he'd better get his butt in gear—he'd been about two years late on that topic.

It was so new to talk openly with his dad, but he was finding him helpful and supportive so far today. "I love her. We've only known each other a few weeks. As much as I'm in a big old hurry to move in with her, get married... I know I tend to rush into things. Maybe we should slow things down a bit."

Paul patted him roughly on the shoulder. "You just might be growing up after all. Keep following those instincts as they tend to lead you in the right direction, but probably good to slow things down a bit. Leave them wanting more; worked for me and your mom." He flashed a clever wink.

He was about to walk away when Asher stopped him for one last question. "What about the apartment over Grandpa's garage? I have a buddy that needs a place."

Kicking a rock absent-mindedly, Paul pondered the situation. "The current tenant actually just moved out. Should be ready in a week or two. Zane?"

Asher nodded. He'd wanted the place for himself, but knew if he lived right next door to Sophie, he may as well move in with her. No, he wanted to be the man she deserved, not a can't cook, can't do his own laundry freeloader.

"Sure thing. I'll write it up; start with six months while he settles in."

Pulling out his phone, Asher shot a quick message to Zane. *Found you some pretty great digs.* He sent the address and Paul's number.

His phone buzzed in response. *Acknowledged. See you next week.*

"Where are you going to live?" His dad asked, eyebrows raised in his traditional expression of, *didn't think this through, did you son?* Phew, and here Asher was thinking his dad just might respect him as an adult. Nah, not there yet. Maybe give it another decade and try again.

A bubble of laughter filled from his diaphragm and moved upward into a bemused chuckle. "Grady's going to have a spare bedroom." He could bum some life skill lessons off of his new friend and irritate the crap out of him while he was at it. Win-win.

Madly, Sophie fired off another text that bounced right back. Pippa was completely off the grid.

If she could just explain. Tearing her fingernails out of her teeth, she stood from the foot of her bed and paced some more. She pulled her phone back out and dialed a different number.

"What up?" Freya answered in delightfully unnatural slang.

"When are you moving back to town?" Sophie cut right to the chase. She wasn't in the mood to mess around.

"Actually, now. I need to fly back to wrap a few things up, but I should be back in a few weeks with my wee worldly possessions."

"I'm thinking of buying a house. Want to be roomies for a few months? I can offer you cheap rent while you settle back into town and use your artist brain to make the place beautiful?" Sophie described the gorgeous house she'd fallen in love with.

Freya's laugh was superb, full and rich from deep in her gut. "I can't believe that place is available. Ask Uncle Paul about it. It was our grandpa's."

"So that's a no?" Sad butterflies flapped their pitiful wings in her gut. Now what? She really wanted that house.

"That's actually a well disguised yes. I would have thought you'd ask Asher rather than me?"

"I want to. But, we're so new. I kind of want to let him romance me a bit first. You know, before we start forever." Smiling to herself, Sophie felt relieved with her plan. That's what she needed. What would make it all okay. Some good old-fashioned courting.

"Let's do it. If Uncle Paul won't sell, see if you can talk him into a six-month lease. I anticipate Asher will have moved in full time by then anyway. I think Uncle Paul was hoping to keep the place in the family." She was quickly discovering that Freya was quite sensible despite her free-spirited ways and was proving to be a pretty great friend.

Sophie wanted to jump for joy but was still too jaded after the day she'd had. Maybe a happy dance once things were sorted out with Pippa. Actually, Pippa had pretty much taught her the happy dance, so it was tough to even consider without her.

Disconnecting the call, Sophie headed straight out to find Paul. He wasn't surprised at her inquiry. Apparently, he had a potential buyer that needed six months anyway, so the timing was perfect. When the time came, she'd give him a better offer than the buyer he had in the wings.

Asher didn't take the news quite so well. Despite the awful morning, or maybe because of it, she needed to be close to him. He was already self-medicating with a swim, so she joined him in the pool. Surfacing in the middle, she waited for him to finish his laps and join her.

"Hey. Didn't expect to see you. Thought you were mad at me." He looked adorable, hair spiked on end as he shook his head and treaded water in front of her. The sadness, the fear in his eyes broke her heart. Had she made him worry that she was bailing?

"Hey. I found a place to rent. Your grandpa's old place. Freya agreed to move in with me for six months." She gaged his reaction.

"Great," he tried to look pleased for her, but his eyes were heavy, the honey in them downright blue.

Treading water a few feet away, she tried to explain her plan. How to make him understand? "I have this amazingly sweet, sexy boyfriend I wanted to ask. But I think he needs a few cooking lessons first." She grinned at him.

He sighed, looking less dejected as he processed what she'd said. "You're not wrong. How about we have tons of sex, of course, and I get to be your boyfriend while I show you just how much I need you forever. Six months. That's it; you know I'm too damn impatient to wait any longer than that. Then, your landlord is selling that place out from under you," he said with a wink.

She sent a huge splash his way. "So, you're the potential buyer? You'll have to fight me for it."

Sleekly moving through the water, she shrieked when he caught up to her and dragged her to him. Wrapping her arms around his neck, she kissed him with all the love she possessed. Holding her up against him as he kept them both afloat, he whispered words of adoration in her ears. Melting, she knew this was right.

Chapter Twenty-Three

All the Days After

D ays passed, and still no response from his sister. Stubborn ass. She wasn't making this easy on him. Hopefully, at least for Lincoln's sake, she hadn't been festering the whole time but was enjoying her honeymoon.

They weren't due to return for another three days, so Asher was surprised when he saw the dust storm coming down the driveway. Coming out when he saw the car, Sophie didn't tolerate waiting in the wings this time.

Pulling up to the house, Pippa stepped cautiously out of the car. She looked pretty bummed. Shit. They must have left before dawn to get here so early.

Waiting for her to speak first, Asher bit his tongue.

Took her a minute, standing in front of the car, arms crossed and eyes red. "I'm sorry I didn't hear you out. I haven't slept much, thinking back on the last few weeks. A few words you said kept echoing in my head, then I thought about some of the details I hadn't paid attention to while I was in full bridezilla mode. It took me a while to settle down and process everything. Poor Lincoln has put up with me the last three weeks, then the last three days... but I needed to get back and talk this out." She took a deep breath before continuing. "I shouldn't judge so quickly."

Asher's heart was breaking with hers. He hated that he'd caused her so much pain. Maybe they should have given her the benefit of the doubt and told her sooner.

Arms folded across his chest, he tried to swallow the heavy sensation. "I'm sorry about before. I am impulsive, and that's led me to some terrible decisions. But I'm not sure I can change that about me. Not sure I want to. If I changed, I might not be the man Sophie fell in love with."

"She... what?" His poor sister. She stared at him, watching for the joke that never came. Her eyes were soft and gooey, desperately hoping he wasn't kidding.

Looking to Lincoln, she raised her eyebrows in question. Asher couldn't see his response, but Pippa's lip stuck out in a weepy pout. Finally, she glanced to Sophie who had her hand stuck in her mouth as she gnawed away at those poor stubby nails.

Dropping her hands, Sophie came running over. Not putting up with Pippa's stiff posture or pouty lip, Sophie threw her arms around her friend. "I love you Pippa. You're my best friend and that's never changing." Pippa softened and let the waterworks flow.

Asher watched as the two cried it out and muttered unintelligible explanations and apologies.

With a final sniffle, Sophie stepped back to stand at Asher's side and wrapped her arm around his waist as she leaned into him. "I'm glad you never let me meet Asher sooner. You were right all along. I fell for him the second I laid eyes on him. Trouble is, I'm not giving him up... Or you."

Lincoln walked and took his place next to Pippa. He tucked her against his side, happy couple mirroring happy couple.

Pippa finally managed to speak, a shaky smile forming on her face. "You guys really love each other?"

With a laugh of relief, Asher kissed the top of Sophie's head and nodded. "Hell yeah. I guess I always knew your best friend was the one for me. Sorry for getting it wrong a few times before I figured out which one." He winked and pulled Sophie tighter against him.

Pippa shook her head at her own foolishness. Apologizing to her friend, her voice shook. "After all the grief I gave you, I was the one that nearly ruined our friendship. I'm sorry."

Weepy, but swiftly transitioning to happy tears, the ladies led the way into the house. Lincoln brewed a fresh pot of coffee, likely exhausted from their early start. Sophie started washing fresh fruit. Pippa pulled out a pan and some bacon.

"Asher, if you're going to be with Sophie, there are a few things you need to get straight first." She shoved the pan at him and aimed him at the stove. "She likes her bacon crispy. Eggs scrambled with cheese."

And Asher's cooking lessons began. The bacon didn't turn out too bad. It was so crispy it melted in your mouth, but Sophie seemed to like it.

Want more delicious Ex-Navy SEAL? Zane and Freya fight an irresistible, inconvenient attraction. Read The Next Day today!

www.CarrieThorne.com

Also By Carrie Thorne

carriethorne.com/novels/

books2read.com/rl/carriethorne

A Demon Hunter Romance

Plucky, yet badass demon hunters in this paranormal romance series.

1. **Six:** Fate sucks. Even demon hunters deserve a little normal.

2. **Wildest:** Bookworm demon hunter begrudgingly joins forces with a werewolf. Need I say more?

3. **Changed:** Who will hunt the hunter?

4. **Echo**: Badass military hero. Flirty, commitment-phobe demon hunter. What if she accidentally falls for him? Saving the world can be so complicated.

5. *And many more are on the way! Vann of course, Noah, Skye, Blayk... did someone say **epic**?*

Foothills Romance

Make yourself at home in the Foothills Romance series set in the Cascade Foothills of Washington State.

1. **All the Days After:** Former Navy SEAL Asher Sutherland can't seem to get a grip on his future, nor can he keep his hands off his sister's best friend.

2. **The Next Day:** Ex-Navy SEAL Zane is completely lost when he gets to Foothills. It may take the intriguing Freya to distract him from his nightmares.

3. **A Day Late:** Grady seems to have it all together, until he falls for completely the wrong woman who just might help him discover it's okay to let go.

4. **A New Day:** Divorced, struggling to find the old Haley that stood up for herself and loved adventure, Haley

Salsborough relents to the idea of a rebound. Professional football player Finn Halseth hit rock bottom, but isn't floundering like everyone seems to think. Neither is looking for anything serious, but damn, it feels so good to break all the rebound rules.

5. **280 Days**: Ryder and Zoe's story is in the works!

A Beachside Romance Series

Despite the serenity of the coastal town of Seaview, Maine, danger always seems to find the McAllister siblings.

1. **Chasing Forever**: Reformed bad boy Chase Anderson returns to his hometown of Seaview, Maine to find the woman of his dreams has a past that will come back to haunt them both.

2. **Running Home:** Payson Roberts is ready to settle down, until her plans are interrupted by the surly, mysterious Ronan McAllister.

3. **Hiding Away:** Natalie is not what she seems. The reserved photographer is lying low in Seaview to hide from her criminal past. Keeping her secret from attorney Aiden McAllister may prove necessary to protect her heart.

Carrie Thorne is living her own happily ever after (with the inevitable ups and downs that go with it!) with her kids, husband, and dogs in the Pacific Northwest, working full time in healthcare, and always wishing the laundry would fold itself. When she's not rocking the world of romantic fiction, she's exploring the outdoors, traveling (or wishing she was), hanging out with her amazing family, or, quite frankly, she's a total introvert and you can usually find her curled up in front of the fire or in the hammock with a romance novel.

Writing romance is Carrie's not-so-guilty pleasure. She believes in writing genuine and strong characters, promoting positive ideals, that love and happily ever afters are for everyone, kindness is everything, and she cannot resist a zinging romance.

www.CarrieThorne.com